BAYOU SECRETS

BAYOU SECRETS

US MARSHALS
BOOK 1

KARI TRUMBO

Inked in Faith
PUBLICATIONS LLC

*Thank you to Devaney L., for helping me see the bayou
and the surrounding area of Louisiana through your eyes.*

A LOOK INSIDE...

A dark red car sped toward her, screeching to a stop in front of her. The other people waiting for the bus dashed out of the way as the back door whipped open. A man rushed her and huge hands encircled her waist. Gray eyes pierced her through his black mask.

She screamed and hit him with her purse, but he yanked her toward the car. The scent of cinnamon filled her nose and her eyes watered. He yanked her close, and her ankle twisted in her heels. She found herself face down on the floor of the car with her knees still on the pavement.

"Get her in! Come on!" yelled the male driver. "They're coming. There's no time!"

ONE

Mia Fairchild stared mesmerized at the news ticker scrolling along the bottom of the screen. She'd ignored the bickering talking heads on the news program. Distraction would mean she'd have to watch longer. Her focus was one name, and one name only. But would her case be big enough to be on television?

US Marshal Jake Thorne paced in the background. He was the one who'd been given the assignment to protect her until she could reach a safe house. Though she felt better with him, she still didn't feel safe. When he'd returned from sitting out in his car, he'd been hopping mad, though that wasn't much different from his usual demeanor. He hadn't shared the reason with her.

They never stayed anywhere long. He usually stood by the window, barking orders for her to keep quiet or stay down. Not that he was mean, just overly efficient. He'd take a bullet for her. There was no question of that. He just didn't like her all that much, and the feeling was mutual.

She'd been scuttled away a week before into the witness protection program after an attempted kidnapping. Jake believed her uncle was behind the whole thing, since he'd been the outward reason for the attempted abduction. Uncle Cole was innocent, and she was the only one who seemed to think so. But how could she help him out now? Wherever she was, she couldn't assist him when she wasn't even allowed to *be* who she was.

"You're not helping me remain calm," she tossed over her shoulder.

Not that she'd been able to fully calm down since she'd almost been stuffed in the back of a red sedan. Though part of that was her fault. Her muscles tensed and she listened to everything around her. If anything good could come of being thrust against her will into the back of a car, that was it. She was alert.

The police and FBI suspected her Uncle Cole was the one behind the attempted kidnapping from the start. He had the most to gain and there were no other suspects. They'd told her not to return to work. Maybe they didn't have bills to pay, but she still needed to make money. Her uncle wouldn't do anything to hurt her. He was the only relative besides her parents she had.

But *someone* had tried to nab her. If it wasn't Uncle Cole, there was some shadowy person out there who'd wanted to ruin her life. Even just for that moment. She tried to push away thoughts of that day, but the endless stream of words on the bottom of the screen did little to prevent the attack on her mind.

"Ignore my pacing. I'm working," he snapped. "Why don't you work on memorizing your new history, *Emily*, or try to remember something about the guys who tried to kidnap you?" He turned away from her and headed for the window.

The stuffy hotel stank of chlorine from the pool, but she tried once again to remember every detail of what happened. That stench mixed with stale twenty-year-old cigarette smoke was too much for her senses. She didn't want to think about the dark stains in the carpet, but even that was more appealing than trying to remember that day. The day she'd gone from accounting assistant to victim.

Emily Miller was her new name. She even had a new birthday. But her history was still up in the air. Jake had given her suggestions, but nothing fit right. He'd said it was something she should come up with on her own, making it easier to remember. That way, it was really part of her.

He'd said she could work out more of her new past once she got to her placement. She might be there a long time. Court trials could take years, especially when there was still an investigation going on.

She'd tried drawing, focusing, relaxing, everything they'd asked her to do. All she could remember was a red sedan, masked men, the smell of cinnamon, and fearing for her life. Raw fear. Like she'd never experienced before. Even trying to think about it made her stomach ache and her fingers quiver.

"If I never see that color car again, it will be too soon." She focused on the news ticker again, but the words blurred as they traveled at breakneck speed across the bottom of the television. Maybe she would spot something about Deerfield Electronics, or even the missing accountant, but only if she paid attention. There had to be a break in the case. Then she could go home. Her uncle would be so glad she kept faith in him.

He'd been framed. She wouldn't believe otherwise, and she would find the person who'd tried to kidnap her.

When the attack happened, she'd put up so much of a fight that nearby men came running to her defense. She'd been thankful for them, but none of them had been much help in giving a good description of either the car or the men.

She hadn't noticed anything inside the vehicle besides the scent. One of her rescuers wasn't even sure the car had been red, making her witness statement to the police weak. All she knew for sure was that someone in her uncle's company was raking in millions in returns that should've gone back to the buyers, and it couldn't be Cole.

Jake had come to the police station as she'd given her statement. He'd been contacted through the FBI to put her into witness protection after she'd reported the fraudulent activity at her job. That's when she found out the crime that she'd reported was actually much older than she thought. The first woman to report the fraud went missing, then was found days later with a suicide note. One Jake claimed didn't make sense with the way she'd died.

"Where will I end up?" She swallowed hard, thinking about Mary and how nice she'd been. Death would not be Emily's fate.

The thought of her friend, now gone, made her homesick. She'd never been away from her mother for more than a few days. Though she was in her twenties, her mom was her best friend. As an only child, she and Mom shared a special friendship. They went shopping together, talked on the phone almost nightly, and never kept secrets. This forced separation would be hard on so many levels.

"I'm working on it. Looks like Zachary, Louisiana."

She hadn't meant to ask that question out loud and she certainly hadn't meant to ask where she would be placed. Her question had been rhetorical, meant for God to answer. He'd kept her alive so far. She'd never stayed for long outside the area surrounding Reno, until now. Only on a few family vacations. "How long will I be there and where is that? I've never heard of it."

"By Baton Rouge." He continued his pacing and ignored the rest of her question. He couldn't answer it anyway, but she had to try. "The contact doesn't know yet if he wants the job. Little does he know, he'll have no choice."

Her mind thought of at least a million reasons that was a bad idea. If this person tossed her out, she'd be alone where she had no friends or family. "What? You're just going to foist me off on someone who doesn't want me there?"

Jake's broad shoulders tensed. He wasn't old, or young, but noticeable in a crowd with slate gray eyes that saw everything. If he weren't so grumpy, he'd be hand-some. He was extremely fit, but too agitated to attract her. Even with the muscle to protect himself, she'd yet to see him without his gun belt.

"A bunch of strangers almost killed me. Why should I trust this guy? Can't I just stay with you? Or better yet, my parents?" Her dad was skilled in home-defense. He'd protect her. She probably should've moved back there in the first place.

"You want to bring these guys into your home? That's

exactly what the outcome would be if you even contact your family. The only reason you didn't end up in that car the first time was because you fought and they picked a bad street to try to abduct you." He held up first one, then another finger to make his point. "Stop trying to think you know better than we do," he growled and cast a pointed glance at her suitcase.

Her mouth dried instantly. She'd hidden something in that suitcase. But he couldn't possibly know about it. She'd done it in secret, when he was outside taking one of his calls. She'd needed it from home. More than her memories. Her bag was supposed to be private. How could he know about the pictures of her and Mom hidden inside?

He strode to the window and tugged the curtain slightly, then peered down at the parking lot. He did that a lot, watching cars as they came and went. They'd already traveled from Reno to Las Vegas, then flown to Texas where they'd rented a car. After that, they drove for hours until they'd stopped at this awful hotel. She wasn't even sure where they were. So, likely no one else knew either.

Jake tensed and closed the curtain so only a hint of light came through. He frowned and continued staring down at the parking lot, narrowing his eyes. His shoulder muscles bunched like a jungle cat ready to pounce.

Just watching him made her worry, and babble. "Of course I don't want them in my home. I don't want them anywhere near me. You're forgetting, we don't know that those guys had anything to do with my job. You're assuming." Though, she'd done just the same at first.

Why else would someone try to kidnap her? Someone at the FBI had to have tipped off someone at Deerfield

Electronics, or her uncle's office was not secure. That was the only way someone could've found out about her report to the police.

He turned so she could see his profile, but he didn't look at her. "Yes, I am. The images of the woman who worked there before you still haunt me. That won't be you. You might not believe you're in danger, but you'd be wrong."

She was so tired of him using that excuse. The news had reported Mary's death was a suicide after she'd gone missing. Case closed.

"No, it won't, because I have no plans to take my own life. I didn't do anything wrong. She was guilty of trying to ruin my uncle's company!" Which had been like a stab in the back. Mary had been her friend. Why were the US Marshals, the FBI, and the local police so intent on pinning this on her uncle when it was clear Mary had something to do with the scheme?

He shook his head, ignoring her tirade. "I've found the best man for the job. He's a bulldog. One hundred percent by the book. Which is why some of the men at his last assignment took it upon themselves to push him off the force. They didn't want him taking a high-ranking position. If he'd become their boss, he'd have cleaned up the whole squad. They didn't want someone who followed all the rules."

Anger made heat rise up in her chest like acid. People always ignored her. "Push him off the force?" Just what kind of man was he sending her to?

"The more I think about it, the more I'm inclined to just drop you on him. If I give him too long, he'll think of excuses why he can't do the job. Not to mention, someone just pulled up and they're a little too twitchy for my taste. I'll feel better when you're in place."

She wouldn't move for just twitchy. This was the worst hotel they'd stayed in to-date. Whoever was out there could be anyone. "No one could follow us here. *We* didn't even know where we were going...did we?" He hadn't been forthcoming about anything except her new name and birthdate. Jake was a need-to-know guy, and she wasn't on his list.

"Yes," was his annoyingly short reply to her question. "I want you to stay here. Only answer the door for me. If someone knocks and you can't see my face, don't answer. I'm going to go check out and come back to get you. Do you understand?" He patted his side as if the gun might suddenly be missing.

She could almost laugh. Almost. "Yes, I haven't done anything against your orders so far." Except those pictures...

He frowned at her and again looked at her bag. She flinched inside. He knew.

After he left, she made sure her one carry-on sized bag was zipped and sat on the bed, ready to go. She checked the news ticker one last time, but it was back to a point she'd seen before. Still nothing. Somehow, the police had managed to keep the media away from the story. It wouldn't be long, and the case would break wide open. But would she ever know, or would she be stuck in backwoods...wherever Zachary, Louisiana was, forever?

If the case took too long, she'd be away from her family longer than she could stand. Her chest already ached after a week of separation. Mom had to be out of her mind with worry. Had they even told her mother?

Jake collected her about fifteen minutes later and,

though it was about eighty degrees, she tugged up the hood on her light sweatshirt to cover her hair and face. They'd colored her hair, but the length was the same, and Jake felt she looked too much the same as before. She got settled in the SUV and tried to surreptitiously find the vehicle that had made Jake so uneasy, but none of them stood out to her. No red sedans in sight.

Emily closed her eyes and leaned back in the chair as the faintest hint of cinnamon wafted through the vents. "What's that?" She popped forward in her seat. "Who's there?" Her skin prickled to life.

Jake had his gun in hand in seconds as he scanned the car. "What's wrong?"

She flipped open the glove compartment to find what could be making that scent. It hadn't been there the whole way to the hotel. Why now? Other than the rental car rule book, it was empty.

"Will you tell me what's wrong?" Jake raised his voice.

"Cinnamon," she squeaked. When had she turned so weak that literally nothing could alarm her? This was all Jake's fault. He'd made her so scared with all his pushing.

He took a deep breath. "I hadn't noticed until you said something."

The slightest glint of silver reflected back at her from inside the vent. "What in the world?" She dug in her backpack and pulled out her tweezers, then pulled out a stick of gum.

Jake tugged an evidence bag from his vest pocket and motioned for her to drop it inside. "If that had been there before we rented this car, the scent would've been gone by now. We also would've smelled it when I used the air conditioning. I hadn't even started the car yet. Someone," he held up the bag, "planted this."

Meaning they knew right where she was and that she'd reported she knew nothing of them but the scent of their gum. They held all the cards.

TWO

Too much quiet meant change was in the air. Like a storm, it threatened in the distance. Ted Owens strode toward the horse barn, kicking up dust, and cringing at the silence of the early morning. Grasshoppers jumped in every direction to avoid him. The driveway was as parched as he was, and just as abandoned.

A bright yellow star painted on the deep red barn seemed to mock him. The bold paint stood out in stark relief high above his head. His father had painted it with pride when both his sons had graduated together from the law enforcement academy. His mother's face had shone with delight. Now, he just wanted to throw a coat of red over it.

If it weren't for his brother, and the hurt it would cause his parents, he would.

Instead, his only recourse was to focus on the task at hand. Five boarded horses needed to be fed, cared for, and exercised. Their wealthy owners from Baton Rouge expected the best. No one else was on the ranch to do the job, so that left the task up to him. He much preferred to be alone anyway. Touching his back pocket, he made sure he'd grabbed his phone. Wouldn't want any surprises, like an owner showing up when he wasn't prepared. That had never happened, and he wouldn't make today the first time.

Snuffles and stomping from the horses inside the barn calmed his frayed nerves. Those were the sounds he'd grown up with. Men might let him down, but the animals wouldn't. They were as comforting as macaroni and cheese on a cool, rainy day. They needed him. Unlike his last job. His last team. His *friends*.

He slid the huge side door open a little harder than he needed to let air flow through, and six tails swished a welcome at the noise. They never seemed to care if he was in a foul mood. Heidi, his own chestnut mare, stood in her stall across from those who rented spaces. Her area was slightly smaller than the others. That fact would've bothered him except she got out more often.

"Morning, ladies and gentlemen." He took a deep breath and headed for the first horse.

According to a letter he'd received early that morning from the new lieutenant of his division on the Baton Rouge police force, the inquiry against him had finally been closed for insufficient evidence. However, despite his request, he wouldn't be reinstated.

They'd claimed the publicity over the case was too much to overcome, even though he was innocent of wrongdoing. He could look forward to the official documents of his release from duty later in the week and could choose to take his retirement right away or let it accrue. They offered him good luck in finding another team. That idea struck him the hardest. No way did he want another team.

He patted the horse's flank. "Looks like you'll all be staying at Hotel Sandy Creek for as long as your owners would like." Because he had nowhere else to go.

Though he had no lasting mark on his record, the evidence against his character would never go away. He wouldn't be able to find another law enforcement job. Leastwise, nowhere near home. No matter that from the moment he'd graduated from high school, he'd had no other plan than becoming an officer with the Baton Rouge PD. Sometimes life was a cruel joke.

The morning feed took a minute to divvy out, then Ted grabbed a curry comb. As usual, he'd start on one end of the barn and finish with his own horse. Each animal preferred to be a little dusty to keep the flies and other bugs from their skin, but he had to make sure to groom them in case one of their owners showed up unannounced. An ungroomed horse tended to look like he didn't care for it.

He had finished one side of a small mare named Molly Red when his cell phone rang in his pocket, making her twitch with unease. He could understand that sentiment. Tugging the phone out, he hit the speakerphone icon. He didn't recognize the number and assumed it was a client or a future one.

"Ted Owens," he answered, then balanced the phone on the top of the stall and continued brushing.

He glanced over the horse to find where he left off, then braced for whoever might be on the other end of the call. His boss had moved. Could it be him? He'd been the placating sort. He'd try to smooth the mess over. It was already smooth sailing for him and his team.

Ted couldn't prevent what had happened from happening again, but he could be prepared in every other area of his life. After a moment of silence, the voice that came was not one he recognized, and he froze for a moment to listen.

"Officer Theodore Owens, this is Jake Thorne, US Marshal. You remember me?"

Ted clenched his jaw. Not at the man, but at his use of the designation. He didn't fit the title *officer* anymore. The words he wanted to say remained in his head, instead of passing his lips. He wouldn't curse and be disrespectful, no matter that he'd like to.

"Yeah, hard to forget basic." They had gone through basic training together for the army reserves. After they were assigned to different units, Ted had lost contact with Jake and hadn't thought about him in years. "I think you've got the wrong Owens. My brother's still an officer. He works in Baton Rouge, though mostly for parades. He'd be the one you want."

His teeth hurt with the effort to remain cordial. Mom and Dad had warned him his attitude in the face of the investigation would break him, especially since he'd quit attending church too, so he didn't see his old friends. Doing his best to be better was difficult, and he wasn't prepared for situations like this. Molly Red sidestepped and puffed, feeling the tension. "Sorry, girl," he whispered, patting the horse's flank.

Jake skipped the trip down memory lane and went right to business. "As a marshal, I'm privy to information others aren't, *Teddy*. I've seen your case. I know you were a scapegoat. I didn't call to beat around the barn. I've got a job for you, and the situation you're in is just about perfect for what I need."

It took all the mental fortitude Ted had not to slam the phone across the barn at Jake's use of the nickname his team had given him. It proved he'd done his research, as he'd said. Jake was still Jake, all business. Ted had appreciated that about him when they'd gone through basic. Both men had tried to be the best. The challenge had made them friends instead of enemies.

He moved to the next stall, bringing the phone with him. The situation wasn't perfect for anyone, especially him, and he wouldn't agree to anything. Clutching the curry tightly, he scraped the comb across the back of Blake, a new addition to his stable, and the horse twitched at Ted's rough handling.

"Sorry, boy." He tried to tamp down his emotions. He was a man. He wasn't supposed to get mad. But the utter injustice of being framed still burned.

"That horse spread you have out there is the cover we need for someone who must stay hidden at all costs."

"I'm not hiding." The defensive words came without thought. Though, maybe he was hiding a little.

Months had gone by since he'd volunteered to talk to anyone. He'd fully expected to be reinstated after the department finished their investigation. "Look. I don't know if you got word yet, but I'm no longer an officer. I was on administrative leave, but now they've closed the case. I'm not reinstated. You'll have to call someone else."

He didn't want to protect anyone out here. There was enough work with the horses, and having someone there might put them in danger. That was a risk he couldn't take. If he had to pay for the value of a horse, he'd have to file bankruptcy. Doing both jobs well would be impossible. Not to mention how bad the injustice burned. To be called to duty now, when he'd been told he wasn't worthy, was the ultimate slap in the face.

"Yes, I'm well aware of the situation. Would it help to know that the Marshals have been keeping a close eye on your case? The precinct's lack of evidence won't go on your record. They're losing a top investigator. All for the sake of following rules... Or not following them." He paused for a moment. "Perhaps you should know that we have a deputy position opening in a few months. Our department appreciates those who get the job done honestly. Doing this job would be a way to get your foot in the door."

A deputy with the US Marshals would be a dream job, a position he never thought he could earn. Especially after his dismissal. But he didn't deserve a leg up. If he *did* deserve it, the BRPD would've found a way to hire him back. His team should've needed him.

The wide expanse of the ranch appeared in his mind's eye—the acres of trees with a ribbon of river right through the middle. There were two large barns, but he only used one, a covered arena, and a huge paddock with a round exercise carrousel for the horses. There was so much land to cover to keep an eye on someone.

His parents had wanted to make the ranch a horse camp but had settled for boarding instead, with his persuasion. The house was large, with four bedrooms, and only he lived there. If he did agree to help, could whoever came keep to themselves? There was plenty of room for one more person. Could he let some stranger into his life —into the mess of his head—temporarily, to make up for what had been taken from him? Would the end result be worth the mental turmoil?

He set the comb aside and picked up a mane and tail

brush, then gently started to detangle Blake's tail. The job relaxed him. "I might be interested. You don't say much." Jake had left him with long silences to let him think. That was the best tactic he could've used. "Talk to me about this person."

"He who speaks more...loses. I don't want to lose this round." Jake chuckled, giving him no further information. Not that he'd really expected him to.

Ted knew he wouldn't tell him much. He was probably under direct orders to keep the principal—whoever needed hiding—as much a secret as possible.

"Why me?" He'd asked that question so often lately. When his sergeant had come to him and told him he was under investigation for evidence tampering, he'd asked that question. Since then, that phrase had been with him almost constantly.

"Why *not* you? You had an exemplary record prior to the investigation. We trained together, so I know what kind of guy you are. I have no control over the ruling, but from the outside, I see no indication of guilt. I can't even find where you handled the tainted evidence."

That had been the sole reason he'd held out hope that the truth would prevail over the testimony of his team. He hadn't touched any of the tainted evidence, yet he'd still paid the price. His hope had been for nothing.

"Sometimes, things happen. They seem bad in the moment. You can make the most of them, or you can wallow in what could've been. Your choice," Jake answered.

Wallowing was exactly what he'd been doing. Though he'd never admit it out loud. His family didn't even talk to him anymore. They were too tired of walking on eggshells when they were around him. He hadn't been off the ranch in months. Sunday dinners at home with his parents and brother were a thing of the distant past. "I'm not agreeing to this, but what are you asking me to do? You've got to throw me something here. I can't just agree to a job without some information."

"To do this, you'll have to get used to staying in the dark. I've got a woman here. She's on a hot list. As in, if the wrong people find her, she won't see tomorrow. Worse, she's a little gutsy and believes she can prove our main suspect is the wrong man." He paused, letting the gravity hit Ted in the chest.

"I *need* her safe until trial. She's our only chance of conviction. It won't be an easy task. She's already disobeyed direct orders to stay hidden. That's why your ranch is perfect. Less chance she'll get herself accidentally killed while trying to save the world. You're trained, armed, ready. They tried to kidnap her once. They won't stop until they have her. She's worth millions to them."

Ted noticed Jake didn't say where "here" was, and he had no plans to ask. Since Jake was a marshal, he could be anywhere. They had nationwide jurisdiction. "Who is this mysterious *they* who want her dead?"

He knew better than to ask her name. He might not ever be told her real name. She would come with a new identity and appearance. His job would be to maintain a safe perimeter around her. And from her.

"The feds are looking into it. International money laundering. Some type of product return racket is going on with the company where she was an accountant. She reported the fraud, both to the FBI and to her uncle who owns part of the company. That's when we think someone on the inside tried to take her out. So, will you do it?"

He set down the comb and stared at the phone, willing himself to come up with the right answer. This was his duty. Protection was in his blood, but could he ignore that he didn't feel dutiful now. "I can't just make a decision like this."

The horses in the nearby stalls stomped and nickered, knowing he was late in getting to them. If he had to watch over this woman, the one source of income that had kept the ranch in the family might be compromised. His horses had to be his duty, not some woman who needed police protection. Anyone could watch her. He didn't fit the bill anymore.

"You've got twenty-four hours." Jake hung up the phone.

THREE

Clutching the handle in the door of the small car did little good. Emily flexed her fingers against the tension. Jake had been driving through the night and they'd only stopped early that morning for him to make a call and get some food. She knew better than to complain about the limited stops. Stopping was stressful.

He pulled onto 110 then got off almost right away on 19. After a short drive, they arrived in the city of Zachary. In the morning light, sleepy, quaint shops and tidy streets seemed welcoming. She loved shopping and city life. The little town might not be as big as she needed... Somewhere to get lost. While Zachary, Louisiana was nothing like Reno, at least she wouldn't be completely isolated with whomever Jake had chosen.

Jake drove around, making many turns, almost as if he were going in circles. Then the turns stopped, and she noticed he'd taken her outside the city limits.

"Wait... Where are we going?" She glanced at the now distant town in her rearview mirror. He'd said Zachary, hadn't he? She had lost her ability to completely focus since the abduction attempt, but that little detail had been important.

"A little ranch, just a few miles outside of Zachary. We're almost there."

Ranches had cows, horses, and work. All the things she knew she'd never like, nor did she know the first thing about them. Ranches were dusty and old. No shopping. She'd been willing to live in a small town, but not so much in the country.

"You're sure this is perfect for me? Because it's not feeling perfect." She resisted the urge to cross her arms and give him more of her mind.

"This isn't about your taste. It's about keeping you alive. You want to be active and help find who tried to kidnap you. You want to run the investigation, pretty much. But if you do that, the only thing you *will* do is get in the way. Listen to Ted and do as he says. All the time. This work we're doing is preventing the people who want to kill you from doing so. What if they know you better than you think?"

They couldn't possibly. Unless they tried to get information out of her uncle. If they bribed or threatened him, he might tell. He was a pencil pusher who wanted to be a full owner but never got the opportunity to buy her father's other partners out. Those partners wanted him gone just as badly.

While he might be occasionally distant and greedy, there was no way he could be behind the money laundering. Jake had the wrong guy. The longer they focused on her uncle, the more likely the real culprit—probably the other partners—would escape. She knew with certainty he was not behind her attempted abduction. Uncle Cole loved her, and he was not one of the men in the red car. All of them had seemed younger and perhaps more blue-collar, though she didn't know why.

"Fine. There's no need to be rude about it. Wouldn't you want to believe in the innocence of a family member?"

He took two seconds to look her in the eye before he focused on driving again. "We aren't talking about my family. One-third of your family doesn't want you to see tomorrow. Whether you believe it or not isn't a factor in my decision." He gripped the steering wheel tightly and glanced in the rearview mirror.

Her attitude wasn't going to make him work any faster. "I'll go where you want me to, but you'd better catch these guys fast." She would never agree to stay out of the case. That might make a liar out of her. More than the hidden pictures of herself and her mother made her. If she stayed on the ranch too long, the country air might kill her faster than the kidnappers.

Emily ignored Jake for a while as fields of a short stubby plant that might be some kind of beans and cotton whizzed by. No one would be able to find her out there, because she couldn't even find herself. Everything looked the same. If she got lost, she was done for.

A red sedan pulled around them and slowed down. Emily unbuckled and slid down in the seat. She hadn't seen the driver but didn't care. A red sedan meant trouble. Jake laid his hand over the horn but didn't press it.

The next second, Jake put his hand behind her head to keep her from bashing it against the glovebox as he slammed on the brakes. Her feet slid around on the floor and she shrieked, losing her balance and reaching for something solid. Jake let her go and held tight to the wheel with both hands as they fishtailed on the uneven shoulder.

"Hold on!" His hands moved so fast as he whipped the wheel first one way, then the other.

Jake slammed the SUV to a stop, and she heard the car rev away. He didn't say anything for a moment, then he took a deep breath. "It was kids. Too young to be involved. They probably saw my out-of-state plates and decided to have a little fun at our expense."

Emily couldn't breathe, and she laid her head on the seat for a minute, unable to move with her shaky legs. When she could compose herself, she choked on tears. "I hate this. I wasn't this terrified at home. I didn't have to worry about every car and men lurking behind every bush. Take me home!"

He slowly shook his head. She'd known that would be his reply, but she had to be heard. What if this move was more dangerous than staying where she'd been? "What do I do when you're gone? I don't know this guy. Do you have any idea how terrifying that is?" The chances of having a connection to her case were so small as to be irrelevant, but that didn't mean he didn't pose other threats.

"If I didn't trust Ted, you wouldn't be going there. He's good. Very good. I'd trust him with my own mother."

She tried not be flippant, but if Jake's mother was anything like him, she would never need this Ted. With shaky fingers, she buckled herself back in, and Jake pulled back onto the road.

"It won't be so bad. He has horses. I don't know if there is one, but try to find a positive. There has to be something out of this you can gain. Maybe you never got to go to horse camp as a kid and this is your chance?"

She rolled her eyes and went back to looking out the window. Maybe horse camp would've been appealing when she was twelve, but not now. She wanted to work, shop with her mom, and get on with her life.

He turned into a driveway that seemed to go on and on, finally stopping in front of a huge ranch-style home. There were two red barns, one with a huge star on the front, and a large fence with a device that looked like an open carousel without horses. The land was mostly fenced, and trees filled in the landscape, penning her in, making her feel all alone.

"Here we are." Jake got out of the SUV. He didn't indicate for her to stay as he had every other time, so she got out, tugging her hood up as she'd quickly learned. A man in dusty jeans came striding from the barn, a pitch-fork in one hand. He didn't need it though, the look on his handsome, stubbly face was terrifying enough.

Jake laughed as he strode toward Ted, holding out his hand. "Ted. Good to talk to you again."

Ted stopped a few feet away and stuck the pitchfork into the hard ground with a loud *clang* and refused the offer of a handshake. "That was the shortest twenty-four hours in history, Jake."

Undaunted, he stepped closer. "We couldn't wait any longer. This is Emily Miller. She's here to work with you. You'll have to train her. I've already told her that she'll need to work. Look like she fits in naturally..." He glanced at her over his shoulder.

Emily found herself a few feet away from the stranger and took a step back. She craned her neck to look up into the cowboy's face. Her newly darkened hair fell around her shoulders as she swiped her hood off. The color annoyed her, and she raked her hair behind her ear where she couldn't see it.

Heat raced up her cheeks at his frank stare, but she couldn't help one of her own. Ted was about as cowboy as they came, with dark chiseled features and short hair that only peeked from below his tan cowboy hat. His jaw was rugged and defined. His hat hung low on his forehead, almost hiding the tempest in his eyes. Ted wasn't happy she was there, but he also wouldn't send her away. She could almost feel his sense of duty in his hard stance.

She wanted to step closer to him because, for all his smoldering eyes, he still seemed warmer than Jake. Ted squinted down at her as if she were little more than a bug, and she took a step back. Goodness, when had her heart learned to do somersaults?

Which was more terrifying? The enemy she didn't know, or the man who would protect her from them?

TED TOOK a deep breath and hung his head. Jake had him, and the marshal knew it. Once she'd been delivered, her life was in his hands. Telling them to go would put her in more danger. He didn't have to work for the Marshals to know that.

"Why did you think of me for this?" he muttered, hoping Emily wouldn't hear him or his doubts. He'd wanted to ask that since Jake had said he'd been following Ted's case.

"You've been on our radar for quite some time. I told my boss you'd be a good addition over a year ago. At that time, you were doing well in your position and hadn't applied anywhere for promotion. So, he didn't want to upset the applecart. Then..." He shrugged.

Then he'd gotten in the worst mess of his career. "I suppose I should be thankful?" He kept the bitterness at bay. He sure didn't feel thankful. If the Marshals had needed him, they could've saved him from the last six months of torture.

"You take it however it helps you get this job done. This one is important, at least according to the feds. We're not specifically handling this investigation, just her protection."

Ted nodded, knowing the drill. Many times, different entities had jurisdiction over different parts of a case. Problems could arise if heads got too big and details weren't shared. "So, who do I report to with any issues?"

"Me." He tugged a card from his breast pocket and handed it over. "Don't call too often. I don't think anyone knows about you, but I don't want them to know, either."

Jake was just going to drop this lady off and wash his hands of her? There was one big issue Jake hadn't handled, the logistics. He was alone out on the ranch other than his very part-time housekeeper and cook who hadn't done either job for him in a long time. He would be alone with this woman.

"I hope you don't plan to have more than one man on duty, because there's no one else here."

Emily stiffened and she crossed her arms as she tossed a glare at Jake. If the situation weren't what it was, he'd laugh at Jake's predicament. The lady was expressive and couldn't hide her emotions. That fact alone would make hiding her more difficult.

"I don't think you'll have any trouble watching her alone. While there's a lot of land out here, most of its yours. Someone would have to come onto your property to get near her. You'd know."

Maybe he'd know. He did have a lot of property and he didn't exactly canvas it frequently. There were many places to hide, so many that he didn't even have to try hard to think of a handful of them. "Your plan seems as holey as a sieve. For wanting her to stay out of reach, you're leaving a lot to chance."

"I don't see it that way. I've put her in the hands of the best officer in Zachary and probably Baton Rouge, too. Oh, and I resent that you thought for one second that I would be looking for your brother...the *parade* captain." Jake snapped.

Ben worked the equine team, which meant he did a lot of horse work. He worked more than parades, but that's what his team were known for. "You said you wanted Officer Owens. That's not my title anymore and you knew it."

Jake smiled with a brief chuckle, showing teeth and a friendliness he certainly hadn't shown in basic. "That's what you think. He's been there the whole time. Just because they don't see that, doesn't mean he's gone."

Emily waved a hand. "Excuse me? That's all great. But...he's not an officer. If someone comes here and tries anything, is he covered to actually do anything? Or does he just wave as they drive away with me?"

The poor woman looked like she hadn't slept well in days. Maybe longer. He doubted she'd eaten much, either, judging by how tiny she looked in the oversized sweatshirt. He wasn't about to school her on law and what rights he was granted as her protector. If Jake hadn't, then he didn't want to scare her with the details.

She probably had no real idea how much danger she

was in. Those he'd met before in witness protection were either frightened out of their senses and could barely function, or they thought the cover went too far and restricted their life. She seemed to be in the latter camp.

"I'm capable of doing the job Jake is asking of me." That didn't mean he wanted to.

"I can see that much, but if you don't want me here then you won't really do the job. You'd be happy to see me go."

He hadn't meant to give her that impression, and her opinion that he would rather see her be kidnapped than do his job cut deep. "I would *never* just let you be taken to get out of a job. That's not even a question."

"Good. It's settled then." Jake held out his hand, and this time he wouldn't leave until Ted shook it. That shake would be binding. Like a contract.

He sighed and reached out. Before their hands met, he caught Emily's eye. She was so closed off. Just like him. She didn't want to be put in this position any more than he did. At least they had one thing in common.

Jake shook his hand once firmly, then headed back to the black Suburban he and Emily had arrived in. He dug in the back and pulled out one single rolling suitcase the size of a child's and set it to the side.

That was it. Her whole life for as long as she had to live with him was in that one tiny bag? His mother carried more than that for a weekend visit. She bit her lip and he realized he'd been staring for a while.

"Ted, I'll be in touch. Only call me if you absolutely need to. Otherwise, wait for contact from me. I've got the technology to hide the call." He turned to Emily and gently held her upper arms like he was talking to a wayward teenager. "Emily. You do as I said. Listen to

Ted. He'll do everything in his power to make sure your uncle stays as far from you as possible. Don't think for a second about becoming a rogue detective. Ted doesn't need that."

Ted internally flinched. He certainly didn't. It would be difficult enough to keep an eye on her all day and get his work done. If she decided to go against him, he'd fail before he ever started.

Emily gave him a sarcastic smile. "I'll do my best. You just need to remember, you can't please all the people, all the time."

FOUR

Ted's chest tightened as Jake's black Suburban drove away. Emily, or whatever her real name was, stood on the driveway where Jake had left her. Her suitcase handle leaned against her thigh, and she held her arm across her stomach, completely out of place and as nervous as a cornered cat.

He couldn't deny she was pretty in her designer jeans, zip-front sweatshirt, and fashion athletic shoes that had never been worn off the pavement by the new look of them. She was attractive and far too feminine to ever be of much help to him on a horse ranch.

"This is all wrong. You aren't supposed to be here. I didn't have a chance to consider all my options. Like whether or not I wanted to do this. *How* I might do this." The words came forth without much thought. He hadn't had to meter what he said for months, since he was his own company for the bulk of the time.

He didn't even have his gun cleaned and ready for use. He hadn't needed it on the ranch in the middle of nowhere. There were no rooms ready for her to sleep in or use. Not that many people visited out on the ranch, but there were people like his mom who would question where this stranger came from. He wasn't the type to just have people appear in his life and move in.

"I can't exactly leave." She stared after the truck, then turned her piercing blue eyes on him. Her dark chocolate hair was fake, he could see that from her eyebrows. Most people wouldn't notice. It was subtle, but her look had been altered. She had a narrow, attractive face that might be easy to camouflage if she wore glasses and her hair was different enough from her natural color. At least he had that going for him.

"I didn't ask you to leave. I'll do this, and do it well, but it's wrong. He shouldn't have just brought you out here. Not without giving me enough time to think and plan. I'm not up for this job. Not after..." His middle name was practically justice, and this smacked of injustice. Especially after just losing his job.

He stepped close to her, grabbing for her bag to move it to the step. She flinched as his hand grazed her leg, and she jumped away a step. She tripped backward on a rock in the driveway and instinct kicked in. He clutched her arm with his free hand to break her fall. A jittery feeling like St. Elmo's fire traveled through him, but the sky was clear and cloudless. Their eyes met and the sizzle increased. He lost his train of thought in her eyes for a moment.

Jake had never told him what happened to Emily to land her in witness protection, but he'd bet—because of her jumpy reaction to him—it had to do with a man. He waited for a moment until she gained her footing again, then let go.

Intentionally calming his voice to take the rough

edge off helped, but that didn't change the tension through his whole body. He had to take this easy, or he'd spook her into running. Protecting her on his ranch would be hard enough. He wanted no part in chasing after her.

"I'm not going to hurt you." He read the hesitance in her eyes at his nearness. If she was going to stay with him and he was going to protect her, she couldn't fear him.

Was it his touch or the situation that had her so jumpy? Jake had to have explained the danger to her. The most hazardous time for either of them was directly after the drop-off. If Jake had been followed, they would know soon.

He headed for the house, keeping track of her footsteps behind him the whole way.

There was only one room he could put her in, even though it hadn't been used in a while. He set her bag at the end of the bed and paused, trying to remember the last time anyone had slept there.

It was the rarely used fourth bedroom in the sprawling ranch house. The smallest of the four, it also had the least appealing view since it was only for guests. The main driveway and the barn could be seen if she bothered to open the curtain. But that would allow her to hear any and every car that drove up, allowing her to react accordingly.

"I hope this is sufficient. At least until I can figure out something better."

"Thank you. I'm sure this will be fine." She backed out of the room before he could even turn to leave. He knew the signs. He was reminding her of something—or someone—she'd rather forget. If not, this would be a long job. Yes, he was a stranger, but Jake had trusted him to protect her. She had to trust him. Her safety depended on it.

"I've got to grab something from my room, then we'll go outside. You can see what I do around here. If your story is that you're here to help, then you'd best know how a horse ranch works. Oh, and change into something you don't mind getting dirty." He indicated her bag.

She flinched once again. That bag wasn't all that heavy. She hadn't brought much with her. For a girl in designer jeans, her whole life had come in a carry-on sized bag. She stepped to the side to let him get by. His ears automatically tuned in to her movements. He'd have to know where she was at all times, so he'd have to get used to that feeling again. Her life was now in his hands. Whether he wanted the job or not.

Ted left her on her own and headed for his room. The whole house felt strange with someone else in it who wasn't family. On a small hidden shelf in the back of his closet, he drew his Colt from its hiding place. With it was the concealed holster he used to use when he was off duty. He clipped it to the inside waistband of his jeans and snapped the strap to hold the gun in place. Just putting it on shifted his frame of mind. Serve and protect.

Emily wouldn't know what to do until he showed her around, so he didn't want her to linger with nothing to do. He hurried back to find her in the living room. She hovered near the family picture his parents had commissioned after he and his brother had graduated. Both of them had just earned jobs in different departments. Their pride in their sons shone on their happy faces, just like Ted and Ben's new badges.

"He didn't tell me you were a cop," Emily mumbled.

Had been a cop. The self-depreciating voice in his

head snickered. "I hope it doesn't make a difference. Because I'm not."

He caught just a hint of confusion over her face before she turned away from him.

"You don't need to change?" She still wore jeans with more design on the pocket than his mother's last needlepoint.

"I don't have anything to change into." She shrugged, but still didn't turn. He was getting mighty tired of talking to her back.

"My mom's pretty tiny. You can check her room for something. Wouldn't want you to wreck the few clothes you have." He led the way to his parents' room, or what used to be.

That gave him a few minutes to make a plan. He'd been dropped in dangerous territory, unprepared. He swiftly considered all the areas of his ranch. Where could people hide out and not be seen? Too many. For as perfect as Jake thought this was, it would only work if she was never found. He couldn't watch almost three hundred acres by himself.

"Where can I find them?" She wrapped her arms around her waist again, making her look even tinier. Maybe Mom's jeans wouldn't fit... He stalled for a minute, hoping he hadn't just talked himself into a corner. She already didn't like him.

"The closet with all Mom's clothes is at the end of the hall on the left of the room. The bathroom is back there too. My room is across from this one. My brother's old room is across from yours. He doesn't live here and hasn't visited in months. We're alone except for my cook, and she lives in a little house out back. You can only get to it through the breezeway. I rarely see her."

He hadn't actually seen the cook in over a week. He'd told her she didn't need to cook for him anymore. He wasn't much company and didn't have an appetite anyway. All that good food was going to waste. He heard her in her little apartment once in a while, but she was mostly quiet. Though he hadn't meant to scare Emily, he could see his words gave no comfort.

She swallowed visibly. "Look. A week ago, someone I didn't know tried to yank me into an unmarked dark red sedan. There were four men. Big enough that I immediately thought they were men. They wore masks. I got close enough to smell cinnamon gum. You think this is hard for you, that I'm here? Trust me, being forced to trust a stranger right now is killing me."

Without waiting for him to respond, she turned on her heel and strode down the hallway toward his parents' former closet.

Her words were a gut punch. When had he ever put his own comfort over that of the victim? She might not look like it at the moment, but that's exactly what she was. And he'd whined about her showing up unannounced. He whipped off his hat, ran his hand through his hair and adjusted it back on. Time to do this right. He was better than this.

Something or someone had saved her from being kidnapped. Whoever had tried, must have done something way worse than just kidnapping. That alone wouldn't warrant the US Marshals involvement. Jake had mentioned some international return scheme. But how could Emily have gotten tangled in corporate fraud?

He wasn't supposed to ask her anything, so he'd have to keep his questions to himself. Yet, she simply didn't seem like the corporate type. More like a retail store owner. Jake would eventually tell him everything they wanted him to know. Though that could be years from now.

Emily might be anyone, but she was only recently Emily Miller. That was all the government thought he needed to know. She gave off a feeling of uncertainty that would draw the attention of others. He'd have to help her come up with a history and help her act naturally in a small town around him.

After what seemed like forever, Emily quietly came out and closed the door to his parents' room. The jeans she'd chosen didn't fit, but a secure belt held them in place. She cocked a hip and tried to give him a cold stare, but she only really managed to look nervous.

"I hope she doesn't mind, I borrowed her boots, too." Emily's glance went right to her feet.

"She wouldn't mind at all. Let me show you the barn. Oh, and sorry for the poor welcome." He lowered his voice slightly. "That's not like me and I have no good excuse."

Since she'd given him a few minutes to consider how he'd maintain both order and get his work done, he could handle the job. The answer was, Emily would help him, giving him time to watch her and keeping her near him all the time. She couldn't just stand around, doing nothing. Not only would that make the days unbearably long for her, they'd be unimaginable for him.

Her eyes softened just slightly, the only giveaway that he was forgiven. "Thanks for that. If it helps, I get it. I wouldn't want someone to drop a stray off on my doorstep either."

He stood and headed for the door, hating that she felt homeless. "I don't see you that way. Let's get back to doing what I was when Jake drove up. Since you don't know, this ranch boards horses. Mostly for people in Baton Rouge who can't keep them where they live. The cost to board here is steep and that's on purpose. We can only hold a few and they get the best care available. Some would call them spoiled." But he preferred well-treated.

He led her out of the house and off the porch into the hot Louisiana summer. She sucked in a breath as they strode off the last step. "Are there always so many grasshoppers?" Her voice squeaked and she shuffled closer to him, tugging her sweatshirt close to her, even with the heat.

He held in a chuckle. "It's been a dry year. Seems they like the dry weather. At least there's less mosquitoes."

He kept walking. There wasn't anything he could do about the bugs, and small talk didn't let him concentrate. Insects were just part of living in Louisiana, meaning she wasn't from the area. Had he truly wished for an end to the silence that morning? Seemed like an age ago.

"You have a lot of land." She quickened her pace again, yet still hung back where he couldn't see her.

He heard her gasp softly, then scuttled until she walked within a foot of him. Almost stepping on his heels. Probably so he'd clear the grasshoppers for her. As if he'd forget the woman was there. Her pretty oval face wasn't easily forgotten. He sidestepped so she wouldn't bump into him as he answered.

"I do, but you should stay right up near the house until I tell you it's okay to wander. Once we determine just how safe you are, we can decide if you can be outside alone. I'll keep watch on all the spots where people might try to get onto the property secretly, but you can go in the barn, the exercise pen, and of course, the house."

Her voice trembled as she shivered. "So I'm not trapped in the house all the time? Jake made me stay in the hotel rooms, away from the windows. The only time I could see faces was on TV."

It was too hot for her to be cold, so confinement made her nervous if her shiver was a giveaway. Not surprising with an attempted kidnapping.

"No, not trapped in the house. But you still can't go wherever you'd like. Zachary is big enough that no one would notice if someone new just showed up. That's good for you, but bad too. We'll never know if you were followed like we would if this was a smaller town. Unless they come right up the driveway." He laughed, but she quickly turned to look like someone could be pulling up the drive that instant. He shook his head and kept going. *Smooth move. Scare her in the first hour.*

He led her into the barn, hoping she would at least like it in there. What town girl didn't go a little gaga over horses? If she had any interest at all, the time might not be so bad for her. Who was he kidding? If she wasn't excited about the horses, there was nothing for her on his ranch.

He'd finished feeding and grooming the boarded horses just before she'd arrived. The horses would need some exercise, either in the ring or out in the pasture. He didn't have to ride each one every day, but he did try to ride the horses frequently so when their owners came to see them, they wouldn't shy away from a saddle or halter.

"I don't think Jake considered the fact that people drive up to my house to see their horses whenever they feel like coming. Mostly on the weekends, but it's not like I'm alone *all* the time." Though, even that had seemed to slow down. Maybe he'd been surlier than he'd thought. "I know their vehicles, but we'll have to be very careful with you here."

"About being alone...is there anyone we could call to stay here too?" She raised her eyebrows in hope, and her oval face softened.

He'd already thought about that while she was changing. Anyone he asked would have to give up working for a while or be put in more danger than he liked. The only option might be his cook, but she'd always resisted staying in what she called 'the big house' with him.

"I wish I could. Jake didn't give me permission to let anyone else in on your secret, and I can't think of a single plausible story off the top of my head where it would make sense to have another person come." If she was in as much danger as Jake said, he certainly didn't want to bring his family into it. Only his brother would be prepared, and he had his own work to do.

Her face tensed back up as she glanced around the barn. Making her first day difficult wouldn't serve to help anyone. Emily wouldn't remember anything he tried to teach her with the stress of arrival.

He strode up to his favorite horse, mostly because she was as sweet as you please. "This is Molly Red, she's older and nice enough that her owner is a seven-year-old girl. Just unlatch the gate, take her by the halter, and lead her out that door." He pointed to where they should go. "I'll lead Sir Kensington first."

She watched him, then did what she was supposed to. For being what appeared to be a city girl, she took directions and didn't complain about the smell of the horses or even ask what a halter was.

A soft mewling came from the front of Molly's stall as

Emily returned. A soft, "Oh!" brought him to her. "Kittens! They won't be hurt in there, will they?"

He sighed as he tried to think of how to deal with another woman in distress. This day just seemed chock-full of them. Another situation to mess up his schedule. But he couldn't leave them in there. Why did it seem like everyone and everything needed him today?

FIVE

Emily took in every movement as Ted carefully picked up four identical gray tabbies and placed them ever so carefully in his cowboy hat. Then he strode through the barn and dug out a shallow indent in a short mound of hay next to a small nook that might have been Ted's office.

"I don't think Molly would intentionally hurt them, but let's not take chances." He pulled out each one gently from his hat, then tucked them all in together on the hay. "Now to find mama so she knows where I moved them."

She couldn't stop staring at the tiny mound of mewling fluff. "I thought if you touched kittens, the mom would abandon them?" Part of her connected with them. Though she'd been the one to leave, she felt abandoned there with Ted.

He had yet to do anything sweet, but this seemed vastly outside of the gruff character he'd shown so far. Was that bulldog bluster all for show? Did Ted...whatever his last name was, really have a big heart? She wanted to believe that. The moment she'd gotten out of the SUV, she felt *almost* safe with him. More than handsome, he was commanding. His presence demanded attention and respect. That would help her learn to trust him. That and watching him handle kittens no bigger than her hand.

Her one long-term boyfriend had been weak. He'd proven time and again that he could be pushed around. Finally, she'd walked away, and he hadn't bothered to fight to keep her, either.

Ted's voice reminded her he was the exact opposite of Carson. "No, she'll leave them alone a while to make sure you won't come back and pester her nest anymore. She may be stubborn and move them back, but she won't abandon her litter. That said, I wouldn't move them at all if I thought they'd be fine in that stall."

He climbed a short ladder in the middle of the barn and stuck his head through the hole in the ceiling to the hay loft. Then, he whistled softly. A moment later, he reappeared with an adult gray tabby rubbing against his head and knocking his hat off as she gripped his shoulders with her claws. The small cat kneaded the fabric of his flannel shirt and purred loudly enough to be heard from feet away.

Ted had strong shoulders. Shoulders that could carry a burden much bigger than a mama cat. The ghost of a smile tugged his lips as he mumbled to the animal. His voice changed when he spoke to the cat, drawing her attention to his jaw, accentuated with a couple days' worth of dark stubble that matched his hair.

He leaned over the nest and the mama jumped down, immediately laying amid the kittens crying for her attention.

"There now. Hush. You take care of them and I'll get something for you," he said as he opened a small fridge just inside his office door. He pushed it shut with his boot and poured a single-serve carton of milk into a bowl. Then he opened what she assumed was his sandwich for lunch and tugged off about half of the lunch meat and dropped it on top of the milk.

As he shoved the sandwich back in the bag, she cleared her throat. "You seem to know her well."

He tossed the sandwich back into the fridge. "Yup, she's been keeping the mouse population to a manageable level for about three years." He stared at the little fluff balls for a moment.

"I'm surprised you don't have more cats around." She hadn't seen any at all that morning. "Usually one feral cat, means lots of them." She'd seen plenty in the alleys back home.

He shrugged. "I don't know where all her kittens go, but I know they won't stay, so I don't bother naming them. When they're old enough, she leads them off and they never come back. I assume she makes sure every farm around here is fully stocked with cats."

She'd always been more of a dog person, but the little balls of fuzz with ears so tiny they quivered were pretty cute. This big guy taking note of, and caring for, a brood of kittens was telling. Maybe Jake had it right. Maybe he had picked the perfect place for her to hide for a while.

"I know you can't ask much of me, but can I ask about you?" She was too curious now to let fear keep her silent. Jake hadn't talked at all the whole week she'd been with him. Maybe Ted would at least provide a little human interaction, something sorely lacking in her life.

He'd relaxed a little before, but her question put him right back on edge. His jaw hardened and he stepped back. She could practically feel him put up his defenses.

"Ask what you want. But you might not like the answers." He swiped his hat off the floor, slapped it against his thigh, then adjusted it back on his head.

"You were a cop? What does that mean? You're too young to retire." He was probably about five years older than her if she had to guess. Determining his age would be difficult since he was so obviously healthy.

He turned his face from her and adjusted his hat once more. "Of course you'd be interested in that. The reason I'm no longer a cop pretty much covers every reason why you shouldn't be here."

She swallowed hard, feeling trapped. Had he done something to someone? Maybe Jake hadn't looked as closely into Ted as she'd thought? She edged a few inches closer to the door.

Ted took a breath. "My last job decided I wasn't fit to wear the badge." He turned and headed for the next stall.

If she'd hoped for clarification to ease her mind, that wasn't it. Had he hurt a civilian? What had she gotten herself into? He said he'd do the job, but if she was in more danger now, Jake needed to know before he got too far away.

The strand of trust she'd clung to quaked inside her. If he couldn't handle a talk, could he handle her life? He had to tell her more. There had to be more to the story than a decision to let an officer 'go.'

"Wait." She pushed past her hesitation and took a few steps toward him. No matter that she'd rather run. "Jake trusts you. He must, or he wouldn't have brought me here.

If you can't be trusted... Why am I here?" She wasn't normally one to speak so plainly. She still wasn't certain her attempted abduction had anything to do with her uncle, and all this seemed completely overblown. But she still didn't want to stay with a bad cop.

Without her, Uncle Cole's company would be destroyed. His arrest was imminent according to Jake. The fraud was already evident in online reviews. She'd found the accounting issue when she'd moved into the bookkeeping area for her uncle after his regular accountant's assistant had quit. Shortly after, his auditor had gone missing. People had asked for refunds on high-cost items. Those funds had been diverted to an offshore account instead.

After looking at the reviews, she realized the production department had created sub-par products. When people asked for legitimate refunds, the company would instead divert the money so their accounts showed a refund had been given, it just wasn't given to the customer who asked for it. She hadn't been able to find any information about that account other than that all the refunds were going there, so as far as she knew, it wasn't connected to her uncle. At least not directly.

Ted made no move to put more distance between them. At least he wasn't running from her. Her questions might make him pause, but he wasn't shy.

"You're here because Jake knows me. Probably better than anyone. You didn't get to see the real guy, just his business side. He's a one-man army. If he says you'll do best here, then I have to believe him. Jake said he was watching my case. I don't know how well, but he knew enough that I doubt he let anything slip."

She led the next horse to the door. This time, she didn't move out of Ted's way to get by to get the last horse. She needed to look him in the eye and know he was trustworthy. "He had to have been following well enough to know you could be trusted."

He managed to circumvent her and went to the last stall. Though she wanted to pressure him to answer, she knew that would be a bad idea. He rested his hand on the latch and took a deep breath. He stood rigid, tense, making her nervous.

"I know you're looking for a reason to trust me. I'd bet that would mean a lot to you right now. I just can't do it. I may not have done what they accused me of doing, but they still didn't want me around. I took an oath to serve and protect. I assumed that oath meant my fellow officers as well. Both me to them and they to me. Call me disillusioned, but I just don't buy it anymore." He pushed away from the stall and led the last horse out.

If Ted had been one of her friends back in Reno, she would've touched his arm or tried to help him by listening. Ted didn't seem to want any of that. He returned to her, then trudged past toward the front of the barn. "Now the real work begins."

"Ted." There had to be more. An understanding between them. If she had to be on alert all the time because she didn't know who her enemies were, she could just as well be at home.

"Yeah?" He stopped and cocked a hip as he glanced over his shoulder at her.

"Was it anything I should worry about? Do I have anything to fear by being here?" Anything other than dark red cars and things that went bump in the night.

"From me? No. I'm no criminal. Just not on the force anymore. It's hard to take on the role of protector so soon after being told I shouldn't have the job." He kept moving and redirected his path into what she assumed was the tack room.

Nothing to fear from him. He was safe. Or, as safe as a guy could be. No matter how long she'd looked, she'd yet to find one she could completely trust. The only man who hadn't let her down was her father. Even Uncle Cole had let her down a time or two.

The barn wasn't all that long, but she didn't want to follow him to the dark corner room where Ted had disappeared. She hadn't felt comfortable earlier alone with him in a room, but she hadn't felt comfortable with Jake or anyone else lately either. She'd have to get over that if the ranch would be her home for now.

Every sound seemed louder without Ted nearby. She could hear distant cars on the road. Birds made noise from somewhere outside. Insects buzzed. But where was Ted? He seemed to take far too long. Hadn't he said she shouldn't be alone or did that mean she had to follow him everywhere he went? Was that assumed and she'd missed it?

Her heart pounded, and suddenly, putting one foot in front of the other was nearly impossible. She swallowed hard and choked on her own breath. The faint smell of cinnamon touched the back of her nose, and she opened her mouth to scream but no sound would come.

She frantically searched the dark corners of the barn from where she stood. When had it gotten dark? It was midday, but the barn was full of shadows. Anyone could be lurking behind a stall or corner.

"Emily? Are you all right?" She heard Ted calling but couldn't respond.

Fear gripped her tighter and tighter in a chokehold. They were following her. She knew it without a doubt.

"Emily?" He poked his head around the corner. Just seeing his face cleared her mind. They wouldn't come when he was here, within sight. She was...safe. Wasn't she?

She slowly followed his path but stopped near the nest of kittens. He'd left the milk close enough that after the mama had nursed her brood back to sleep, she'd managed to consume every bit of what Ted had left her. The cat's green eyes inspected Emily and she began to purr once again. The cat probably expected anyone who stopped long enough to notice her to pet her.

Since there was no one else around, that meant Ted had the cat trained to expect attention. The guy had wounds she couldn't heal. He'd been treated poorly, but that didn't mean he took it out on anyone else. Not even a scrawny barn cat.

"So, you think I'm okay?" she whispered. "I don't know why he'd mess with you. Just a silly old gray barn cat. And he'll let all your kittens fly to the wind, too." She reached out and ran her finger gently under the cat's chin. The mama closed her eyes and tilted her jaw, moving Emily's hand naturally where the cat wanted attention most.

Ted appeared at her side. "Why would I mess with her? Because if I didn't, who would?" He reached down, his long fingers covering the cat's back as he gently massaged down her spine. The cat turned toward him and made a soft noise that wasn't quite a meow, deep in her throat.

Emily's insides stopped quivering as she watched the burly, manly cowboy pet a tiny cat. He was gentle with her, caring even. "Is it the same with me? Are you taking care of me because no one else would?"

He met her eyes and their cool blue shocked her. "I expect. I'll show you what you need to do next."

SIX

All afternoon while Emily followed Ted around the ranch, she tried to remember all the things he told her. By the evening, she couldn't think of a single thing he'd said. All that came to mind were throbbing muscles and a scent that seemed to cling to her no matter how many times she washed her hands.

Now that she'd finished her first day of unpaid manual labor, she needed a shower and a nap, though that would never come. Sleep had been difficult before the incident. Now it was impossible. Every time she closed her eyes her mind would try to reassemble the scene, but there wasn't enough information. Her imagination tried to fill in what it didn't know, often leaving her terrified. Far too agitated to ever sleep.

She trudged into her room and collected the few things she would need for a shower and glanced through her bag. Ted had mentioned twice that she hadn't brought much. Jake hadn't allowed her to. Too much of what she'd owned was connected to her mother or seemed personal.

He'd told her not to bring anything she couldn't leave behind if she had to rush.

Three outfits and two pairs of shoes were all she had left. At least now, when she didn't have to be out in the barn with Ted, she could do laundry. Three outfits would be more than enough if she never saw anyone.

She stifled a yawn and made her way to the bathroom. Her stomach growled, but she ignored it. Food had no business near her until she scraped off the layer of dust, dirt, and sweat coating her skin. Then she'd feel human again. Mostly.

After a long, hot shower, Emily wrapped her hair up in a towel and sat on her bed. Her suitcase lay open next to her. She riffled though the contents, knowing what was there and still hoping to find something else. Though she'd loved to shop at every boutique in Reno, the outfits she'd brought were out of date and hardly worn.

To her own eyes, she didn't look at all like Mia Fairchild anymore. No more light blonde hair, or trendy clothes, and no designer shoes. Emily Miller was supposed to be a blend-in country girl. She was supposed to be a natural on a ranch. Maybe she'd at least gotten that part right, though her protesting muscles screamed otherwise.

Everything else Jake had asked of her, she'd fought him. He'd tried to scare her with threats of the last accountant winding up dead. All the news outlets had said it was a suicide to cover up guilt. Her story was the closest Deerfield Electronics had come to being in the news. The only reason the case had been mentioned was because the body did not look like a suicide at first.

The media had never even hinted at the full extent of

the fraud. Deerfield Electronics had pinned all the allegations of theft on the now-dead accountant. If the accountant was the source, there was no need to be in hiding. She simply needed to find proof to tie the money laundering—the account she'd found—to the dead accountant. Then she could go home, and her uncle could be exonerated.

Jake had asked if she had any incriminating information with her, but that depended on what was considered *bringing*. She had nothing physical. Her power was in her recall. She'd committed the foreign account number to memory. All she had to do was find a computer with internet access and she could keep hunting for the true culprit.

When Jake had met her at the police station after she'd made her statement about the attempted kidnapping, he'd whisked her off almost immediately. He hadn't even allowed her to say goodbye to her family. With a dire warning about not talking or making eye contact with anyone, he'd rounded her up. She'd grabbed a few outfits and they'd hit the road.

Emily pulled two pictures from her bag that she'd taken a year before. They were selfie-style with her mother. She stared at them, touching her mother's face, and an ache clenched at her heart. Jake wasn't supposed to have known about them, but she suspected he'd found out with the way he'd scowled at her bag.

She'd desperately needed some way to connect to her mother. When he'd been out taking a call, she'd crept down to the hotel office in Las Vegas. There, she'd printed out the few pictures where she'd saved them on the cloud. She'd never been away from Mom for so long.

Jake had warned her not to call her mother or any other person, but a photo couldn't hurt. The temptation to ignore his warning was heavy. He'd claimed Deerfield was a big enough company that they could be watching her mother's phone, or even her own. Especially since those phones were purchased by the company from her father's account. They'd taken her phone away right in the police office for evidence.

His warning still rang in her ears, though she'd tried to ignore it. He'd glanced over to her after they'd spent hours driving, closed in together in the car with nothing to talk about but her case. "If you call, you'll put your mom in danger. Don't do it. I know you miss her but the better you are about staying away, hiding who you are completely, the more likely you'll survive until trial. Your mom wants to see you again, alive, so don't be tempted to ignore my orders."

Jake really was a no-nonsense guy. But she'd still eluded him and printed the pictures. The only thing that kept her from calling was that Jake may have found her while doing it. He hadn't checked her bags, and no one but the hotel front desk person saw her. Yet so many times over the last few days she'd felt like he knew what she'd done.

She laid the pictures on the bed beside her and tears welled in her eyes. Mom would be scared, not knowing where she was. How would she feel if she'd called Emily's phone and gotten no answer? Emily had lived on her own for years, but never more than a few days had gone by without talking together.

Mom would want to know about where she was, who she was with, what had happened... all the things she was told to keep to herself. She tugged out the burner phone Jake had given her and took a quick picture of her room and a silly selfie in front of the window. Then she propped the pictures of her mom over the framed pictures on the dresser. Now the room felt more like home.

Everyone said she looked like her mother. Though not right now. Her usual light blonde hair was dyed a deep brown. She usually wore it down, like her mother, but since she'd colored it, she'd started putting her hair up in a loose bun. The color bothered her, and she didn't want to see it at all. She wound it up in a loose bun now for that reason.

The house seemed very quiet, and she popped out into the hallway to see if Ted was finished with his own shower yet. They had both worked hard, but he'd let her have dibs on the first shower. She heard the water running and let herself breathe. Even though he eased her mind, being near him still had her on edge. Another few minutes until she had to feel on guard again.

He'd been as prickly as a porcupine all afternoon. With him occupied, she could take some pictures of the rest of the house to show Mom later. The living room was quaint with an old country charm. The large, overstuffed furniture had gingham print with matching pillows and looked comfy. Next to the living room was a sweet country kitchen with a coat tree by the door that resembled a real tree. The floor plan was all open, making the room feel huge. She stood back and got the whole area in one shot.

Jake had noticed first that the police hadn't taken her phone when he picked her up. He'd deposited it into evidence, then gotten her the cheap burner. When he confiscated her wallet and locked up all her identifying information, he'd told her she would probably never see it again and had her back everything up then and there. Then he'd created a new ID for her.

A text came through and she glanced at her phone, unsure of who could possibly have the number? Was it safe to even look? She peered around the room to make sure she was still alone. Her mom's number flashed across the notifications.

Dad had to have found the phone. He was a tech mastermind and wouldn't stop until he found her. The text was short and to the point:

Sweetie, where are you? We're worried sick.

Jake had promised he would get word to Mom that she was all right. But he probably wouldn't do that until he made it home. Depending on if he'd hopped on a plane out of Lafayette or if he drove back to Las Vegas, he may not get back for another day. She'd realized in the shower that he'd driven around a lot between Reno and Louisiana, just to keep her—and anyone following them—confused. Mom would be worried sick by then.

She went into her room and closed the door. Ted wouldn't invade her privacy by barging in. If she was going to break the rules again, it wouldn't be where she could get caught. There was still the possibility all of this was a big misunderstanding. Women were kidnapped and trafficked every day. Just because some car had targeted her right after she'd told the FBI about Deerfield, didn't mean the attempted kidnapping was them.

How could anyone from her uncle's company know she'd filed a report? She hadn't told anyone about her contact with the FBI. The only way someone could've known was if they followed her when she reported it, or if someone had traced her keystrokes when she'd been at work. Or if they'd tracked her phone.

She glanced down at the burner, wanting to reach out to her mother, but was it safe? Her heart raced, and distantly, she heard the water of Ted's shower stop. She only had a few minutes to decide, and she might not have another chance.

Glancing toward the door, she bit her lip, then opened up the text. Quickly, she typed up a reply letting her know she was fine and would have a lot to tell her soon. She stared at the text for a minute and her stomach clenched. Yes, she'd disobeyed Jake and printed the pictures. She'd ignored the FBI rules before the attempted kidnapping too. But what could one text hurt? It wasn't like her kidnappers could track this phone.

After she'd reported the fraud, she'd been put in touch with an FBI agent. He'd told her to lay low, change her routine daily. Don't go into work. A new job was necessary. She'd reasoned she couldn't leave her uncle to deal with the accounting mess. Not when his first accountant had let him down so badly and the person she'd replaced had quit.

On her way to work three days later, the dark red sedan had appeared at her bus stop. But she'd been careful otherwise, and nothing else had happened. If she sent the text, she would be violating a direct order. She could put herself, and now Ted, in danger. Printing the pictures hadn't taken this much decision power. She hadn't cared about Jake because he would have her moved before anyone could find them. That wasn't the case now. She wasn't a moving target anymore.

She laid down the phone and stood up to pace. The room was too small to go far in either direction. Ted seemed capable of handling anything, but was she? She wanted to think so, yet this hadn't been easy. Her parents had spoiled her, and being away from them and the life she knew was hard. Reporting the fraud had been the right thing to do, but the consequence seemed to affect her more than the one committing the crime. Especially since they seemed sure the criminal was still active, not dead.

There was a knock on her door, and she froze, unsure of what she should do. If she tucked her phone away, she would look guilty. Emily grabbed her phone off the bed and opened her mouth to make him wait, but the door swung open in the next second.

Ted stood there, his hair damp, a button-up jean shirt and dark wash jeans clinging to his just showered frame. He zeroed in on her phone immediately and strode into the room, plucking it from her fingers before she could hit send.

"I was calling you. Have been for a few minutes. I figured when you didn't answer, you were up to something or someone had gotten in here. What do you think you're doing?" He stared at the screen. "If you're important enough to a federal case that you're in witness protection, then you shouldn't be contacting people. I can't believe Jake didn't take your phone." He stuck it in his shirt pocket with a deep frown creasing his brow.

She wanted to correct him, to tell him the phone wasn't the one she'd had. This one had to be safe, but her voice wouldn't work. Not when Ted was obviously so furious. She backed away another step and gripped the top edge of the dresser for support.

Ted fresh from the shower was even better than in his work jeans. She forced herself to stare at his pocket where the edge of her phone protruded, instead of him. Without that phone, she was sunk.

Ted stepped forward as her reality came into glaring focus, smelling like Old Spice. "Understand this. You don't know who your kidnappers were. They could be neighbors. Someone could, even now, be making friends with your family to try and find you. You could've been followed. Don't think for a second that these people are stupid. They aren't." He stepped back out of her space then glanced at the photos of her and Mom together.

He took a deep breath. "I wouldn't have guessed you were a blonde, and the hope is that no one else who meets you does either. We can't have these out. Until you go to trial, everyone who comes up that driveway is a suspect and you've got to play your part. You can't announce who you are to everyone." He collected the photos and put them in her top drawer, then closed it. At least he hadn't taken them.

She was sick of being a prisoner when the real thief was either dead or walking free. "You don't understand. My mother is my best friend. I wasn't the type to make friends easily, but my mom was always there for me. She's worried. Not only that, the threat has been... how would you cops put it? Neutralized? The last accountant committed suicide, and Uncle Cole said that she was behind everything."

Ted's eyes softened just slightly, and the hint that he was human under all those rules became evident for the barest of moments. "I understand your frustration. You're probably lonelier now than you've ever been. The case is far from over, judging by the little information Jake gave me." He glanced around the room as if looking for other contraband, then zeroed in on her again with those blue eyes that left her more than a little off-balance.

"You don't want your mom in this situation, so don't put her there." He leaned against the wall. "I think you'll find your role easier if we come up with your story together. You need to become Emily Miller. Who are you, why are you here, what is your past?"

Emily glanced into the full-length mirror on the wall. Even just a change in hair color had made her feel like she wasn't herself. Coming up with a history for this new person she was supposed to be would make it easier to bear. "Okay. We can do that. I'll trust that Jake will contact my mom, at least for now."

He smiled and stepped aside so she could leave her room, but he didn't reach to give back her phone. "Don't worry. Even if she does text, I won't tell you."

SEVEN

Emily found the cupboards in the open kitchen relatively bare as she opened each one in search of supper. Outside of a few cans of gourmet looking soup that had been there a long time, he'd been eating like a bachelor. So much for the cook Ted mentioned earlier. Maybe she didn't shop? Had he even said his cook was a woman? She'd assumed so, but the thought that she was out there with two men alone was even more frightening.

She glanced over her shoulder, an action she found herself doing a lot lately. Her nerves jangled, not knowing just where he was. Her fears weren't just of kidnappers, but of her protector, too. Ted was a formidable man and wouldn't let her just do as she pleased to try to help her uncle. Not like she'd hoped. He wouldn't hurt her, that was evident. But he was more like Jake than she'd thought he'd be.

That didn't explain why she felt nervous about scanning his cupboards, but she still did. It was a subtle invasion of his privacy and made her nervous. No matter that Ted wouldn't mind her looking for something to cook. She still found herself tense, waiting for him to come down the hallway to catch her.

Why couldn't she be normal and relax? As she closed the cabinet door, she flinched at the noise. If she took a moment to examine herself, her main fear was acting up because he'd caught her trying to text her mother. She'd done something untrustworthy.

Time to be more careful, Mia. The agreement to work with him was no more than temporary, but that's how it had to be. Her mother needed to hear from her, and there had to be a way to start building the case against her uncle's former accountant. The only one who might know what had happened would be the woman who had quit. She might hold all the answers.

"There's not much for food in the cupboards. I wasn't prepared." Ted's voice came from behind her, making her jump. A nervous laugh tumbled from her lips before she could stop it. He'd scared her even knowing he was coming.

He cocked his head slightly as he came nearer, confusion knotted his brows at her reaction. "I didn't mean to startle you."

She took a breath and forced herself to settle down. "It's fine. I was just focusing on the cupboards and didn't hear you." And maybe a little too much on the issue with her uncle.

"It will take me some time to figure out how I'm either going to get you to the store or leave you here while I go."

"Leave me behind?" Her heart kicked into high gear. "As in... alone?" There were things she could do, but she hadn't been left to her own devices in over a week. What if someone found her? Ever since the attempt to kidnap her, she'd been unable to make decisions. Be safe and do what they asked, or take risks and save her uncle?

He opened a cupboard next to her and his arm brushed hers, sending tingles of awareness through her. That certainly wasn't helping her think straight.

"I'd rather not have you alone. Neither option works well. My cook is a bad choice since she isn't good at protecting anything but sugar cookies and doesn't even know you're here. I think I'd feel much better if I gave you a few self-defense courses before I leave you all on your own. I can't exactly give you those tonight. We need food in the near future."

She laughed but didn't reply. If Ted left her alone for an hour so he could go shopping, she could look through his room and get her phone back. But first, she had to get her heart under control. There was nothing to fear. No one really wanted her. She'd never been so jumpy. Jake and Ted had cultivated fear in her, and she would believe it was just that until she was proven otherwise.

Trying to look as calm as possible, she leaned against the counter. "Jake let me go shopping with him in Las Vegas, for toiletries and incidentals, not that I got much. He didn't give me time to look at anything or ever leave his sight... but I was out in the open." She shrugged, hoping he would see she wasn't concerned. "So, he let me go shopping with him, but I think I'm fine here. Your choice. You live in the middle of nowhere." She shrugged, hoping she looked like she wasn't trying to sway his decision.

He *had* to go shopping. They would starve on what he had in the house. If she could tap into his internet, she could also find out if anything had been released to the media yet. The more ideas came to mind, the calmer she was about staying.

His brow furrowed in obvious skepticism. "If you were safe to leave alone, Jake wouldn't have driven across states to get you here."

He wasn't going to do it. She could feel her freedom slipping away by the inch. Staying with Ted wasn't bad. Staying under lock and key was. "Well, if it was good enough for Jake—" she pointed out.

"Jake is Jake. He'll do things differently from me. I could have my mom come over, but I hate to ask her. If something happened, I don't want her in danger. I'd honestly rather keep her in the dark." He gave her a knowing glance and scratched his chin.

Her stomach knotted slightly, and she fought the knee-jerk reaction to defend herself. Was he insinuating she didn't care about her mom because of the text? Wanting to check in with her mother wasn't being dangerous, it was respecting her mother's feelings. No one else would see a text to her mother. The feds had tried to convince her someone might tap her phone, but that was insanity with the new device. No one wanted to know who she called or texted. They would be bored. Mom was the only one.

"I guess we better get your story worked out, then I'll get pizza takeout. We can do a little grocery shopping after that. The fewer times I have to bring you into town, the better. But I'm just not ready to leave you alone. Not yet."

His lack of trust bothered her, no matter how justified it was. This was her home for the foreseeable future. There had to be something she could say to make him understand she needed a little freedom. She stood taller. "I thought you said I wasn't a prisoner?" Staying chained to him sure felt like jail, though mostly because she didn't know him at all.

"You're not. You're staying alive so you can go to trial. There's a big difference. Let's sit." He motioned to the couch.

She followed him out of the big kitchen that took up one corner of the house. The area encompassed a kitchen, dining area, and living room and was all open. A sofa acted as the barrier in what looked like the middle of the room where the polished tile met carpet. He dropped onto one end of the sofa, and she stayed to the other.

"So, the name they gave you is Emily Miller. You're on a ranch, so your new history has to include either horses or me. Whatever you did before, avoid it in your story."

She laughed. "I was an accountant for a very short time. It shouldn't be hard to avoid that in my new history. As far as the ranch... You saw me earlier. I know nothing. Maybe colors? The horses are brown—"

"Chestnut," he corrected, his eyes laughing. That was new. He had soft crinkles beside them when he did that. Did he smile often, or had he just been grumpy all day because she'd been dropped on his doorstep without warning?

"Gray?" She raised her eyebrows, trying to joke with him and hoping she got it wrong.

"Dapple." He chuckled.

She found she liked him a lot better in this mood than how he'd been before. Her mind flew to the horses she'd led that morning. There hadn't been many.

"And white with red spots?"

He laughed outright. For the first time since she'd shown up unannounced, he seemed fully relaxed. Her appearance on his huge ranch had ruined whatever he normally did in the middle of nowhere, Louisiana. But maybe he didn't mind as much as it seemed. His laugh was welcome and set her at ease.

"Paint." he replied. "You'll learn, I have no doubt. That's the best part about your arrival. You're smart enough to learn anything fast. But in the meantime, we better center your story around me, not the ranch."

Did he really believe she was that adaptable, or teachable? Even Uncle Cole, who loved her, hadn't thought she was completely capable until she'd shown him how much she could do. Could Ted learn that much about her in eight hours? She'd tried her best to work with him earlier and ended up with a few badly placed blisters from pitching hay.

"I guess. You're the expert."

He nodded at her approving words. "I think it might be a good idea to pick up some really weak reading glasses. After seeing your picture, the dark hair doesn't change you enough, especially with it pulled back like you do. They'll recognize you." He leaned forward, squinting in thought and making heat rush to her cheeks at his frank analysis. "I'm not going to let anything happen to you, but I need your help, too. What else? You've come here to be with me. Why? How did we meet?"

She chewed her lip for a moment. What would be a plausible reason for her to be staying with a man she didn't know? Or did she have to act like she knew him well? "I've got it. I have a fiancé who is going to start a horse ranch. He sent me here to learn from the best. Maybe you're old friends?"

Ted laughed again as he shook his head. Warmth spread over her face. Was he laughing at her or did he like her idea?

"I could be wrong, but I don't think people will believe any man with a brain would send his pretty fiancée to live with a single man. That will be our biggest obstacle. How do we explain your presence in a way that won't make people think too long and hard?"

She found herself focusing on his compliment instead of the problem. She was a homebody. No one thought she was pretty. The believability of why she was there, sleeping in the same house with a single man, hadn't occurred to her. The situation had bothered her for other reasons, but not that one.

The cook was there in her own little house, so the locals wouldn't think they were alone. But that didn't change the fact that she *felt* alone with him. Up until then, she'd been too worried about other things: like every noisy truck that drove by on the road, just far enough away that she couldn't see them. Or other things, like learning how to clean stalls and let the horses out. Like convincing Ted she didn't want to ride just yet... Too many things.

She tried again. "Let's say my grandmother, Anna Miller, knows your mother from way back. They've kept in touch, and she arranged for me to come stay with you for a summer. You don't really want me here at all and I don't really want to be here, but... Grandma." She shrugged. "Better?"

He slowly nodded. "I like that. My mom knows everyone, and people would think it's likely she would have friends outside the area."

"How old are you?" She really looked at him, with the slight crow's feet by his eyes, yet no gray in his hair, she couldn't put an age on him.

"Thirty-two. Why?" He tucked his chin and gave her a questioning glance with just a hint of a smile.

Admitting she'd just been curious would be embarrassing. Curiosity over Ted could land her in trouble. "I'm twenty-eight, but people usually guess I'm much younger. I should create a new age for myself, one that will go with the story that my grandmother sent me here. People are not going to believe that a twenty-eight-year-old woman let her grandmother dictate her life for her."

"That's true, but I also don't want people saying I'm taking advantage of a child. Let's just do our best to keep you away from anyone who might ask questions. If it wouldn't put my parents in danger, I'd ask them to come and stay here with you. I can't do that until I'm sure there's no danger to them."

"What about this cook you keep mentioning? I'm not really alone when she's out here."

He nodded his agreement. "Unfortunately for Clara, who is actually my mom's cook, she can't know what's really going on. At least she's not directly in the house and probably won't be in imminent danger."

She swallowed hard at the words *imminent danger*. Why did everyone believe Uncle Cole would try to kill her? She just wanted to go home. Guilt whispered in the back of her mind. At least she could go home to escape the rumors and trouble eventually.

When this all got sorted out, Ted would be the one who would have to deal with the talk long-term. People wouldn't forget. Some would never hear about her and would believe whatever story she and Ted created for the rest of his life. That was a burden to leave behind. "So, we're back to the original question. How do we get groceries out here if I can't be seen?"

He smiled and turned toward her, his excitement to tell his idea palpable. "Do you like dogs?"

"Better than cats." She laughed, though the barn cat was sweet.

"Then we'll have to tell my brother about this, the truth. He's an officer who lives in Zachary but works in Baton Rouge. Better, he has my dog temporarily."

She wasn't sure how a dog was going to solve their problems. Even with a dog, she'd still be alone unless he was planning to leave her with his brother.

He continued without waiting for her to ask questions. "Usually, with a protection order, there are two people hired to watch. One for day and one for night. If anything happens, I'll try to bring him here as my second."

"Why does he have your dog?" Though the dog wouldn't be like a person, she would feel much safer with it there. They could hear things humans didn't, like sedans driving up the driveway.

"He had Captain while I was waiting to hear back from my last job. The team didn't ask for him back. He *is* retired, so I'd hoped they wouldn't. He's trained in water rescue, which you won't need, but he's also protective."

"Your brother... or your dog?" she joked, knowing the answer.

"I'll tell him you said that. My brother is Ben, the dog is Captain. I'll go call my brother and let him know we're coming and ordering pizza. You can stay with him while I go and get groceries. Then we'll bring Captain home."

She breathed a sigh of relief. She wouldn't have to rely so much on Ted with Captain around, and he might trust her with a few minutes alone. Time when she could sneak in and get her phone. Then it wouldn't take long to get online and start looking for information. Who knew a dog could bring so much opportunity?

EIGHT

The evening pressed in on them, and Ted still had to disguise Emily before they could leave. He finished the call with his brother, telling Ben about Emily and keeping as much secret as he could. He returned to the living room where Emily waited for him.

She'd pulled her hair back as usual and, not for the first time, he wondered if it would look better down. The dark hair around her face would help her disguise, but if she didn't want to do it, he wouldn't make her.

He finished the call with Ben and frowned as he handed his ball cap over to her. She had been willing to wear it, but something bothered him. There was an unnamed tension about the whole situation. Something he couldn't name or place, and he hated any unknowns in the situation. He adjusted the cap so her ears didn't stick out. Being close to her rattled his insides. He'd noticed she was short before, but standing right next to her, he felt like a giant.

Emily cringed slightly and backed away a step. "I'm

sorry. It's just so hard to be near any man. I keep thinking about the abduction and what might've happened. Before..." She trailed off, but he couldn't let her say more. He couldn't know her past, not even what had happened the day before.

If he knew nothing, the person after her couldn't get information from him if they ever captured him to get to her. "It's not that I don't want to know, or that I'm not curious. It just puts you in greater danger if I do. You're Emily Miller who likes horses and has a nosy grandmother. That's what I need to know about you right now."

He tried to keep his voice level, knowing that sometimes he was gruffer than he wanted to be. That was just part of being a cop. He was supposed to be in charge. His DNA didn't seem to know he wasn't employed anymore.

Emily glanced up at him, her eyes plaintive for him to understand. "I just didn't want you to think it was you. It's not. I'll just try to forget that other part of me for a while, the part that really *is* me. It's hard. This is all so new. I can do it though." She straightened, tried to smile and failed, but didn't back away from him further.

"Good, you'll need that. That dedication to do the right thing is exactly what they teach you when you start training to be an officer. You would've made a good one." Not that she would ever try or that he would know. He certainly hadn't been a resounding success.

After years of work, striving to do his best for the people in his precinct, finally making it to investigator, the hard work was gone in an instant. Everything fell apart when he'd been disciplined right out of his position. Released from duty for a crime he didn't commit.

"My brother will tell you the same. You'll probably be more comfortable with him." He turned away from her.

His face must have betrayed him, because she'd looked shocked for a moment, then concerned.

"I've only known you for a day and I can tell you must have done your job well. I doubt he'll make me more comfortable than I am with you," she offered.

He ignored her statement and glanced over her to make certain she was as concealed as she could be, even for the quick walk between his truck and Ben's front door. The conversation wasn't going anywhere, and he'd like to end it. "Let's go. Ben's waiting."

His pickup sat parked just outside and she climbed in, already looking mostly like she belonged there. The terrified city girl Jake had dropped off now seemed more relaxed after most of a day of getting used to him and not being a prisoner in a hotel room with Jake.

"Tell me about Ben," she asked as she buckled herself in.

Of the two brothers, Ben was the one who got along with women best. Ted would rather not say anything about his twin. But if he kept information about Ben to himself, he would only worry her. That didn't make him want to give her any information beyond his name. People were always more fascinated by his brother, but women especially.

"He's my twin, though he'll tell you he's older. We both live for horses and ranching. He's on the Baton Rouge PD Mounted Patrol. I don't see him all that much." Especially since Ben still had to work with the guys who'd let him down by not coming to his defense. He didn't want to be between his brother and his brother's team. Ben still had to trust those people with his life. Family had to come second.

Her eyes lit up and he fought the mild jealousy that

always stabbed him when people were more interested in Ben's horse than in him. As stupid as it was, he wanted Emily to find him fascinating. He was the one who had to protect her and share his home. He didn't want anyone to mess that up. Not even Ben.

"I've never seen a real officer on horseback, other than in historical reenactments. What does he do?" Other than the brief moment of excitement, she didn't seem overly curious. Just inquisitive.

He wanted to ignore the question and just move on but at least she was talking. "He mostly works crowds and community involvement. He makes his horse dance. It's an important job..."

Though he'd joked and often *felt* like Ben's job was a waste. He'd gone from investigation to what seemed on the outside like a mostly pomp job. Ted's desire for rank and for respect didn't mesh with Ben's. Not that they needed to have the same career goals.

"Horses dance?" She raised her eyebrows at him, and he wanted to laugh. Emily was one of those people who could ask a full question just by looking at him. "Outside of the Lipizzaner Stallion commercials I saw as a kid, I didn't really think that was a thing."

"Yes, they dance in order to stop people in crowds. It's not for show, though sometimes his unit will do demonstrations for kids."

She rolled her eyes, then glanced away. "I guess I can ask him more when I meet him. I'm curious."

Whether she'd sensed his agitation or just decided to shift away, he couldn't tell, but he was thankful for it. There was no safe way to respond to her question. If he offered more, she'd learn he didn't think much of his brother's choice. If he said nothing, she would simply be more curious. He didn't want her to take an interest in his brother. She wouldn't be around long anyway.

"Maybe focus on Captain. He'll be the one staying with you."

She laughed. "Don't worry about that. I'm sure Captain and I will get along fine. I didn't say I wanted to be his BFF. I just want to know what he does."

He didn't chuckle, because he didn't want her to think more of his reaction than it warranted. Though her teasing was funny. For some reason, her reassurance that she wasn't interested in his brother beyond his job eased his mind.

He never drove with anyone in his pickup, and having her there in his house—and now in his truck—was like having a wife he hadn't planned for. He had to protect her like one, which made him reevaluate their plan.

"Instead of your grandmother story, what if we tell people we're married? When you leave, I can just say we went too fast. You got cold feet. Whatever. We could test it tonight with just Ben." People would be more likely to believe that story, and they wouldn't talk about her staying at his house. Plus, then she couldn't get attached to his brother.

"Married?" Her voice quivered slightly, then she took a deep breath but didn't look at him. "I guess I can do that. If I get too tense when you're near me, you'll have warn me with a look though. I'm still not comfortable getting near anyone. I don't even like the idea of staying with your brother for an hour. I'd rather stay with you."

"Good." He let the word escape a little too fast and her questioning gaze forced him to explain himself. "I mean, it's good that you don't just immediately trust people. He's not going to hurt you though. You don't have to worry about him, and you don't have to go near him. Let's go inside. The pizza should've been delivered a few minutes ago." He parked in front of his brother's one-story home.

"You made him pay for it?" She laughed as she climbed out of the truck.

"What else are brothers for?" Besides paying for pizza and keeping his dog.

He'd missed Captain. He hadn't realized how much until he faced seeing his partner again.

He led her to the door and his brother answered. Though many people couldn't point out exactly what was different—whether it was the way they stood or how they dressed—people could usually tell the brothers apart even though they were identical.

"Ben, this is Emily. She's my wife... for now. I'll explain later."

Ben chuckled as he stood aside to let them in. "Interesting, since she wasn't your wife when you called me a half hour ago. Guess it's good I paid for the pizza. Cheapest wedding gift ever."

Captain, his huge dark German shepherd, sat at attention just inside the door, his tail thumping. The dog was about nine years old and had started to show some gray around his muzzle, but he still obeyed commands without hesitation.

"Captain, come." Ted ordered.

The dog came forward, and Ted held out Emily's hand for Captain to sniff. The dog whined slightly, then licked her palm.

"Once he gets the command to protect you, he'll do it until he's told he's off duty. He has specific commands for that. For now, just get used to him. I'll be back soon."

"Wait!" She scrambled toward him and reached for his arm, then stopped before she actually touched him. "Aren't you going to stay? You need to eat."

He'd like to believe she cared about his hunger, but he suspected she didn't want to be alone with a stranger. Understandable after what she'd been through, but he couldn't wait any longer. "I can't. Save me a few slices and I'll eat later tonight after I pick you up. I just want to get you back home."

EMILY WATCHED as Ted drove away and Captain whined at her side, nudging her thigh. For being a dog who wasn't on duty, he certainly seemed demanding of her. Her chest ached with the stress. She hadn't realized just how comfortable she'd become with Ted until he'd walked away. No matter how much Ben looked like his brother, he wasn't.

"Captain wants you away from the window. He's smart and is already worried about your safety. He can probably sense your nerves." Ben's voice came from a few feet behind her. At least he'd known to give her space.

If he could sense that, he was an exceptional dog. She'd tried to hide how she felt from Ben. After getting dropped with Ted and now being left with Ben, she was at her limit for strangers. She could feel him nearing her and her body reacted immediately.

"I really need you to stay back." She clenched her fists and crossed her arms. No matter how she tried, she couldn't get over the fear. Men had yanked her into a car.

Captain nudged her toward the kitchen and her stomach growled. He was far too smart for his own good.

"Why don't you eat a little if you can and just talk to me. I'll sit back and listen."

Ben tried to hide the fact that he was staring at a car outside, but she was too nervous of his every move and motive not to notice. "What are you looking at?" She turned around again, and this time Captain barked at her, nipped at the loose knee of her jeans, and tugged her toward the kitchen.

"That car pulled up and parked shortly after you did, and they haven't left. I know all of my neighbors' cars. That's not one of them."

Any desire she'd had to eat ceased and she dropped down onto the nearest sofa. "You think they followed us?"

"Why would someone follow you?" His eyebrow rose in a challenge.

She hated that Ted hadn't told her what was safe to talk about and what wasn't. Especially if someone had followed them. Wouldn't Ted have noticed? How had she never seen the car before?

"It's a little coup. Two people inside. Men." Ben stood at the window and surveyed his neighborhood like he wasn't checking out the one odd car in the street. "One of them is on his phone."

Could they be calling to tell someone where she was or was it a coincidence? Her fear and flight response were almost immediate. How could she ever help Uncle Cole if she didn't stop being so afraid?

"Are they just sitting there?" she asked, slouching lower on her kitchen chair.

Captain rested his large head on her lap and searched her face with his big eyes.

"Yes, which means there's not much I can do. I can't call in a disturbance or even suspicious activity until they do something. You should probably eat, then stay in the kitchen. You'll be out of sight there and it's not good to stress on an empty stomach."

Food had never been a big deal before, but now she didn't want to. Maybe hoping Ted would leave her behind was a bad idea. If he had, there would be no one to help. At least with Ben there, he could watch those men if there was a threat. Alone, she would just have to sit back and hope the situation was nothing.

"You're sure there's nothing we can do?" She gnawed her lip instead of the slice of pizza in the box in front of her.

He tossed a reassuring smile over his shoulder that came across cockier than he probably intended... maybe, she wasn't so sure about him yet. "I've got the situation in control."

Emily grabbed a few slices of deep-dish pizza from the box. Captain laid right on top of her feet, holding her in place. The kitchen was nothing like the one at the ranch. Where Ted's was open to the whole house, Ben had a narrow kitchen that felt small and cramped. A big screen door offered most of the light in the room along with a small window above the sink. She hated moving the dog to hunt for the light switch.

Everything was dim, but the pizza wouldn't offer much of a surprise, and with the shadowy darkness she could stay out of sight. She'd just finished her first slice when the window above the sink exploded, sending glass flying everywhere.

"Emily!" Ben called from the front room.

She hit the floor and covered her head while Captain growled at something nearby. She couldn't see anything under the table except the dog. The *click* of Ben's service handgun as he cocked it, sent tremors up her spine.

Glass crunched under Ben's feet as he made his way to the window.

"Sorry, Mr. Owens!" A boy's voice floated to her from across the yard. "I'll go get my dad!"

He sighed. "You're safe. Tommy just hit a foul ball through my window. At least he was honest about it."

She heard him do something with his gun, then holstered it. Glass pricked her hands where she pressed against the floor to get up, then she moved Captain from his spot. When Ben returned, he made a growling sound low in his throat. "With the distraction, the car left. I still don't know if they were just hanging out there or if they had to do with you."

Her chest constricted and she slumped back into the chair. Where was Ted?

NINE

After he'd returned from buying groceries to pick up Emily and Captain, she'd seemed more subdued. Certainly less talkative. The broken window had distracted Ben and he'd spent the whole time Ted was there talking with a neighbor. He hadn't wanted to ask her when she was in such a rush to leave, but now that they were alone, he could broach the topic.

"Anything happen that I should know about?"

She rested her hand on Captain's head where he laid it on her lap. The move was telling. Captain could tell Emily needed him and was willing to break the rule of laying down in his truck in order to comfort her. He'd tell the dog to lay down on the floor of the pickup when they got moving, but he wanted to focus on Emily, not driving.

"There was a car that parked outside Ben's house just after you left to go shopping. It was blue, with two male passengers. He didn't recognize them and they didn't do anything. They weren't blocking anyone, not making too much noise, just sitting there. He couldn't tell if they were watching his house or waiting for one of his neighbors.

They left about a half hour before you came. As soon as Ben left the front window to see about the broken one in the back... they left."

The days following drop-off were always the most dangerous, and scary. He knew that the mind could play tricks, making connections where there were none. He'd been telling himself that since she'd arrived. Was this one of those, or real?

"We'll get home and ride the perimeter together before it gets dark. Just to make sure no one has been on the property. It'll put your mind at ease."

She snorted. "I don't think anything is going to calm me tonight. Not after that baseball came flying at me through the window. I thought it was a... I don't know what I thought it was. But my mind didn't immediately rush to *baseball*."

"If it makes you feel any better. Mine wouldn't have either." If he could be sure his touch calmed her, he'd touch her arm. He'd been tempted to. But she'd made it clear touch made her uncomfortable. Maybe now that Captain was there, she wouldn't feel so worried about being alone with him. "Captain will come with us. You should know where it's safe to ride and where people could access my property. Watch him for clues. He'll scent any danger before you'll see it."

She'd avoided riding earlier in the day when it was hot, but now the sun would set completely before they got home. There were no excuses left. She'd never ridden before, but she'd never scooped out a stall either, and she'd survived.

"I can do this. I need to. Just learning will be good for my cover." She nodded and stroked Captain's ears. He raised his head and immediately laid on the floor, settling over her feet.

"Good." He patted Captain's head to give his approval. "I'll teach you his commands tonight once we're back in the house. He's yours while you're here. He'll be a last line of defense against anyone."

She gave a slight nervous smile and shuddered. "If they get through you first."

"I'll give them all I've got." His oath to serve and protect was now an oath for one very important lady. He couldn't let her down.

The drive went quickly, and Emily helped him put away the groceries. She was much more efficient than he'd ever been. She logged what he'd purchased quickly and then made a meal plan for the week, writing everything down daily-planner style.

"How did you keep track of all that?" He handed her the last can of peas.

She smiled as she set the can neatly next to its mates on the shelf, then taped the meal plan inside the cabinet full of drinking glasses. "I was an accountant in my former life, if only for a few months."

He sucked his breath and ducked his head for a moment. "I'm not supposed to know that, Em."

Her eyes widened and she turned a slight shade of pink. He hadn't meant to embarrass her any more than he'd meant to use a nickname. He'd already known, but she wasn't supposed to so casually let her past slip.

"Let's get this riding business done, then come back here and try to relax. I won't get any sleep tonight if I don't." She crossed her arms and stepped away from him.

A few minutes later in the barn, he showed her how to saddle Molly Red and helped her mount. She looked mighty uneasy in the saddle, then he whistled to Captain. Within a moment, the dog loped up and sat next to her horse. As he'd suspected, the dog calmed her down.

This would have to be his quickest ride around the perimeter he'd made in a long time, but it had to be done. If someone had watched Ben's house while Emily was there, he couldn't assume they didn't know where she was staying. Nor could he brush it off as coincidence without proof. If she couldn't stay with him on his ranch or with Ben, where would she go?

His land was mostly flat, but heavily treed and a little swampy in areas. He relied on Captain and his horse, Heidi, to get a scent of anything strange. They didn't alert him in any way as they rode but he wouldn't let his guard down until they returned to the house.

Emily pointed to a group of trees. "That looks like a place someone could hide a truck."

He nodded his agreement. "It would be if they could drive through my fence. That area's fairly well-protected, but the trees make it hard to see any distance. I'm not saying it's not possible, but unlikely. If you ever ride alone for any reason, take Captain. In fact, just don't do anything without him."

He reined in. "I had planned to teach you some defensive moves once you were comfortable here, but I think we should start tomorrow, like I mentioned earlier."

He hated to push her, but until he heard word from Jake, she had to stay there with him. Danger or not. The longer he was around her tension, the more he tended to believe the men in that car were behind something. He'd wanted to brush it off as coincidence, but Ben knew the cars in his area. He knew his neighbors well.

"I think that's a great idea. But not today. This ride

has been more relaxing than I expected it would be, and I'm ready to call it a night."

He'd let her, but he had already decided he needed to stay up a while longer and figure out what could be done to protect his ranch, and his new *wife*.

A BRIGHT, sunny day filtered down where Emily stood on the sidewalk outside her apartment. A construction crew worked on a sewer entry about thirty yards away, laughing and talking. She was early to the bus stop, nervous about a meeting with Uncle Cole later that day.

A dark red car sped toward her, screeching to a stop in front of her. The other people waiting for the bus dashed out of the way as the back door whipped open. A man rushed her and huge hands encircled her waist. Gray eyes pierced her through his black mask.

She screamed and hit him with her purse, but he yanked her toward the car. The scent of cinnamon filled her nose and her eyes watered. He yanked her close, and her ankle twisted in her heels. She found herself face down on the floor of the car with her knees still on the pavement.

"Get her in! Come on!" yelled the male driver. "They're coming. There's no time!"

Construction workers who'd been patching the pavement stormed the car, surrounding it. She could hear them yelling and one of them tugged her back to her feet, pulling her away from the car. Mr. Cinnamon held tight to her computer bag. He tugged it, pulling her toward him and the open door again. The construction worker stepped forward and punched Cinnamon in the nose.

"I called the cops!" said one of the other construction workers.

Her limbs trembled and she couldn't thank them. The words just wouldn't come.

"You're fine now. Shh."

Except the construction worker hadn't said that, her mind protested. He'd told her she'd better be more careful and carry some mace with her. Then he'd walked away... The daze of sleep slowly let her go.

"It's just a nightmare. Wake up now." Ted's soothing voice broke through the dream.

She forced her eyes open and the memory evaporated. She found herself sitting up in bed, with the blankets everywhere. Poor Captain's eyes were worried, and he whimpered as he pressed his cold nose into her calf. All at once, she realized she was in Ted's arms. He was holding her and soothing her.

And it was working.

He was touching her, and her skin didn't burn with apprehension as it had every time she'd been near a man since that day. Was she finally getting over the trauma or was Ted just special?

"Do you need to talk about it? Sometimes dreams don't come back after you fully explore them, even though you might not want to." He didn't let her go and his voice was so soothing.

They sat on her bed, and she should feel totally uncomfortable about that, but she didn't. Tackling her dream, however, made her vastly uncomfortable. "All I can remember that makes any difference is the smell. The car they used had some type of air freshener or something that made the whole thing smell like gum. I won't forget that smell and I can't stand it now."

Though it wasn't cold in the room, Ted backed away from her and draped a blanket around her shoulders. "I can tell it must have been horrible. You started screaming and I thought someone was breaking into your room. Scared the life out of me."

She fought the urge to apologize. Her feelings were hers, there was nothing to be sorry about. "I go from being terrified that someone really does want me dead, to convinced the attempted kidnapping was just a fluke. I happened to be in the wrong place at the wrong time."

"What made you go to the police again after?" Ted moved from the bed to a nearby chair.

The move made her feel separated from him again, and she wished he'd return. Even the difference of a few feet made her speak louder than she wanted, no one spoke secrets so loudly.

"I..." That was hard to explain. She'd been frightened, but her mother had convinced her to go to the police. Even though Mom hadn't known she'd been there the week before reporting the fraud. "I was encouraged by my mom. She takes care of me. I'm an only child. Which is why I was trying to text her."

"I know. I'm from the South. We're all close to our mamas here, or so everyone says. I think she gave you good advice." His eyes were trained on her like she was the most important person in the world and he couldn't get enough of looking at her.

No one had ever looked at her that way before. "You're making me nervous." She felt her cheeks grow hot under his gaze.

"I don't mean to. I should let you get back to sleep."

She shook her head, and though she yawned, she knew she would get no sleep the rest of the night. "I can't.

If I close my eyes, I'll be right back in that dream. I've tried before."

He glanced at the door, then the clock. "Guess I'd better brew us both some coffee then. It's going to be a long night."

TEN

The following night, Captain's heavy form slept butted up against Emily's door all night long. If he'd heard anything, he hadn't let her know. Ted had told her to keep the dog with her, but she couldn't sleep with him in her room. He snored and she wasn't used to his weight next to her.

After so many hotel rooms, and now here, she was slowly getting used to sleeping away from her own bed. Exhaustion had struck her so hard that she'd collapsed as soon as her head hit the pillow. Once down, she'd slept deeply for the first time since finding the accounting issue at her uncle's tech company.

The job had seemed so routine, boring. The end-of-the-month spreadsheets had to be done, but she'd noticed an oddity under some of the big returns. The bank accounts used to pay for the goods were not the same as the ones used to receive the refund. She'd dug deeper over prior months and found there was an account in Brazil that received the refunds. At first, complaints had been handled with duplicate payments—one to the Brazilian account and the other to the original purchaser. After a few weeks, the original account was simply left hanging while the Brazilian account got the money.

She'd asked her uncle about the former accountant and how poorly she'd done her job, pointing out the discrepancies as proof. Uncle Cole had told her not to talk about her. He'd said she'd committed suicide shortly after quitting. The way he'd made it sound, the bookkeeper felt so guilty about her crimes that she'd taken her own life.

Emily had hunted through emails and documents, finally finding the old accountant's information. With that, she could eventually dig for evidence to clear her uncle's name. As she waited for word from Jake or on the news, those few things were all she had to go on.

She ran some water into the coffee pot, scooped coffee into the filter, then let it percolate. Oddly, she felt at peace in the home that wasn't hers, unlike anything she'd known before. She glanced out the window at the huge red barn. The trees stood sentinel all around, giving the house a protected feeling.

Captain nuzzled her hand, reminding her that Ted should be up to let out the dog. He probably wasn't one to usually sleep in. But after she'd woken him the night before, then kept him up for almost twenty-four hours straight, he was most likely used to more sleep than he'd gotten.

"I'd bet you need to go outside?" She glanced down at Captain. His large chocolate eyes never left her. He'd stayed by her side from the moment she'd opened her door that morning.

He whined slightly and nuzzled her palm again. Emily couldn't see anyone out front, and the yard had been silent the whole time she'd been awake. Ted had assured her Captain would hear something before she did, so opening the door to let him outside would be safe. She'd never bothered worrying about what others thought before, but Ted had taken her in when he didn't want to. She had to at least *try* to follow what he said and be the best pretend wife she could be.

Her stomach did a strange flip at the idea of being anyone's wife, much less the tall and handsome former cop turned cowboy.

An older woman sat on the front step and turned to glance at her with a soft smile and a raised eyebrow.

"You are not the one I was expecting to let Captain out this morning." She had long dark hair that she wore in two braids down the back of her rounded shoulders.

"I..."

"No need to explain, child. Theodore told me as much as I need to know when he called last night. His secrets are my secrets... and yours." She smiled softly and went back to snapping beans.

She heard Ted dragging his feet behind her from his room. He looked like he'd only gotten a few winks of sleep, with his tousled hair and his jaw shadowed with dark stubble. She did her best to avert her eyes from what seemed like a far too personal display, though he was fully clothed. His basic tee and cotton sleep pants seemed intimate after just thinking of him as her husband.

"I... uh, think I'll go outside with Captain. The coffee is there if you need it." She'd need some herself once Ted was dressed for the day. She hadn't planned to go with the dog outside and didn't care to sit with the strange cook, but in the wide-open house, there was nowhere else to go.

He gave something that sounded like a grunt, and she closed the door behind her. In the short span the woman had disappeared, and Captain rushed toward her with his nose to the ground, then veered off and raced toward the back of the house. She sat on the porch, enjoying the feeling of being alone for a minute.

A little while later, Ted appeared, now in jeans, with a steaming mug in hand. He handed it to her. "I didn't figure you'd made this only for my benefit."

She hadn't, but she might have if she'd known he'd obviously slept so poorly. "Up late?"

He nodded, taking a bracing sip from his own cup of still scalding-hot coffee. "I needed to make a plan. I don't like going into a situation unprepared. This caught me unawares. We were both too tired to go over any defensive moves last night, but you need to learn them."

Had she said anything while she was dreaming to make him think she was in danger? The thought of being that vulnerable shuddered through her. "I'm sorry. Jake was the one who decided to surprise you." She'd hated that part of his plan from the start.

Ted shrugged. "He seemed to think this was the perfect place for you. You're here now, so let's make sure everything works out as he hopes."

She noticed he didn't say out loud that he would make sure she stayed alive. That was the biggest hope of all.

"I'm thinking I'll put you in the exercise arena today. It's fenced in, but Captain can walk right along with you. That fence will make it harder for anyone to get to you and see you. I wasn't worried about them coming up here until you saw those guys in the car at Ben's. He sent me pictures. He was right. Hard to tell if they were doing anything."

She took a tentative sip of her own coffee so she

wouldn't have to respond right away. The car had made her nervous, but she wouldn't live in fear. That wouldn't solve the case. She'd wondered if Ted and Ben would talk after she'd gone to bed. What had he told Ben about her? Of the two brothers, Ben may have been more confident, but she preferred to stay with Ted. He was more of a bear and protector. He understood her need to be left alone sometimes and held others. Just recalling his arms around her forced her gaze away from him. What was she thinking?

The men in the car could've just been waiting for someone else. Both men had talked on the phone while they sat in the street. She hated that something as innocent as parking a vehicle could be suspicious, all because of her.

She changed the subject. "You'll have to show me what to do in the exercise arena."

Captain came bounding back to the front step, his tongue lolling out to one side. "I'll get this guy fed and watered," he stroked Captain's head, "then we'll feed the horses. After that, I'll show you the excitement that is the arena."

She couldn't miss his sarcasm and hoped that his tone meant she would have a much more boring day than yesterday.

TED LEFT Emily with Captain to walk circles in the ring. It was the slowest way to exercise the horses, but it made sure they learned pacing and kept them moving while they weren't cropping grass. Some of the horses hadn't had a visit from their owners in quite a few months. He could only do his best to keep them ready. If the horse didn't treat their owner the same when they only visited four times a year, he couldn't help that.

His phone buzzed. He'd normally ignore it, but that was another thing that had to change with Emily there. Though, he didn't resent the change as much as he'd thought he would.

"Ted here," he answered.

"It's Jake. Just calling to see how the first few days went. She's a bit out of her element there with you, but that's good. They may not look for her rurally."

Ted paused, wanting to brook the subject slowly. An upfront warning might come as an insult. He didn't really think Jake had messed up.

"Out of her element is an understatement. She doesn't even know the difference between hay and straw, but at least the mix-up was easy to fix."

Jake laughed for a moment. "Other than first time on-the-job confusion, was everything quiet?" he pressed.

"About that..." He considered just how he could tell Jake about the phone and the car at Ben's. Sandy Creek Ranch might not be as perfect as Jake thought. "You may have been followed. I'll keep you advised."

Jake cleared his throat. "I didn't see anyone. Is there any way someone could've tracked her?"

She'd worked for a tech company and her uncle was at least part owner according to what he'd gleaned between Emily's bursts of sharing her past and what Jake had told him. "She still had a phone. It could've been tracked, and she did try to make a text the first day she was here, though I stopped her. If they managed to hack it and she left on the location settings while you were traveling... it might have acted like a beacon."

Jake grumbled something incoherent and the phone muffled. "She told me she would not try to contact her parents. I searched her purse for any other devices."

"I don't know how they may have found her, but I think they did. I wish you'd given me a choice about this. She's a handful, and I'm out here alone." He didn't want Jake thinking he was doing anything wrong, but he had the same issue with their living arrangement that everyone else would.

"You'll do your job. Just like I knew you would. You'll follow every rule, just like you always do. You'd have taken this job anyway, even if I'd given you weeks to decide, because she was in danger and had nowhere else to go. She *still* has nowhere else to go."

Ted opened his mouth to reply but slapped it shut again just as quickly as Emily screamed from outside. "I've got to go." He slammed the phone down on the small desk in his barn office and ran for the door. Emily wasn't far away.

Captain barked and growled. The noise was more menacing than he'd sounded in years. Ted drew his gun as he made it to the door. His training kicked in and he hid his body behind the doorframe, then took in the scene in a glance. There was a white car with two occupants. One driver, one heading toward Emily. His weapon would do no good. The man was too close, and he might hit Emily.

The man reached out his hand to Emily and grabbed her wrist. She screamed as Captain chomped into his arm.

"Get out of here!" She screamed as she scrambled away to the other side of the arena. Captain released the man's arm as he stood his ground in front of her. The attacker clamored back into the car and gunned away. A whimper drew both Emily and Ted to Captain's side. A small trickle of blood dripped down one side of his mouth. Ted gently pulled on Captain's lips until he could see the cause. He'd been holding onto the man's arm so tightly that when he pulled away, it had tugged loose one of Captain's teeth.

"I'll have to have Clara take him into the vet." Ted scratched Captain's neck softly as he glanced up at Emily. "You okay?" He knew she wasn't. These attackers were more brazen than he'd ever expected. Who just came to the front door? Yet he hadn't recognized the man, and the driver had left the car running and didn't get out. All the hallmarks of an unwelcome guest.

Emily rubbed her wrist. It was red with actual finger marks on her pale skin. Anger built deep and hot at the sight. He wasn't supposed to let anyone touch her.

"I'll be fine, just shaken up." Though her voice was so unsteady, he doubted she would be fine. She needed some way to calm down and relax so she could think. She'd gotten closest to the men, and if she could think rationally, then she could give him a statement. Cops often made their best reports if they were given twenty-four hours for their brains to rest and process everything they'd seen. She would be no different.

Any dog injury was a fairly urgent matter. They had so many germs in their mouths that the resident veterinarian at the precinct told them to err on the said of caution. If the dog is bleeding, get them treated. First, he had to quickly get Emily safe and secure.

"Come with me." He stood, and she followed, her body trembling with shock. He put his hand on her back to help reassure her, and she didn't flinch this time. Somehow, that helped him too. He was doing the right thing, even if she'd been found on his watch.

Captain followed, luckily without a limp. He could've easily been run over. He watched the dog as he followed to see if anything else looked wrong.

Emily had seen his parents' room when she'd found his mother's clothes, but he doubted she'd seen their bathroom. It was usually closed and completely interior, with no windows, giving the feeling of ultimate privacy. That would comfort her. She also seemed like the kind of girl who would be relieved in a big bath, much like his mother had when he was younger. Which was why the bathroom had a huge soaking tub. He hoped between the security and the tub, Emily would be right again soon.

He led her back there and opened the door. She glanced at him skeptically until she stepped close enough to see the huge room with Italian tile from floor to ceiling. The tub was bigger than some hot tubs he'd seen, but with three spigots, it filled fast enough.

"Wow..." Emily stared, unable to move.

"Why don't you get a change of clothes and relax. Lock yourself in until you feel better. I'll be around if you need me, but I'll bet you won't." He felt his cheeks heat.

She laughed and rested her hand on his arm. He couldn't believe she'd actually chosen to touch him. After just a few days, she knew him enough to trust him. "Thank you, Ted. I don't know how you knew exactly what I needed, but you did. I'm amazed and impressed. You really are a great investigator to figure that out." She smiled at him, then released his arm to go back to her room.

Captain whined as he watched her leave. He didn't

know what to do. His gaze swung from Emily back to him. "At ease, partner."

The dog visibly relaxed and followed him back to the kitchen. He'd have to clean out Captain's mouth and check him over before Clara took him in. If the tooth was too loose, it might have to be pulled. If Captain was out, he couldn't watch Emily.

He pulled out his phone and dialed the Lane Regional Medical Center. He let the registration desk know that someone could be coming in with a dog bite to the arm and if they did, Baton Rouge police officer Ben Owens wanted to question him. He then sent a text, telling Ben what had happened.

Jake would want to know, but he hated to call and tell him. Emily had only been there a few days and he'd already been faced with two potential situations. The car at Ben's could've been a coincidence, but the white car could not. There would be no reason for someone to come up and grab Emily.

Later, he'd have to ask Emily all sorts of questions about the car and the man that might ruin the little trust she had in him. His chest ached and he hoped she took a good long bath. The longer she was in there, the longer they could pretend he was worth trusting.

When they were done talking, he'd have to call Jake and admit that her stay should be over.

ELEVEN

The only company Ted was fit for was a tall glass of iced tea. He'd lit a small outdoor lamp that was supposed to keep the mosquitoes away, and Captain thumped his tail from under Ted's chair. The semidarkness that surrounded the front porch fit his mood. He'd been so sure he was a good cop. His team hadn't found evidence against him that wasn't there. Yet, his failure with Emily proved *they* were right. He wasn't a good cop.

He clenched his fist and closed his eyes, feeling watched even though he'd already checked around the house. With Captain. Twice. Emily was safe in the master bath, since there was no way in or out except the door, but he'd still let her down. He'd tried to focus on her. Yet, life had still gotten in the way.

She had to stay safe. He couldn't let Jake or Emily down again. He'd already failed his team in Baton Rouge. Though he'd thought for certain he hadn't handled the evidence, he must have for them to be able to fire him. There were channels police departments had to follow.

They were subject to public scrutiny. No one had come to his defense. Except Jake Thorne, and in a very unexpected way. Not even his own brother.

Jake had offered him a dream job, but only if he could perform. Success was mandatory. Not just for the job offer, but because he couldn't live with himself if anything happened to Emily while she was under his protection. If he couldn't do this, he may as well rip up his credentials and plan for a life on the ranch. Alone. Where he couldn't hurt anyone else.

Tipping his chair back against the house, he searched the stars for answers. The only one that stood out, even on a night full of stars, was the one painted on the front of his barn. Maybe he should give up. That's what all the signs pointed to.

Horses snuffled quietly in the nearby barn. His current life was not exactly what he'd intended. But was that God's plan? Could he be meant for something other than to serve and protect? A deep need welled inside him to keep Emily safe. But was he the man for that job or was he just trying to atone for his own mistakes?

The door swung open softly and the fruity smell of feminine soap kissed his senses. A very pleasant change from the aroma of hay and citronella. Emily laid a gentle hand on his shoulder.

"You okay? And Captain?" She searched for the dog, finally finding him lying under Ted's seat. She made her way to the deck chair next to his and sat, her hands braced at the side of her knees, clutching the wood seat like she was on a roller coaster, not a front porch.

She had on leggings with a long, loose tank top that showed her slender arms. The slightly blueish bruise on her wrist had faded, but he still wanted to growl when he saw it. Her hair was fresh from the bath, and she'd done nothing except run a comb through it.

He liked how good she looked naturally. Except for the hair color. She would look even better without the dye. The brief image he'd gotten of her with her almost white-blonde hair stuck in his memory. He squeezed his eyes shut momentarily. Her natural color was supposed to be a mystery. Except in that photo she'd brought, the one he couldn't erase from his mind.

"Yeah, maybe. Captain is sore. I brought him back to see Clara and she pronounced it fine. Not even wiggly. His gums were just sensitive, and he needs a tooth cleaning at his old age."

Captain sighed loudly under his chair, though it may have been a snore. Emily laughed. "I guess you know how he feels about being called old."

He wanted to laugh along with her, to let go of his worry, but he couldn't. How had those men made it up the driveway without anyone hearing and without Captain alerting? His dog even barked at the boarders when they came, which was why he'd kept the dog with Ben for a while. Only a car Captain knew well should've been able to get all the way to the house and up to the fence. Yet, Captain had attacked when he saw Emily in danger.

Emily waited for him to reply, then looked bashful for a moment and went on. "Your cook is also a vet?" She leaned forward and gently petted Captain's ears.

He'd made her uncomfortable. He had to get his own feelings under control. "Not a vet, but she's really good with animals and she can cook a mean mac and cheese."

Emily laughed and gave him a slight nod, letting the night surround them without talking for a few minutes.

"You can't let this get to you, Ted. I'm fine. Nothing happened." She held out her arm in the dim light. The hand-sized mark where she'd been gripped and tugged was still red and a little swollen, even in just the candle-light. "A little beat up, but none the worse for wear." She laughed. Her damp hair swung down in front of her face.

He took her arm for a moment and ran his thumb over the slightly raised area. Her skin tensed beneath his touch and was so much softer than his own. Unexpected. "They never should've gotten near you again. I'm going to have to call Jake and have him to find you somewhere else to stay. We're going to have to find a way to move you without anyone knowing. Somewhere safer than here." He hated that the door of a new career offer would be closing, but he refused to risk her life for his own gain.

She tugged her hand back and scowled for a moment in the lamplight. "I don't want to leave. I'm tired of running. I ran from Reno, then to Las Vegas, then here. So much running. This will never go away until we face it. I'm tired of being pawned off to strangers for the sake of *safety*."

He wasn't supposed to know any of that, but she didn't need a reprimand when she just wanted a listening ear. That he could do.

"I can't promise he'll let you stay. I think those guys tracked the phone he gave you. I'm going to mail it back to Jake in the hopes of drawing them away from you." He prayed that would work. But now that they'd seen her here, they would be fools not to stick around long enough to verify if it was actually her or just her phone in transit.

"I'm sorry. I shouldn't have touched it. I just needed... connection." She sighed. "I still do. It's like my heart hurts."

He needed that same connection, though he hated to admit it. A huge part of being an investigator was his team, especially his direct partner. Though, Ted hadn't heard from *him* at all since the administrative leave had started. Mark was surely with a new partner by now. He missed the comradery from both his time in the military and on the force.

"Connection is fine when you get home. You just might have to live without it for a little while." He wished he could help her find what she needed, even for the relatively short time she would be with him.

"Easy for you to say, you like to live out here away from everyone." Emily slapped at her arm. "That noise...? Like an electric hum? We get that back home some years. Cicadas, right? And what are these bugs biting me?" She scratched at the spot.

He was so used to the cicadas he didn't even think about them or their racket anymore. And mosquitoes were an annoying part of life, but one he simply accepted. His ranch was on a small, slow-moving river that was part swamp, part bayou. The humidity and rain in Louisiana made for hordes of them. Since the weather had been drier that summer, the mosquitoes weren't even as bad as usual.

"Want to move back inside?" The hum of all the insects, which he'd just ignored until then, came vividly into focus.

Captain thumped his tail again as if Ted had asked him instead of Emily.

"I think Captain has let it be known where he would like to be." Emily laughed.

She stood and offered a hand to help him out of the chair. The action surprised him yet again, since even the day before, she'd said having him nearby made her nervous. He grasped her hand and stood, then almost lost his footing as he stood up too close to her. He didn't want to invade her space, but there wasn't room between her and the chair for him. She stepped back, and he searched her eyes for the unease he expected to find. Instead, they twinkled with... laughter? She was made of stronger stuff than he'd thought. That was certain.

How could this amazing woman be so calm after the day she'd had? He took a deep breath and made sure his feet were solid before whistling to Captain to come out. He put out the lantern, then skirted around Emily to open the door for her.

When they got inside, Emily curled in a relaxed ball on his couch with her legs tucked under her. She'd finally made herself at home, which was perfect. Captain jumped up next to her and laid his head on her ankle. The scene was so calming, like family. "I'm glad you're comfortable here."

She smiled and stroked Captain's ears. "I hope you can find a way for me to stay. I don't want to go. I know I'm not fit for country life, but that might be because I'm jumpy. Every noise that's different from what I'm used to makes me tense."

"Ah, that's why the cicadas bothered you. They *are* really loud if you're not used to them, and they do have almost a mechanical engine sound."

Was that how he'd missed the little car? He was used to the insect noise, but could they block the sound of a car? He'd have to pay much better attention.

"They didn't bother me, but other things do. The distant sound of cars instead of the constant hum. It makes each one louder, more menacing. Every single vehicle is a different person. In the city, the noise of most cars is indistinguishable from any other." She took a deep breath. "The quiet can be just as unnerving as the noise that interrupts it."

She glanced out the window and smiled softly. "There are good things though. I never in my life thought I'd see a real-life lightening bug—as my grandma used to call them. She told me about them. And just like she said, they're calming the way they seem to float through the air."

He followed the direction of her gaze, as about a half dozen spots of greenish light blinked softly along the line of rhododendrons beside the front walk. He'd always enjoyed them. From the time he was young enough to catch them in a jar, all the way until now when they provided the perfect calm to a rough day.

An SUV pulled up outside, blinding the little bug light display, and Ted reached for his gun. Captain barked and jumped off the sofa, positioning himself in front of Emily. Ted hadn't been expecting anyone. No one had called, and his clients never showed up after dark. He went to the window but didn't recognize the truck parked outside.

He took a deep breath. An attacker wouldn't come to the front door and knock. Though these particular criminals had been pretty brazen. Emily tucked herself tighter into the couch but didn't run. He made his way around to the door.

"Ted Owens? It's Jake. Open up."

Ted let out a long breath and laughed as the tension left his body. Jake was an officer through and through. He opened the door and Jake came inside. He wore jeans and a button-up cotton shirt with pointed-toe cowboy boots. From their time together in the service, Ted knew Jake was originally from Texas and had never quite left.

"I decided to turn around and come back after talking to you yesterday. I don't have anywhere else I can place Emily right now and it's urgent that she is safe. That means helping where I can."

Ted motioned for him to sit, then went to the fridge to get him a glass of tea. "That was yesterday. They tried again today. I think you need to take Emily's phone with you."

"That was my plan. I'll wait to leave until tomorrow morning. Most of the time when we have a direct protect order, there would be two officers watching the one in protection. One at night, one during the day. I'll take the night watch tonight. I have a decoy out in my car, and it'll look like there's two of us leaving when only one came. If I have the phone with me, it might fool anyone if they aren't able to watch the house itself too closely. Too bad you don't have a garage." Jake accepted the drink with a nod. "But secondarily, we have to get someone else here to help you."

Emily glanced at him but didn't seem near as at ease with Jake. She'd stayed with him for days, yet Jake seemed to bother her. She reached for the comfort of Captain as Jake made himself comfortable on the other end of the couch. That fact brought some of his assurance back. She hadn't wanted to trust him but did. She wanted to stay with him.

"Did you see anyone when you drove in?" Ted took a position in the middle of the room, where he could easily watch the driveway out the front window.

Jake shook his head. "It's dark though, and there are

no lights on the road or anywhere until I got up to the house."

Jake pursed his lips. "We were hoping that when Emily's uncle picked a new accountant, we could incite them into becoming an inside plant. That's the best way to get evidence. Cole Fairchild never does as we assume though."

Ted forced his face to stay free of shock. Jake had just slipped up in a major way. Ted wasn't supposed to know real names. Especially not surnames. He now had enough to find out who Emily really was, if he wanted to break the rules. Jake was right, though. He was by the book. While the information wouldn't ever be forgotten, he'd make sure no one else ever knew the knowledge he held.

Emily sat up straighter in her seat. "You assume my uncle is behind all this, but he's not. There's someone else in the company pulling all the strings, or they're dead. My uncle is innocent. He helped me get that job. There's no reason he would put me in that position, then try to hurt me."

Jake took a deep breath. "I know you want to believe the best of your uncle, but he's not the man you think he is. He certainly is innocent until proven guilty. I don't doubt that there's more than one person in on this scheme. But I would bet your uncle's hands aren't clean after seeing who he hired to replace you. The new accountant is a dirty, disbarred lawyer from Las Vegas. It was probably easier to cut in the accountant than to try to keep them quiet or kill them off after losing three."

Emily gasped and Ted wished Jake would tone down his tactics. "Please remember one of those accountants is in the room." Ted leveled a pointed gaze at him.

"I'm well aware. An accountant who must remain alive and well-protected. Where's that phone?"

Ted left the room to go get it, though he hated leaving Emily alone with Jake. When he returned, they were both silent. He tossed the phone to Jake. "It's fully charged. Are you heading back to wherever it was you started to take them off the scent?"

He nodded. "Understand. This might only buy you a day or two, or none at all if they're really savvy and watching closer than we think. Be careful where you go, and don't let her out of your sight. It would be best if she doesn't even leave the house."

He didn't need to glance at Emily to know how she would take that news. His house had just become another prison. He wished he could keep her in sight at all times, but he had to sleep. At least for one night, while Jake was there, they would have eyes on the outside.

TWELVE

Emily woke with the sun to help Ted. He wanted to make sure Jake got off the property without anyone seeing him. Ted went out right away to saddle up so he could ride along the driveway and make sure there were no cars or men hidden in the trees, but that would leave her alone at the house. She hated the unease she felt without Ted or Captain nearby. She'd stayed with Jake and he was a fine officer. But he wasn't Ted.

Jake sat at the kitchen table, drinking coffee. She slowed her footsteps, hoping Ted would be nearby, but neither he nor Captain were there. She diverted her path to the coffee maker. With Jake there, she couldn't risk going outside. If Ted wasn't there to take her, she couldn't go. He probably wouldn't let her go even if Ted was.

"Ted told me last night he was waiting to teach you defensive maneuvers until you had a few minutes where you weren't on high alert, but that time is now. He's asking Clara to do the required tasks on the ranch today so he can stay in here and train with you. I don't need to tell you how important this is."

Shivers tingled up her arms. If she'd known some way to defend herself at first, she might have been able to get away on her own. She may never have been pulled into the car at all. "I know."

"I believe this is the perfect place for you. Ted is better than he thinks he is. An officer, no matter what rank or division they're in, has a gut instinct they learn to follow. My gut tells me this is absolutely right. *He* is absolutely right."

She would call it faith, but he'd never made any mention of beliefs. "I believe you're right but if he doesn't..."

He nodded but gave away nothing. The man was a closed book and she suspected he'd learned to be that way.

"Are you married, Jake?" She hoped he had someone with whom he could relax and be himself. If he didn't, he may forever lose who he really was in the act of putting up his wall of protection. His self-defense would bring him nothing but loneliness.

"No, ma'am." He paced to the window and pulled the curtain as she'd seen him do so often at the hotels on the way to Zachary.

"I hope that changes for you. Someday."

He laughed shortly. "Not with the hours and travel, but thank you. Here comes Ted."

He'd brushed her off so easily, yet who didn't long for someone to share their life with? The idea brought her up short. Who would she live her life with? Would she be old and lonely, just like she was predicting for Jake?

The door swung open and Captain burst in, his

tongue lolling as he rushed for his water dish. Ted tapped his boots over the rug and caught her gaze for a moment before he focused on Jake.

"The road is clear. You'd best get gone before that changes."

"You've got everything you need? You might not get another chance to have someone else I trust watching Emily." Jake stood his ground.

Ted shook his head. "We'll be busy today but staying here should make this easier."

"Then stay here as much as you can." He tipped his hat and left.

In his absence, the room felt charged, the silence almost deafening. There was so much to say and nowhere to start.

Emily took a breath and broke the silence. "If he came back, he probably never contacted my mother." Mom would be frantic. It had been over a week since they'd spoken, and she'd never let a full day go between texts.

"You can't worry about her right now. She's an adult and can handle a little stress. Jake will get a hold of her by whatever means is safe when he gets back to his office. She'll know that you're protected. You just have to give him time."

She accepted his reply but didn't agree. He didn't know how much her mother worried. "I did give him time. He gave his word."

Ted sighed and sat next to her. "Em, he's under a lot of pressure. I'm sure he didn't want to come back. That phone was a hazard. Give him the chance to protect you."

Waiting was infuriating, and she hated that her mother had to wait longer, partly because of her own lack of foresight. "Did you see anything out there?"

He accepted the change in topic without any sign he'd noticed. "I didn't see any tracks leading off the driveway. At least they don't seem to be wandering the property yet."

She heaved a sarcastic laugh. "Because driving right up to the house is better." She glanced down at her arm. The red marks were gone, but she only had to look to feel the stranger's hands on her again. Just like the first time. Though, this time he hadn't been masked and she didn't recognize him from Uncle Cole's company. "I won't sit back and wait for them to come back."

He sat down, and Captain laid down in front of his chair. "I don't expect you to just sit and take whatever life throws at you. I do expect you to understand that none of this is without purpose."

She bristled and turned her face away. "So, I'm learning to bide my time?"

"Yes. Not everything can happen in the timeline you'd like it to. I had to learn that too when I was put on administrative leave."

She whipped back to face him. This was new information. If he was willing to talk about it, then it was time to tell her what this was all about. "What happened?"

He sighed, and his eyes unfocused from the room. "I guess if I want you to trust me, I'll have to trust you, too. But I'm more concerned it'll do the opposite." He took a deep breath and scrubbed his hand down his face.

His discomfort rolled off him like waves, and she almost wished she hadn't pushed the subject. He would tell her when he was ready. Maybe. Ted was hard and cold on the outside, but what he showed when his personality came out was far different. She opened her mouth to stop him, but he didn't look up at her as he started talking.

"I was working on a big case involving a local doctor and some reports of abuse and misconduct. The evidence was fragile, as medical things usually are. So, even though I'm usually one of the guys that handles evidence collection, on this case I handed it over to a forensics team. I stuck with the human side, witness statements, things like that. About a month in, the doctor's lawyer filed a motion to dismiss the case because of evidence tampering, against me. I thought it was slam dunk, since I never handled the evidence."

He paused for a moment, lost in the past. "They never found out who put my name on the reports, but they couldn't conclusively discount the charge. I was dismissed, as was the case. The doctor got away. He left the area about three days ago."

"The day I arrived," she whispered, now understanding why he'd been so gruff. "You didn't do anything wrong."

He shook his head but wouldn't look her in the eye. "I must have. No conclusive evidence was ever found to prove my innocence, and my team didn't back me up."

"But there was none to prove your guilt, either," she reminded him. "Didn't Jake just say last night, innocent until proven guilty. That's how the justice system is supposed to work."

His jaw hardened. "Maybe, but not always. And certainly not in the court of public opinion."

"I trust you." She stared him straight in the eyes, though he still wouldn't meet hers. Without even testing her theory, she found it was true. Of all the people she'd talked to, from the federal agents to her uncle, the one she trusted the most was Ted.

"Thank you for that." He stood and offered his hand

to help her up. "Come with me. I want to show you something."

His dark eyes crinkled slightly, and she was happy for the change of subject. She slid on a pair of flipflops and followed him out to the barn. Even with his report that the road was safe, she still kept an ear open and an eye over her shoulder.

He brought her into the barn and over to his office, away from the horses. The mother cat lay in her little nest with her brood, content and safe.

"Pick up Cat."

"You named her Cat?" She couldn't help but laugh. "That's original." She bent and snuggled the soft barn cat in her arms.

Ted ignored her chiding. "Good. When she's close to you, it's easy to hold her, right?" He eyed her, complete seriousness over his features.

"Yes, I mean, she's sharp, but not heavy." Emily shifted the cat slightly as Cat's claws kneaded her arm.

"Okay, hold her around the waist and stretch out your arms about a foot from your body."

"What?" She changed her hold and held the animal out, as instructed. Cat went limp, almost like jelly, and started to slide through her grip. Emily quickly groped for the cat and pulled her back up against her stomach. "Okay, what was that for?"

"When something is solid, maybe not rigid, but solid, it's easy to hold."

Clarity dawned. "So, you want me to be like a cat when I'm attacked."

"In more ways than one, yes." He nodded, reaching for the cat. Their hands brushed as she gave Cat to her owner, and that strange jolt trembled up her arm.

He put the cat back in her nest and led Emily back out of the barn to the house. Within a few minutes, he'd pushed all the furniture against the wall so there was plenty of room in the living room. The space was huge. Ted took Captain to his room and closed him inside.

"I don't want him coming to your defense. I'm going to get beat up enough without getting bitten by accident. Captain is a great judge of character, but he knows he needs to protect you and he will. Even against me."

She couldn't imagine a scenario where the dog would ever need to do that. She strode to the middle of one end of the room, her heart pounding hard. She'd never been an active person, and that fact would be obvious to Ted soon. She didn't want him to think of her as weak. If he did, he'd never let her out of his sight.

"I've never done anything like this."

"I wouldn't expect that you had." He stretched his shoulder muscles and she hoped he would take as much care with her as he'd taken with the kittens.

"I mean...I don't run. I usually wear heels. I worked in retail until my uncle needed my help. Gym class in high school was a long time ago." She babbled on then bit her lip and hoped he didn't laugh at her.

"I would have guessed just that. You're slender, but don't have runner's muscles. Trim without an athletic body."

He'd noticed how she looked? For some reason that warmed her insides even more than the thought of exercise. "Oh, I didn't realize you'd figured that out already." Heat raced from her middle all the way to her cheeks.

"I was an investigator. I make deductions based on facts." He leaned and stretched his hamstrings.

"Right. Facts." She should've known better than to

think he'd noticed *her*. No one ever noticed her, beyond making the assumption she was stupid because she liked clothes. She was too attached to her family, too skinny, too plain. That's what they all said. Maybe they were right, but turning away from her mother and father didn't seem the way to go either.

"So, what do I do?"

"Both times you've been attacked from the front. So, I'll teach you what you can do first from the front, then from behind. He came within a few feet of her and crouched slightly like he might pounce, his arms wide and raised to waist height like he might tackle her.

"The first thing I—and any attacker—will do is try to get a handhold on you. You had people come to your rescue the first time and Captain the second time. With this, or a combination of both, you may not need to rely on either."

She replicated his stance.

"Good. Now, when I reach for you, I want you to thrust your elbow down and then around in a half circle, bringing it back to center. My arm won't bend that way and if you're fast enough, I'll be forced to release you out of instinct." He showed her the movement first, then came at her before she could even think.

His hand connected with her arm, and she shoved her elbow down, then swung her fist out and back in position.

"Good, you're free, run!" Ted charged toward her. She turned and the next second he had her around the waist. A strange mixture of excitement and a little fear of the unknown knotted through her as Ted yanked her against his chest. Though he was trying to simulate an attack, she didn't believe it.

"Now, remember the cat in the barn," he said into

her ear.

All she could think of was purring. "Yes?"

"Go limp, like the cat. Make it difficult for me to hold you. Just remember that your legs should still hold you upright, you'll need to run. When you go limp, oftentimes your attacker will loosen his hold to adjust his grasp. Use that against him. Wait for him to do that, then bash him with the back of your head."

"I can't do that to you!" She refused to hurt the man who was her last line of defense. What if she sent him to the hospital?

"I'll know it's coming and get out of the way. Do it. I need to know you can." He tightened his hold on her. Slightly lifting her off her feet, then set her down.

If he'd been trying to raise her fear factor, he'd done it. She forced herself to go limp like the cat and a moment later, Ted loosened his grip. She almost fell and he tightened again.

"See, that's why you have to relax your upper body, but try to maintain the tension below your waist. Try again, you're doing great."

His praise fortified her, and she took a deep breath, taking in his scent and his strength. "I can do this."

He gripped her again, and she focused on relaxing her whole upper half, even to her knees, but her feet were ready to run. She felt him release her and she sprang into action, tossing her head back, then charging forward. He was right, he'd moved in time and her head didn't connect with anything, but she'd gotten away.

She turned to face him, trying to get her breathing under control. "How did I do?"

"As long as we can keep you in shoes that aren't flipflops, I think you've got a good shot. The other thing you can do as a last resort is to grind your heel into his feet if you're wearing boots or any hard shoe, especially the pointy ones."

She giggled. "I don't think I'll be wearing any heels in the barn."

He chuckled and glanced at her hands. "You can use your nails, too. Aim for tender parts, eyes, nose, neck. If you're facing him, a judicious knee can work, but be careful with that. Most men are ready for that attack. Once they have a hold of your knee, you're caught. You can't really do the arm move with your leg."

He had a point. She would've immediately thought a knee to the groin was the first option, but if an attacker was ready for that, it was better to do the unexpected. She pursed her lips. "Now I feel ready to prove my uncle is innocent."

Ted blew out a long breath, then set to arranging the furniture back where it belonged. His phone rang and he answered with a short, "Hello."

"Raymond?" He rubbed his eyes and sighed. "Thanks."

Ted hung up the phone and glanced at her. "Well, that car yesterday was not your attackers. It was the new owner of Molly Red. He didn't realize he should call first, and he wanted to stop you when you were leading the horse around. He's sorry for being so aggressive. Ben checked out the story. He was a jerk, but he's not with Deerfield."

She pursed her lips and stood taller. "It's also possible the guys outside of Ben's weren't doing anything either. We could be worried over nothing. They didn't follow me. I'm safe here. I refuse to believe otherwise until I'm proven wrong." And she hoped she never was.

THIRTEEN

A harsh growl woke Emily from a sound sleep. It felt like only a handful of minutes had passed since she'd gone to bed. In her stupor, she reached for the dog. When had she let Captain into her room? He stood on her bed, over her, growling at the window.

The thin lace curtain blew lightly in the soft breeze. Emily blinked to clear her eyes and patted Captain's side. "It's okay, boy. There's nothing there. It's just the curtain. The wind must have picked up a little. That's all." Her fuzzy brain questioned if she'd opened the window, but she couldn't remember.

Captain ignored her and barked loudly. The house shuddered slightly as a door slammed at the end of the hall. Emily grimaced as Ted's footfalls raced toward her room. Another night of poor sleep for him, and all her fault. If she weren't here, his life would be back to normal. Yet she'd practically begged him to let her stay.

Her door swung open and banged against the wall. Ted burst in, his gun drawn, pointed down. His gaze caught her first, but only for a moment before he swept the entire room. Ted aimed at the window and side-stepped along the wall toward it. Silent as a cat. Even Captain quieted now that Ted was there. Finally, he moved the wispy curtain aside to reveal a missing screen.

Emily's heart clenched, then raced. Her head spun. Of course she hadn't opened the window, she was supposed to stay locked in. Someone had been within feet of her while she slept. The ruse of the phone hadn't worked. She couldn't form words, though she had a million questions.

"I'll get the screen put back on. You take Captain and go out into the living room. Don't move from there."

Before she made it all the way, her whole body began to tremble. She'd refused to allow herself to believe someone wanted her dead, but now she couldn't deny it. There was no way this could've been anything but harmful intent. They didn't just want to kidnap her and find out what she knew, they wanted her to disappear in the dead of night.

Once she sat, Captain laid his head on her lap, his huge brown eyes begging for approval. "You did well." She ruffled his ears but couldn't quit shaking. He nuzzled in closer, his cold nose against her arm. His huge brown eyes begged her to trust him.

Ted strode out of her bedroom and holstered his gun. He'd slept in his clothes, prepared. "I've put the screen back on. From now on, we keep the windows closed, locked, and braced. We're also going to move you to the basement where the windows are too small to gain access."

She had yet to go downstairs but hated the idea already. Everywhere she went she was a prisoner, and her world was getting smaller and smaller. She'd gone from living on her own, doing what she wanted, to watching her every step, now under lock and key.

"I don't remember opening the window... You really think I should be in the basement?" She didn't want to argue with him, especially in the middle of the night, but the decision seemed rash. Especially if they could lock the windows.

"I should've locked the windows before and made certain they were locked every night. I'm failing at this." He raked his hand through his hair. Frustration roughened his voice.

Emily stood and slowly approached him. She'd asked a lot of him, and asking him to listen to her right now didn't need to be another thing to add to the list. She could sleep for one night in the basement, but something would have to give soon. She was in desperate need of interaction. Her emotional bucket had only a few drops left.

She reached out and took his hand, as much for her own support as for him.

"You're shaking." He squeezed her hand tighter, and his eyes widened. "I'm sorry, Em."

She found herself in his arms, but unsure how she got there. Had she stepped into his warm embrace, or had he pulled her close? Whatever the way, she was there, and his arms were strong and protective.

The fear she'd experienced whenever men were around since her first attempted kidnapping was gone. She'd only had it for about an hour with Ted, as if she'd known somewhere deep inside that despite his gruff exterior, he was not only trustworthy, but a genuinely good man.

Emily rested her head against his chest as the fatigue of all the stress hit her. For just a moment, she forgot about men chasing her and she breathed a normal breath. He chuckled slightly, rumbling low in her ear, and he loosened his grip on her. She wasn't ready to let him go, but there again, she had no right to ask even more of him. Not even comfort.

"I'll help you move some bedding and whatever else you need downstairs. We'll talk about a more permanent solution tomorrow after we've both had more sleep." He stepped away from her.

Emily crossed her arms to keep him from seeing that she was still shaking. She doubted she would get much sleep at all. "I should keep Captain with me?" She hoped the dog would stay with her. It was bad enough being relegated to a different floor than the man who was supposed to protect her, but to be without the dog too would be torture.

"Of course. He's yours. While you're here."

She was already growing to love the dog, and maybe his owner wasn't so bad either. "Good. I hate basements and I don't want to be alone."

He exhaled slowly and nodded his understanding. "You won't be. There are two rooms down there. A living room and a game room. Both have sofas. You'll go into the living room, because the sofa is newer and more comfortable. I'll be in the game room. I'm not leaving you alone again."

From now on, she wouldn't fight him or try to go behind his back. They had to work together to keep those men away, and maybe to solve her uncle's case. Once they found the real criminals, she could go home, testify, and spend a week with her mother catching up.

The thought didn't settle her as much as she thought it would. What would happen to Ted? Would he come to her trial? Would he stand by her? Doubtful. He had his own life to live. She wasn't even sure if Jake would allow Ted to see her after the trial.

"You don't have to do that. If they can't get in, then you'll be uncomfortable for nothing." He had yet to move, and she liked that he didn't want to leave her space any more than she wanted him to go. The closer he stood, the calmer she felt.

He shrugged. "That may be, but you're my job right now."

She finally stepped back and tried not to let the words slice her. A job. She was only a job. His comfort wasn't because there was anything between them, he just didn't want her to go into hysterics. She'd thought because he understood her ultra-girly need to soak in a huge tub with bubbles earlier that he somehow understood her.

"Right. Job. I'll go get my pillow and blankets. No need for help. I can make my own bed, been doing it for years." She dodged around him to go to her room.

When she reached the door, she paused. The room had a different feel now. It wasn't private or comforting. Someone had taken off her screen and may have come inside if not for Captain. He *may* have come inside, and Captain scared him back out.

"You sure you don't want me to go in there to get your things? I understand." Ted's voice was calm directly behind her, his presence strong and reassuring at her shoulder.

He wasn't pushing her to do anything, nor was he coddling her. Why did the guy who understood her ridiculous need to be both a strong woman *and* a scaredy cat once in a while, also have to be the one hired to protect her? She'd never be able to look at him without thinking of abductions.

"I..." Her voice quit altogether.

"I've always found it interesting that the psalmist talks about the valley of the shadow of death and fearing no evil. Fear is perfectly justified without faith. That's what that means. Without God, we fear the shadow of death. With faith, we have the ability—the blessing —not to."

Emily wanted to hug him again to thank him for understanding. The room felt like that shadow.

"Just take Captain downstairs and get comfortable with him, then learn where all the lights are. If you need one on tonight, I'll deal with it." He said no more and gently moved her to the side as he entered her room.

He seemed to have no issue with strangers breaking into his house, or if he did, he covered his anger better than she did. He wasted no movements as he folded all of her blankets at once in quarters, then topped the huge sandwich with her pillow. He turned and heat climbed up her neck and settled in her cheeks at the realization that she'd been staring instead of doing what he'd told her to do. He sure wasn't hard on the eyes.

Ted smiled softly. "I'll just get my bedding and meet you downstairs." He prodded her verbally to get going and Captain whined from behind her.

She didn't understand how Captain seemed to understand every word out of Ted's mouth, but it sure seemed as if he did. The dog was more intelligent than some people she'd met. She wasn't sure where the basement was, since Ted hadn't shown her. However, Captain did, and he bounded toward the back of the kitchen.

There she found a door she'd thought was a pantry. A well-lit, carpeted stairwell led down to a wide-open room with two sectional sofas and a large television mounted on the wall. Lamps sat on every end table and graced each corner. The color palette was brown in every imaginable hue.

The room was unexpected, as basements were rare in Reno and even more rare in Louisiana. Baton Rouge just saw too much rain. The water table was too high, and frankly there wasn't much need. She took a deep breath, expecting the carpet to hold a musty smell, but she couldn't detect anything, though the temperature was much cooler.

Ted shuffled down the stairs behind her. "If you're wondering how this marvel was accomplished, my great-grandfather was from the north, where cellars are more common. He wanted one because if he was going to try to grow anything, he wanted it to keep for months. So, he moved dirt. A lot of dirt. To build up the area. He raised the grade around the vicinity of the house by four feet. That's why the porch seems higher than most. He still couldn't bury the house any deeper in the ground than what he'd added."

She glanced around the room to the cinderblock walls. "Your grandfather did not build this." Unless he had when he was a very old man.

"No. He didn't. This home was built by my parents, who shored up the whole area even more, though there's still three feet of basement sticking out of the ground. They had to tear down the original house."

Emily took her blankets from his arms then claimed her spot on one of the sectionals. "Why, did it flood?"

Most of the state of Louisiana was below sea level. Having a basement seemed crazy.

Ted headed through the room and back to an open doorway, then paused. "No. It burned down when lightning struck. I'll be here if you need anything."

He pulled a curtain between the two areas, separating them but not completely. Emily sighed, punching her pillow back into shape, then arranged her blankets. No matter how nice and comfortable Ted's basement seemed, she hated them. They were dark holes and she always felt trapped.

Captain jumped up at her feet and got comfortable, laying his big head on her calf. She fixed her blankets to accommodate him, then patted his head. "I hope I don't have to hear you growl again for a long time."

Emily laid her head down and closed her eyes, but morning couldn't come fast enough.

THE SOFA in the game room wasn't really fit for sleeping. It had a twill fabric that was rough and left embedded grid patterns on anyone who sat too long. By six a.m., Ted was finished trying to sleep and just gave up.

After he folded up his blankets, he got his phone and sent Jake a text, letting him know there had been a break-in at his house. This one couldn't be shrugged off. The phone ruse hadn't worked. Someone was paying far too close attention to his house. It simply wasn't safe to keep Emily there any longer, as much as he hated to admit that fact after seeing her curled up so comfortably in his living room just the evening before.

Ted sighed as he hit send on the text. Emily belonged

somewhere safe, but that didn't make the decision easy. When she left, he'd never see her again. That was part of the process. Part of why he could never know her real name. But when he'd held her, though he hadn't really intended to, he'd felt...alive.

His whole purpose had always been to serve and protect, and she was the answer. Yet, what did that mean when the job was done? The Lord always seemed to make matters clear to everyone else. But not him, not anymore. His way was a muddy mess. Would his purpose in life be over after Emily made it to trial?

That seemed crazy, but Jake's request to watch Emily had been a strange one to begin with. This wasn't usually how witness protection was handled unless there was a specific order of protection. His house had never been registered as a safe house. He could offer to watch over people for Jake forever, but he discarded the thought as soon as it came. This job felt right, but he hadn't done all that well at it, and he had no desire to watch anyone but Emily.

Jake sent him a reply giving him permission to ask his brother Ben to help if possible, making Emily's case a full protection order. There was still nowhere else for Emily to go and no way to get her safely anywhere else even if they did. He suggested following through with putting her on lockdown, completely secure, if Ted thought that was the best course of action.

Emily would hate that, and would probably hate him too, if he even made the suggestion. She'd already balked at staying in the basement because she felt caged. He couldn't blame her. *He* even felt caged, what with being unable to ride like he usually did, unable to go to town, and even his job had suffered. He'd done little with the horses except feed them and ride his own. Clara had done the rest and she would not be willing to keep that up indefinitely.

Having his brother around would be a good idea, not just for another pair of eyes on Emily. Though, he could only help when he wasn't on duty. Ben would also put distance between him and Emily that had to stay there. When he'd held her, he felt right. He could get far too used to that, making not only his job of protecting her harder, but also saying goodbye.

Ben would provide the reminder that Emily was supposed to be his job. There could be nothing lasting between them. She made a wonderful addition to his house, but she would never choose to stay. He had to remember that, or get lost in her sweet stubbornness.

He quickly shot off a text to Ben, asking for him to come stay out at the ranch and that he would explain why when Ben got there. There was too much to explain in a text and he wasn't certain anything was secure anymore. He couldn't shake the feeling that these men were always one step ahead. Like they had a man inside listening to everything. That wasn't possible, not with Emily's phone gone. Unless she'd brought something else from home with her and hadn't told him...

He crept from the game room and slowly tiptoed toward the stairs. Emily slept, completely silent curled on the sofa. Captain laid at her feet and only shifted his head slightly as Ted went by. She wouldn't have deceived him again. Not after all she'd been through. Yet, he couldn't shake the need to check her room.

When he made it all the way up the stairs and into the room she'd stayed in, he turned on the light. She hadn't changed much of anything inside. He immediately glanced at the window. Those who weren't supposed to know she was there, obviously did. They knew more about her than he did.

Anger nipped at his nerves. He wanted to know more about her, but he was following the rules. He *always* followed the rules, and what did it get him? He tugged open her top drawer and the picture of Emily and her mother had disappeared. He pushed aside everything, trying to find them, knowing deeply that she wouldn't have moved them.

There was very little in the drawer, only a few pairs of socks and a few other pieces. He put everything back sort of the way it had been in the drawer and closed it. After going through two more drawers, he remembered she had very little in the way of clothing or anything. He opened her suitcase, but it was completely empty. There were no electronic devices that he could find. And no pictures.

So how did these attackers know what was going on? And how had they made it all the way into her room, found the pictures, and left? His skin crawled with the thought of someone being in his house and so near her, especially near enough to her to look for the pictures without getting bitten by Captain. Thank the Lord, his brother would be there soon. He needed help to get this situation in hand.

He stared around the bedroom and couldn't help feeling like someone was looking over his shoulder. Somehow, they were getting information. The only way to be completely certain they couldn't collect it was if they couldn't get close enough. Hopefully Ben would get the text and could come right out by first light. He would have to go for a ride in the morning. There was a theory to test, and he couldn't leave Emily alone to do it.

FOURTEEN

There was nothing worse than grumbling through the night about being awake only to find out she must have slept at some point. Emily tossed her blankets over the back of the couch without bothering to fold them. She glowered at the mess for a moment before stomping up the stairs, Captain whining at her heels.

He would need to go out soon, but she wasn't ready to do chores or anything else. What she wanted was an argument. She needed to let off all her pent-up anger at the injustice of being locked up when her attacker was free. Free to continue to chase her. It wasn't Ted's fault but getting a few hours of sleep gave her energy, and she needed to get a few things off her mind.

Ted had managed to leave, and she hadn't known it. Hadn't heard a sound. So she must have fallen asleep, but her mind sure felt like it had been active all night. Mostly with thoughts of the walls caving in on her. The brown walls were almost the same color as dirt, and that was nightmare fuel. Trying to sleep downstairs had only made her distaste grow. The whole night had left her feeling like strange men in masks who smelled like cinnamon gum were hanging over her bed, shoveling dirt on her.

She slammed open the kitchen cabinet where she'd remembered putting the fresh coffee. Captain whimpered and belly-crawled under the table. Emily frowned and tried to rein in her pique. It wasn't Captain's fault she couldn't stand where she was in life. Well, not everything was so bad. At least she'd met Ted.

"You going to tear off the doors on my cabinets?" Ted chuckled behind her.

She grabbed a heavy mug and tossed it at him. He caught it easily and strode toward her. The hair on her neck prickled to life, but she knew Ted wouldn't be mad.

"Careful. You make a mess, you get to clean it up." He set the cup down on the counter next to her. He smelled of hay and hard work. He had to have gotten up very early, since it was barely six. He'd had Clara work the whole day before, but she was older, and he'd probably had a lot of catching up to do for taking a day off. A day he'd been forced to take off because of her.

"Didn't you sleep?" She ran water in the carafe and waited for his reply. Complaining to Ted about her predicament would only make his stress worse. As much as she needed the release, this wasn't Ted's fault. She'd just have to deal with her anger and resentment at being held hostage, while the criminals were free, without talking to Ted.

"Not after your visitor last night."

"I don't know that it was anyone. A bird could've hit the screen and knocked it in. If it were a person, wouldn't they have dropped the screen on the outside?" She hoped her overzealous mind had come up with at least one plausible excuse for her window to have been breached in the middle of the night that didn't lead to her almost abduction...again.

"A bird?" His eyebrow rose and he didn't have to say more.

It was a silly, but possible, scenario. While she hated that she sounded naive, that was preferable to admitting she might be in danger. Because then she had to admit she couldn't help Cole if she was running for her life. "Yes, maybe it was simply a poorly timed accident. Maybe they are gone, chasing after Jake with the phone like we planned. You never know."

The coffee machine burbled loudly, and Emily didn't want to talk over it. She already felt silly for even hoping she could go outside. As it was, she doubted Ted would let her go anywhere out of his line of sight. The ranch that had seemed so big and welcoming a few days ago, now felt tiny. She should've taken him up on the offer to ride that first night. If she'd known she would only get one chance, she would've.

"I'm sorry, Emily. I know you're looking for any excuse you possibly can to get me to let you sleep back up here. I know you hate the basement, but I have to think about your safety."

Despite her promise to herself not to dump on Ted, his immediate, almost practiced response left her fuming. How was this even a little fair? She might be stuck here months with only the basement walls to look at?

"You don't understand. I don't ever just sit around inside. I go shopping. I talk on my phone. I have never gone this long without talking to my mother. I need to see people. I need to talk. I need to be outside, go visiting, do work, walk, anything but sit here and pretend like this is normal. Because it's not." Maybe she should've asked for decaf. She tapped her fingers on the counter, wanting nothing more than for the pot to fill so she could take her mug to the table, sit, and try not to cry.

He held back from her and that made her even madder. Just the day before he'd comforted her. Maybe that's what her sudden emotionality boiled down to. She wanted him to hold her again.

"I need to talk to my mom. Can I send her a letter? Anything?"

He slowly shook his head, though his eyes were apologetic. "I can't let you talk to your mom. No matter what. Not any way." He sliced the air with his hand like his decision was final.

"No one at Deerfield Electronics knows my family except my uncle and my father," she offered. He was innocent, so even if Uncle Cole found out later that she'd called, it wouldn't matter.

"If that were true, it would be all the more reason you shouldn't call." Ted didn't raise his voice, but he didn't need to. She could see his pupils dilate and his hand tense.

"What do you mean, 'if that were true'? It *is* true. I didn't know or talk to anyone at Deerfield. Uncle Cole even handled my new hire paperwork so no one would accuse him of nepotism when he hired me." She gripped the counter as her knees weakened. Did Ted know something about her mother that Jake hadn't told her?

"Unless you threw away the pictures you brought of you and your mom, they're gone. They were taken."

Gone? Her last connection to her mother was gone? She felt a deep ache grow in her chest. "No." Coffee forgotten, she ran to her door and stopped dead in the doorway, still unable to force herself to go inside. "Did you tell Jake they were there? He had to have taken them."

"I didn't. He didn't take your photos. Jake's on your side, even if it doesn't feel like it." He came beside her but didn't reach out. She appreciated that he understood when she needed him to keep back. Because if he touched her just then, she would cry. Someone had severed her last connection.

"You believe them? You believe Jake when he says my uncle is part of all this? He's not. He's a good man. I'll make sure everyone knows it when I go back to testify. You have to let Jake know what I did. Let him know that my mother is now in danger. I can't believe they're gone." She wanted to sob, but what good would that do? If she could only call her. "Maybe they can bring her here? Maybe there's hope..." Now she needed him. Would he figure it out?

"I will. But I can't guarantee that they'll want her here. Nor can I promise you'll make it to testify if we can't keep you safe. That means you can't talk to your mom or anyone else. At least not yet. You must sleep where they can't reach you. You must keep Captain with you. You know all of this."

He didn't need to say the rest. If she'd listened to Jake from the beginning, there would be no photos or phone. She'd set a target on her mother and herself. "It doesn't mean I like it."

She shrugged past him and tugged the coffee pot off the warmer, then poured herself a cup. Maybe that's what she needed to think more clearly, because so far, her brain wasn't cooperating.

Ted took a deep breath and grabbed a cup, then poured some for himself. "I'm sorry, Em. I already asked

Jake to find somewhere else for you, but there is nowhere. He suggested complete lockdown."

"No!" Her heart rattled in her chest, and she set the coffee down before she spilled it. "How could this possibly get stricter? I told you I would do what you said. I agree to stay with you at all times. I have no phone anymore, despite the fact that it would help if I ever got separated from you. I accept that I can't go shopping or do anything. What else could you do besides put me in a cell?"

Ted stepped forward, reaching for her hand. She let him take it, even though she shouldn't. He was forbidden, too. Just as much as calling her mom or anything else. His touch made her skin come to life. She dearly hoped she wasn't reaching out to him only because she was so desperate for someone to talk to. He was too good for that.

"I hear you. I'm listening. I'm trying."

She nodded and took a deep breath. "I needed to get that off my chest."

"I know. My brother sent me a text this morning. I asked him to come stay here and help me. He will, but he can't tonight. Soon, though. Once he's here, you'll have a bit more freedom."

Emily gave in to the urge and pulled herself into his arms whether he wanted it or not. She needed personal contact. "Thank you. I appreciate everything you've done for me. I know this isn't easy. I know you didn't ask for this and I can be independent."

He chuckled. "That's for sure." But he didn't push her away, instead he rested his chin on her head, as if completely comfortable to let her stay as long as she'd like.

She bit her lip and counted to ten. Since he was in such

an agreeable mood, could she get him to agree to a phone? While he was right, she had to stay hidden. Her uncle *was* innocent, and her parents didn't know anyone from his company. There was absolutely no way for information to get back to anyone at Deerfield. She could warn her mother about what had happened and have them increase security at their home. And if they got separated, she could contact him.

"Would you consider letting me have a phone that was new? Just a throw-away one without a contract? So I could call you if I ever needed to? Like the one from Jake, but with no connection to my past?"

She said a little prayer that he would, because talking to her mom was becoming her biggest need of all. Mom would know what to do about Uncle Cole and be able to help her find evidence. But, perhaps more importantly, she could tell Emily what all these sudden feelings were for Ted. Was it just because he was her protector, or could it possibly be more?

***

TED'S HEART clapped against his ribcage like a Clydesdale's hooves on pavement. He hadn't planned to end up with her in his arms again. Though, maybe she needed him. In which case, he wouldn't deny her affection. But at what cost?

She had promised to follow the rules. Having her own phone *would* help if they ever got separated. She might even need it to call the police. He could put in his number, his brother's, and Jakes. That would also let him know if she called anyone else. The number would show on her phone. But was he giving in just because he was starting to feel something for her and wanted to do what he could for her?

"I have to finish work for the day first. Then we can talk about phones and what we're going to do around here. Unfortunately, I can't have your help outside anymore. You'll have to stay in here with Captain."

She stepped out of his embrace and glanced at the huge dog hiding under the table. "He didn't alert when they drove up to the fence. He didn't alert until they were in my room. Are you sure this is a good idea? Because I'm not."

He understood her frustration, but she could've slept through Captain's bark. Her sleep had been disrupted for days and she was tired.

"But he *did* alert last night once the window was out. You said he was growling over you when you woke up." He wasn't going to let her insinuate his dog hadn't done the job. Maybe *he'd* failed, but Captain hadn't. "It was also his first night with you. He was still bonding with you since he'd slept by the door the night before." Captain had actually done really well considering the short amount of time they'd had together.

"You're sure it wasn't just a bird and you misplaced my pictures?" She raised her eyebrows and gave him an almost pitiful look somewhere between hope and worry.

"I'm sorry, Em. There's no way. The screen wasn't bent or lying flat on the floor like it would be if something hit it with force and knocked it inside. The screen was lying outside on the ground against the house. Someone was trying to come in your window. Quietly. Because of the shored-up foundation for the basement, they were able to look right inside."

She slowly shook her head, eyes unfocused. "I can't

think about that. I have enough images in my head when I dream. I don't like staying here alone. Can I go with you out to the barn if I stay with you? Captain will be right by my side. I won't leave."

He wanted her with him and hated that she was obviously terrified after the last few days. While her argument would've sounded to anyone else like a bid for freedom, he could see she wanted to stay with people, where it was safer. If she stayed next to him, she would be just as safe outside with him as she was in the house.

"So, you like using the pitchfork, then?"

She flinched and held up her hands. Her palms were still raw, and a few blisters had burst. He had the strangest urge to kiss them. Ted shook his head and headed for the bathroom before he gave in to his desires. Where she was concerned, he didn't seem to have any willpower at all.

The lines of sight were open in the barn and there were only two exits. He could reasonably watch her in there. If someone came, there was nowhere to hide. If someone breeched the barn and took him out, she was gone. Then again, if someone drove up while he was outside, Captain was her only defense. Lose, lose. If something happened and Jake asked him if he'd followed the rules, what would he answer?

He grabbed a jar of salve and brought it back out to her. "I didn't know you'd hurt your hands. This should help." He handed her the container.

She smiled at him, and he let himself enjoy her gratitude. A moment later, she pursed her lips, and he wondered what she had on her mind. What was she thinking that she wouldn't tell him?

"I'm going to head back outside shortly. If you're

coming, you'd best get changed and make sure you've eaten."

She slicked a thin layer of salve over her hands. "I'll be ready when you are."

He was pretty sure he would never be as ready as he needed to be. For anything.

FIFTEEN

The blisters on Emily's hands would be huge. She kept her fingers clenched to keep from looking at them. If she didn't look, Ted wouldn't notice. She'd said she wanted to help, to get out of the house. He'd taken her completely at her word, so she couldn't look weak now. She had never worked so hard in her life. With her legs quivering and her hands throbbing, she was ready for a hot shower and a rest. But she'd stuck with it, which meant she hadn't been alone all day.

After a slow walk up to the front step with Captain on her heels, she stopped short at the door. A note fluttered in the breeze, taped near the knob. She pulled it off and shivered as a gust of wind brushed over the damp skin of her forehead and neck. Captain whined and nudged her knee.

She shouldn't open it. The note wasn't her business. Unless it was from the men watching her. She glanced over her shoulder to see if Ted followed. He'd kept her by his side all day and had checked the yard before letting her walk to the house alone with Captain. He'd insisted that if they needed to talk about her phone, her schedule, or anything important, they had to do it in the barn. He hadn't explained why, and she hadn't asked. Now, his new rule made sense. She felt watched even standing right outside the house.

Ted came out of the barn, whistling a soft tune. He slid the huge door closed and the *clack* as it drove home made her jump. She couldn't move. Not without knowing if those men had invaded her life yet again. She'd needed just one whole day to herself. She didn't know anything she hadn't already shared with the FBI. Why couldn't they just leave her alone? She couldn't make anything worse for them now.

"What's that?" Ted took two steps at a time up the short porch and stood behind her. His strong presence drove away the jittery feeling of unease.

"Probably nothing. This was taped to the door." She handed it to him. Even a day ago, she would've wanted to know exactly what was in the note. What it said. How was she affected? Now, she wanted Ted to handle it. If it wasn't about her, that was even better. He was an expert at these situations, no matter how poorly he thought of himself.

He tore open the tape closing it and chuckled, immediately diffusing her worry.

"It was my mom. She came to the house to get a pair of shoes for a party tomorrow. I thought I saw Captain look outside earlier, but he didn't growl. He's trained not to bark unless there's imminent danger."

Ted knelt down and patted Captain. "And I just figured out why he didn't alert when that car came up the first day he was here. It wasn't the same year, but it was the same make and model car my mom drives. I didn't even think about it, but the cars probably sound the same and look similar enough that Captain didn't realize it wasn't her. As soon as he recognized the owner of the car wasn't someone he knew, he barked."

She nodded and leaned down, giving the dog a scratch behind the ears. Captain flopped onto the porch and rolled on his back, enjoying all the attention. She hadn't thought she was much of an animal person until Captain. Mom's dog was spoiled and often took her attention. She almost resented Mom's dog.

"I miss parties." The mention of one stoked a longing for freedom and company. "Is that why your brother couldn't come right away?" She hadn't meant to worry him, but Ted's hand stalled over Captain's belly.

He held his hand to his lips and glanced around, his eyes suddenly hard. He mouthed the words, *In the barn.*

She'd forgotten. Important topics in the barn only. "Sorry," she whispered. While she wanted to clear her uncle's name, she was no spy or detective. Ted and his family definitely had more of those tools than she did.

He reached over and grasped her hand for a moment, whispering, "Let's talk in the barn." He jerked his head slightly toward it. She nodded and followed him back out, keeping her mouth shut. His hand in hers made her flinch, and she hoped he didn't notice the added blisters.

When they reached the barn, he made room for her in his office so she could sit. "I know this seems like overkill. But my gut tells me that somehow, they're listening in the house. That may have been a big reason they broke into your room. Think hard. Is there anything else you know that you haven't told anyone? Anything, even silly? I can't figure out why they're trying to kidnap you, and not..." He swallowed audibly.

She'd wondered the same thing. If it was just a matter of silencing her, then they would have killed her when they had the chance. Why kidnap her? Why this game of cat and mouse? They'd already taken her computer, so what was it about her that mattered? Was it only to instill fear? She didn't know anything other than what she'd told the FBI.

"I told them everything I knew. Jake tried many times to get me to try to remember things about the first kidnapping attempt, but honestly, I wasn't much help. Every time I try to remember anything, I get more confused. Is it a real memory or am I creating memories because people want more information?"

He leaned his hip against the wall and tilted his head to keep the sun from his eyes as it poured though the side window. "I want you to go inside, change to go shopping, and say nothing." Then he laughed. "Better yet, we'll test out a theory. I'll put my trail cameras up in the windows before we go. Casually mention having a picnic with me this evening but change the place we're going to have it as you talk your way through each room."

She nodded her understanding. "In my room, I'll say something like the picnic will be so nice in the back yard. I hope the bugs don't eat me alive. I'll look so ugly."

He examined her face and brushed her hair behind her ear. Heat set up a homestead in her cheeks. Did he have to check out every bite on her face? She fought the urge to scratch when she suddenly felt itchy everywhere. The bugs seemed to get worse by the day.

"I don't think it's possible for you to look ugly." He finally stopped examining her cheeks and caught her eyes. She watched his Adam's apple bob as he swallowed hard.

Now it was her turn to swallow. She'd never had

anyone say anything like that to her before. "I'm certainly not used to anything around here. The bugs...or the men."

He flashed a quick smile. "Any place you are, is as good as what you make of it. Be it bugs or men." His back straightened as he turned toward the door of the office. "I certainly didn't plan to be back living out here at my parents' house. That snuck up on me."

She'd been curious about that from the beginning, especially since his parents were not old. "Why *are* you out here? And why are they not? Your parents' room is full." When she'd found his mother's clothes and boots, the closet had been tight with all the clothes still hanging there.

He glanced at his boots and kicked a pebble into the wall. "When I was put on administrative leave, I wasn't much fun to be around. I didn't want to talk to anyone or see anyone. Mom and Dad decided to trade houses with me."

"Trade? So, they're living at your house?"

He nodded. "I offered to stay out here and keep the horses company, they stay at my house where it's comfortable in town and they don't have to be near me and my grumpy attitude..."

She laughed, loving that he was willing to open up with her. "And did Captain live with you there?"

The dog perked up his ears at the mention of his name, and Emily reached down to scratch him.

"That's right. He's been retired for a year, and I brought him home. The department stipulates when you adopt one of their dogs that you take the best care of it. They wanted him to go with Ben because he knows the rules."

"He hasn't seemed all that difficult to take care of."

Ted ran his hand through his hair and let out a sigh. "He's a pretty big reminder of what I lost. That's why I don't put him in his vest, even though I should if I'm using his commands."

She'd heard him whistle a few times, but she'd yet to learn any real commands for Captain. He just did as he was told. "What's wrong with him? Why did he retire?" He didn't look that old.

"He has mild arthritis in his hips. If I could stand for him to wear it, the vest gives me a handle when I need to help him up in the morning. It would be cruel to make him keep his paces. There are other reasons, too. When he wears the vest, he thinks he has to be at work. It wears him out."

Ted really loved his dog. She could see that in the way he talked about him. But did he feel that way about his home? She'd assumed the ranch was where he wanted to be. "When this is all done, will you trade back?"

Curiosity might kill the cat, and she would never know him, never live anywhere with him outside of the wide-open Sandy Creek Ranch. Yet, curious, she was.

"I don't know. Jake told me if I did this job well, he might have an opening for me as a deputy marshal. I don't know where that would take me. I might not be able to stay in Zachary at all. Or maybe I will. This on-the-job training hasn't been easy."

He'd have to give up his family, and she could relate to that. "That's a hard choice."

"There are others that are harder." He glanced at her again with such depth it took her breath away. He wanted her to understand something without saying the words, but she felt unversed in the language. Sparks flew between them, but did he feel them? Was he trying to tell her he felt the same or was she grasping at straws?

"I'll go get changed and blather away as I walk through the house. I'll keep notes on which area for the picnic I say in which room, so if they show up on a trail camera, you'll know which room I was in."

"Good, then we'll know which room has the potential listening device in it."

She laughed and pushed away from her seat. She was ready to put on clean clothes and partake in some retail therapy, not to mention get away from the ranch for a little while.

"What's so funny?"

"I can't wait to tell my mom about all this espionage." And everything else she'd stored up in her heart lately.

***

TED WATCHED Emily as she rushed away. A sinking feeling in the pit of his gut came as a dire warning. Emily desperately wanted to talk to her mother. Probably enough to ignore his warning and put them in danger. Again. Yet, he could understand her hesitation to believe her own uncle was behind the theft and attempted kidnapping. And maybe murder. She may have her head in the clouds, but at least he could understand why.

It was the murder of the accountant that bothered him the most. Since Jake had filled him in on so many other details, he'd finally just let him tell the whole story. Now he knew exactly why the feds wanted her safe. She had to go to trial, because unless they could get an insider to snitch...they'd never pull enough evidence for conviction. The murderer might never even go to trial.

As Ted strode through the house, he tried to make note of all the places he could put trail cameras. He'd checked Emily's room after the break-in but hadn't found anything. There was a possibility the attackers had known their every move by guess, but more likely they'd managed somehow to plant a listening device in his home. If he had something that belonged to the person who planted it, he could probably get Captain to sniff out the device. Though, he hadn't been used in that capacity since he'd started training.

He heard Emily talking to herself as she walked through the house. Little snippets of her voice floated to him while he shaved. Everything he'd asked of her, she'd done so far. Even the strange things like talking outside and chatting with herself as she walked through the house. She wasn't just lying down and letting him handle the security, she wanted to take part. He loved that she met every challenge with fervor, even the situations that scared her.

Emily waited for him in the living room. She wore the same jeans she'd worn the day she arrived and a pink fitted tee that would probably really set off her blond hair, but made the brown look rich, like chocolate. For a change, she wore it down, and he held back the compliment he wanted to give her. He'd probably done enough of that today. Without a word, he nodded and led her to the door. He pointed to Captain's bed, near the sofa. The dog sat and held his head high like a sentinel. Ted had no doubt the dog would be there when they returned.

Once she climbed into the truck and he got settled in, he breathed a sigh. If his theory was right, they would be able to be gone all afternoon because her attackers would be in the dark about where they were. All the trouble would be worth it if they got one afternoon of peace.

Emily faced out the window, away from him. She'd been preoccupied all day, ever since they'd talked about getting her a phone.

"I appreciate that we've been able to work together today." He hoped she would take that to mean he didn't want her keeping secrets from him. He wanted her, frankly, needed her, to trust him.

She grimaced slightly. "I hope I didn't overdo it. They probably think I've taken leave of my senses if they were listening."

"I guess if they are listening from more than one room, they'll know we're on to them. I asked you to do it so I could narrow down which room they'd planted a device by where they showed up on my trail camera."

She nodded. "It's a smart idea. I just felt stupid."

"No need for that. You did great." He couldn't keep his gaze from taking in all of her. She was smart, independent, and beautiful. But the state would require her to go back home to testify. He had to stop thinking about her.

"Is the cell phone store in the mall?" She bit her lip.

While she seemed hesitant, he noticed a gleam in her eye. Hadn't she said she missed shopping? "It just happens to be, yes."

"Would you be willing to take me to a few stores? I just..." She frowned and shook her head. "Never mind. It's a terrible idea."

He hated that she couldn't at least do one thing she wanted. The chance they would be followed into a mall was slim. There would be too many security cameras. It would be the worst possible place to try to kidnap her. Then again, they'd tried on a busy street, too.

"I think, if we're careful, we can go to a store or two." Though he hated the idea of leaving them both vulnerable. Not only that, but he'd also have to pay attention to every face and try to gauge their reaction to her.

"Really?" She opened her purse and shuffled through a few things in her wallet. "Jake didn't leave me with much...but if I can find it." She sounded so excited.

"You can't use any credit cards from before. Cash is safe." He tried to focus on the road, but it was hard. He wanted to see the smile she kept hiding by looking through her purse.

"I have one cash card that Jake gave me with my new name on it. I don't carry anything that would identify me as Mia."

His chest tightened. No. He wasn't supposed to know her real name. He loved that she trusted him and felt comfortable with him enough to let that vital information slip, but she couldn't do it again. What if the listening device was in his truck? Even as he thought that, his mind held tight to the precious information. *Mia.*

"I'm not supposed to know that. Don't tell me anything from your past... I can't know."

She sighed and her shoulders fell. "I'm sorry. I'm just so tired. I was always the girl accused of being honest to a fault. The little girl that was never invited to parties because I was too good to do anything wrong. I guess I'm paying for that now."

He gripped the steering wheel tightly. "That's not how life works. No one keeps score to punish you for being honest. You did the right thing. I'm glad you did."

She blessed him with a brief smile. "I suppose if I hadn't told the truth, I never would've met you."

If she hadn't told the truth, he'd still be talking to

horses every morning and hating where he'd landed in life. Her honesty had pulled him out of despair, and he hadn't even noticed it was gone, or how far he'd sunk. Somewhere over the last few days he'd gone from mild resentment over being asked to do a job he didn't want, to finding he was thankful for it. Without Emily, he'd still be wallowing.

He stuffed that down deep to think about it later. Emily didn't need to hear about his troubles. She had enough of her own. Today would be a day she could relax, at least for a few hours. "I'm sure glad you did."

SIXTEEN

Only a scattered handful of cars sat parked outside the large doors to the main mall entrance. Ted scanned the front of the building to find the area with the least cars. The shopping center didn't look overly busy from the parking lot, thankfully. Ted pulled into a spot as close to the doors as possible.

Normally, he'd have chosen a spot in the back and walked since he'd rather avoid people completely. But if anything happened inside, he wanted to be able to get Emily out and into the truck without having to think about where he'd parked. Nor did he want to have to pull her through a crowd to do it.

Emily fidgeted next to him, almost as jittery as he felt. As they made their way through the lot, she stretched out her hand, weaving her fingers through his. She'd never done anything like that, and he wasn't sure how he should react. He didn't want her to think the action wasn't welcome, nor did he want to look too deeply into it. Slowing his steps for a moment, he waited for her to either explain or let him remain stumped.

"Because we're married." She shrugged, answering his unasked question.

"I see." He didn't bother to question her further. If he asked any more, she would assume he minded that she'd reached out to him. Which he didn't. Instead, he pulled her close and draped his arm over her shoulder, tucking her close to his side.

He could have everyone convinced Emily was only his as long as she would let him. Like this, he could keep an eye on her easier. Most men they encountered would ignore her since she was obviously with him. Pride puffed his chest a little as he pushed through the shopping center door and held it for Emily.

He tried to force himself to relax. This was only a mall, and he'd been coming here his whole life. He held her hand as they walked down the mall. The farther they went, the more annoyed he felt.

Men noticed her. Almost all of them in some capacity or another. Some just nodded, others smiled. At least she didn't seem to take note of their approval. The real issue was, there was no way for him to tell if they were just appreciating a pretty face or if they recognized her. If his job was to forget about those who weren't a threat, he couldn't. Now more than ever he wanted to get done with the shopping and get her back home where he could control the environment.

After a quick check of the mall directory, he launched them in the direction of the small cellular store. Two men followed close behind but turned off into a footwear store. He held tight to her hand and tugged her along. Hopefully no one else noticed how rushed he felt.

"Did I do something wrong?" Emily tried to slow the pace, and he dropped her hand, placing his instead on her back to get her to move faster.

"No, nothing. I just didn't realize how many people would be at the mall today." It hadn't seemed like so many until they were inside, and he was trying to inspect every face. There didn't appear to be many women in the mall at all, which was strange. Was he only noticing the men because of the danger, or just ignoring the women?

"This...is a lot?" She paused to glance over her shoulder and raised her eyebrows at him.

Would his concern worry her, or make her think he was overly protective? He'd already told her he thought she was pretty. He didn't need to reiterate it by explaining that having every guy within a quarter mile stare at her was giving him anger issues.

"Let's just get this taken care of, then we can stop at two clothing stores." He held up his fingers. There would be no more than that. A compromise would have to be good enough. His nerves couldn't take more.

"I'll make that work." She smiled, heading right for the contract-free phones.

Jake had offered him a stipend to use for anything Emily needed, this would go toward that. So far, he'd only had to buy her food. There just wasn't much a girl needed out in the country. Except a protector who could actually do the job. He sighed and followed her lead while trying to watch the door and everyone around them.

She reached over and laid a cool hand on top of his. "Hey? You okay? We don't have to go to the clothing stores if this is just too much stress. I figured it was too good to be true."

The sadness in her eyes ate at him. He couldn't let

her down. She'd given up everything after the attempted kidnapping. He'd brought her here to relieve some of her tension, not cause more. Someone else should give for a change. Meaning him. He made a conscious effort to loosen up so she wouldn't know how anxious he was.

He shook his head. "No, I'm sorry. I wanted you to have a day without stress and I'm ruining it by being the thing that's stressful. Let's pick out a phone."

She laughed and selected a plain smartphone. "You're forgiven. Since I hope I won't have this long, let's just get one that's basic, functional. I don't need more." She handed him a small box with the phone locked inside.

"Are you sure? Almost seems too easy." He glanced at the front of the box but frankly didn't care as long as it made calls and gave Emily a little much-needed joy.

"Do I get to pick which clothing store we go into?" Her impish smile made his chest tighten. He'd never seen her look like that.

"Sure. Let me pay for this and get it set up." She followed him to the counter and managed to keep an eye on the store and the front without looking overly obvious. She'd make a good undercover officer with a little training. Though she'd never said she wanted to do anything of the sort.

He quickly paid, then she slid the paper bag handles over her arm as she led the way out of the store. "I saw the perfect place on the directory when you were looking for the mobile store. It should have everything from dresses, to jeans, to shoes."

"Wait." He stopped her in the middle of the hall, almost causing a traffic jam. "Just how much do you want to buy?" He realized after he'd said it just how much like a real husband he sounded. He hadn't meant to, only that he didn't want to be in the store for hours.

She laughed. "Not much. I don't have a whole lot of money and not enough room in my suitcase. Sometimes, just looking is plenty. Shoes are my weakness."

He'd thought the phone would be her weakness. Shoes he could handle. Shoes wouldn't let anyone know where she was. The lack of space in her bag was just the reminder he needed to keep this professional. She wasn't staying. "Lead the way."

He hoped there would be someplace he could sit and keep an eye on her while she did her hunting. Didn't stores usually have benches where poor, beleaguered husbands could take a load off while their wives tried on mountains of clothing and shoes? He'd never thought he'd be in those ranks. Though his status wasn't real.

The store was massive. With intertwined departments. People seemed to be hiding behind every rack of clothes. Emily didn't notice, but he couldn't get off high alert. One young man popped out from behind a mannequin to ask Emily if she needed anything and almost got accidentally punched. Ted just couldn't keep a handle on his adrenaline.

She dragged him through the shoes, then to dresses. Everywhere they went, pockets of people waited around talking, getting in the way, obscuring his line of sight. He couldn't sit, nor could he crowd her without feeling like an overprotective bear.

Emily tugged him along to the jeans section and shoved him down in a chair. "Behave." She pointed at him like a discouraged teacher, but her voice teased. "I'll only be a few minutes. We haven't seen anyone I recognize, and I'm finally enjoying myself. If any crazed kidnapper is going to follow me in here, then I'm a goner, because it means they'll try anything," she whispered quietly enough he could barely hear her.

He hated the feeling in his gut at even the joking mention of Emily dying. There were at least four cameras mounted to poles within the vicinity, he noted as he glanced around. No one would ever try something where there would be so much evidence. Would they?

Emily was trying to get him to relax again, without coming right out and saying it. He hadn't tried to make his fears known, but she saw the evidence just the same. He had to try, for her, to be calm and let her have a few minutes of freedom.

A short time later, she ducked into a changing room with a stack of clothes and started humming a song out of tune. He recognized it as one from the radio a few years before. If anyone else had been humming like that, it would've annoyed him. With Emily, it was...endearing.

Her bare feet below the door shimmied and shifted in constant movement as she tried on various clothes. Though he may have felt guilty watching anyone else, he had been asked by Jake to watch her every move, and he wasn't about to let her out of his sight after the last few days. Her feet weren't going anywhere without his knowledge.

She stuck her head out of the changing room door. "I need a second opinion."

He tried to keep his face passive. "Is that so?" His chest ached with laughter that he wouldn't allow to burst free.

She opened the door and came out in a pair of jeans that looked like they'd been sewn just for her. She turned this way and that, trying to see herself from every angle in the three-way mirror. Her face scrunched in adorable consternation. "I just don't know if these are right."

The laughter died as he sucked his breath in, then whistled softly as he let it out. He'd always been a bit of a sucker for a nice pair of jeans. "They're fine. I think we should go."

She glanced at him and her happiness slid away like he'd just dumped her candy on the ground. "Fine. Let me get changed." Her shoulders drooped as she strode back and tugged the curtain closed behind her.

He hadn't meant to kill her fun. He searched the area, since he'd been ignoring their surroundings, and found no one wandering through the changing area. Odd, since the whole store seemed busier than the rest of the mall. There hadn't been any point they'd been alone so far, but now the lack of people seemed sinister.

He stood and investigated as far away as he dared without losing sight of Emily's changing room. A few people were over in housewares, but the clothing section was quiet. His heart wanted to believe that something had finally gone right for Emily for a few minutes, one he hadn't managed to ruin. His mind discounted that immediately and wondered what was going on to distract people away from the changing rooms where people usually congregated.

Emily appeared at his side, empty-handed.

"Aren't you going to get your jeans?" He'd told her they were fine. Didn't she believe his opinion? Or maybe it hadn't really mattered. He was only a guy, and a distracted one at that.

"No. Let's just go." Her eyes were a little glassy and she blinked rapidly as she shoved past him.

FINE. She swallowed hard and pressed her lips together to try to keep the tears away. Why had she thought for a second he would care about her clothes or how she looked? He'd been agreeable to holding her hand because it meshed with his suggestion to act as a married couple. It wasn't because he felt the strange pull to her as she felt for him.

He was just too hurt by people to let her in. She was a career move to him. If he succeeded in protecting her, then he could have a job as an officer again. A means to an end. Though, wasn't she always? Hadn't she constantly filled in when others failed? Not really important enough to consider, except in an emergency. Like when her uncle's accountant had quit after the head accountant didn't show up, he'd thought of her to fill in.

Uncle Cole hadn't even ever offered her the job permanently. Even after she'd found the information that would save his company from thieves. She'd found the evidence of money laundering and had reported it to him right away. Yet, as far as she knew, he wasn't trying to contact her. Only her mother had tried. He had to know she was missing since she hadn't come to work. If her mother had found her number, why hadn't he asked for it, too?

Ted hung one step behind her, which was just fine. She didn't want him asking questions when she was about to cry. If he even touched her, she'd lose all ability to hold it together. He didn't need to know how much his lack of an opinion of her hurt.

She made it all the way back out to his truck, and he unlocked it remotely as he closed the gap between them.

She climbed in before he could even reach the truck and turned away from him to buckle her seat belt.

He took a deep breath as he settled into the driver's seat. "You want to tell me what's wrong?" He made no move to drive away.

"Nothing." She hated being that person who didn't want to talk, but she didn't want to cry either. Which meant he had to deal with her brushing him off. He couldn't even let her have a few relaxing hours. At least he'd shown her the bathtub. When they got home, she would lock herself in his parents' room, then lock the bathroom door and soak until she didn't care about Ted anymore.

"Really? Because you seemed pretty upbeat, then..." He let the sentence trail off.

She whipped around to face him. "You know what? I wanted your opinion. That's all. I wanted to hear that you thought I looked good. I felt good for a few seconds and then, I didn't. Fine isn't good. Grandma's green bean casserole is *fine*. I don't want to be just fine." Especially to him. Why couldn't he see that she wanted him to think of her as more than fine? How had he managed to get past her wall so easily? She hadn't wanted to talk to him. She shouldn't be telling him anything.

His eyebrows bunched together, and his lips parted slightly. "I like my grandmother's green bean casserole."

She sighed. "Let's just go home." That word knocked the heat right out of her argument. *Home.* His home. Not hers. She didn't belong and wouldn't. When she locked herself behind closed doors, she would call her mother to find out how the case was moving. Ted needed her out of his hair and his life. For good. He didn't want her there. If she could move the case on faster, then he could get his job and send her home. Where she belonged.

She'd be happy eventually.

"Can I look at my phone?"

He snorted. "It's in the bag. Go ahead. Just remember what you promised me."

She'd never actually given her word. So why did she feel so guilty about even thinking of breaking it?

SEVENTEEN

Back at home, Emily rushed off with her phone before Ted could ask her much about it. If he didn't touch it, he couldn't check her phone activity. She could delete any calls or texts before she showed her face again. She rushed toward his parents' bathroom.

"I'll be busy for a while. Just...going to take a bath."

He seemed distracted and barely nodded a response.

The tub would take at least ten minutes to fill. It was very deep, and if she didn't turn the water on all the way it would take even longer. The noise would be loud enough that Ted would never hear her talking. She plugged the drain and set the tap water to the right temperature. She grabbed her phone and quickly sent her mother a text, letting her know she had a new number and to please answer when she called.

After ten minutes, the tub was almost full, and she'd seen no response from her mother. Finally, a text came through. *Your mom is busy and can't take a call right now. I'll let her know you're fine. – Cole.*

She almost dropped her new phone into the tub. Why would her uncle have her mother's phone, and why would her mother ever let him answer for her? Cole was innocent, she believed that. Yet, she couldn't deny that having him respond was odd, even...suspicious.

Mom had been missing her, would be frantic by now waiting to hear from her. So why wouldn't she answer unless something was wrong. And Cole was there. Cole never stayed long enough to get comfortable in their home, and he'd never answer her mother's phone.

Was it possible Jake and Ted had been right the whole time? Had she been wrong to trust and believe in him? If so, she'd just sent a text to the prime suspect in her kidnapping with her area code and three-digit city code. Uncle Cole would now know for sure where she was. If anyone had been fooled by her change in phone number, she'd just ruined the ruse.

"What have I done?" She could hardly speak.

She stared at the steaming water of the tub and now couldn't even think about a bath. The connection to her past was open like a door and she felt watched. Ted didn't deserve this.

One thing was certain. She couldn't tell Ted about the text. He'd either be furious or disappointed, and she couldn't handle either from him. She highlighted the text and deleted it.

WATER RUNNING in the back of the house gave Ted the first hint that Emily was safely locked away in his parents' bathroom. She'd been reserved on the way home, giving him short answers. Not that he'd been the best company.

He tried to ignore his need to go find out what was really bothering her and why she was so bothered by the words he'd used. She had said she was angry about the word he'd used to tell her how good she looked. Fine wasn't an insult. At least not to him. There had to be more to her anger and sensitivity.

He couldn't deny that it bothered him when she ignored him. He didn't want to be the reason she stopped trusting again. He'd meant she looked fine, what else was he supposed to say? She had to have been angered by his insistence they leave and being perturbed the entire time they were out. He'd ruined her fun.

Stewing over Emily wouldn't get far though, because she was in the bath and he couldn't talk to her. Once she was out, they could figure this mess out. In the meantime, she was safely locked in the best room in the house. He could go and check all the memory cards on the trail cameras they'd placed before they left. If any of them had images, he'd know where to look for listening devices.

Captain raced ahead of him. Even with his sore hip, he had the energy of a puppy sometimes. As Ted collected all the cards, Captain got in some good exercise. He'd been locked in the house for the last few hours and was glad to get outside to run.

Back in the house, his laptop waited on the kitchen counter. He pulled up a stool and popped in the first memory card from the various mounted cameras. He always kept the cards color coded, so he knew which camera the pictures came from. The blue card, which he'd faced to show the whole front of the house and the driveway, corresponded with Emily talking in the living room. He found nothing but three pictures that seemed to have been tripped by dragon flies.

He pressed the card and it popped out, then replaced it with the black one. This was the card that corresponded with Emily talking in her room. There were dozens of pictures, but he couldn't immediately see anything.

His cameras were sensitive and could've been set off by the wind, but that wasn't likely, given the few pictures on the last one. When he zoomed in on the pictures, two men hid in the trees near the back of the house where she'd joked about having a picnic. One even held a green can that might have been bug spray. She'd mentioned the mosquitoes.

Hair on the back of his neck prickled to life. There had to be a device in her room. They must have planted it when they'd removed the screen. Maybe the goal hadn't been to kill her but to find out what she knew?

He'd move her immediately to his parents' room. She would be as safe there as in the basement and she would feel more comfortable. That room had the added safety of the bathroom as a secure area should they need it. The only thing that made the basement safer was that the windows were too small for anyone to come through. But they were also the easiest to open if they wanted to plant more devices.

Emily's pleasant lavender scent preceded her by a few seconds. He tensed, knowing she would be there shortly and knowing there would be a battle ahead. But this time, he had a way of compromising that might make everyone happier. And he wouldn't renege on his compromise this time.

She appeared a moment later, scrunching her wet hair in a towel. She wore her comfortable leggings again, one of the few outfits she had. Guilt for rushing her out of the store nibbled at him again. She'd needed a few things and he'd rushed her. She might not get to go again soon.

"That was a short bath. I expected you to be in there longer. To soak and enjoy yourself...relax."

She glanced away, an oddly guilty look covering her features for a moment. "I didn't realize you would notice."

He couldn't seem to pay her the right kind of attention, no matter what he tried. He'd thought he was being sensitive after his blunder earlier. He couldn't seem to overcome his own words.

"I'm sorry you weren't able to get anything at the store. You needed clothes, and I got in the way." So what if he didn't understand why she was angry? The whole ordeal had been stressful on her, and he'd added to it.

She sighed and let the towel she'd used to dry her hair fall around her shoulders. "I shouldn't have put that on you. I have no right to expect compliments from you. I shouldn't have put you in that position. Your protection should be enough. From now on, it will be."

His stomach clenched uncomfortably. She was saying just what needed to be said. They had to maintain a distance. There shouldn't be anything between them for her safety. Yet he wished he could argue. "You're right, of course. That's best. I'm still sorry you didn't get anything and that I didn't help."

She closed her eyes and turned away. "Did you find anything on the cameras?"

There had been a white car at Ben's, then the white car came up to the house but turned out to be nothing. Now, he wasn't sure what the men in the pictures were driving. Only two relatively blurry men had appeared where they shouldn't be. None of the camaras caught their approach.

"Yes. I think there's a device in your room, judging by what I found."

"I've been thinking a lot about that night, the night Captain woke me. Over and over, really." She still didn't turn to face him, as if she couldn't. He hated that she'd started avoiding him again. He'd liked that he was the only one she trusted.

"Have you come up with something, a memory?"

"No, nothing like that. Except, I'm certain I left Captain outside my room that night, just like I did the first night. I wasn't used to him yet, and when he moves on the bed, it wakes me up. When I woke up, he was standing over me. There's no way he could've opened my door, and I don't sleepwalk."

They had more than just come into his house. They'd done more than stolen Emily's pictures and possibly planted a device. They had gone beyond, into his home, doing...who could guess. Fury wrapped itself around him. He'd promised to protect Emily and Jake had been certain his house was perfect. Now, strangers had walked through his home.

"I would speculate that they came in while I slept, went through my drawers for information and came away with the pictures. When they couldn't find anything else, they planned to take me out the front because they couldn't get me out the window without waking me. That's when they opened my bedroom to clear the way for a quick escape and met with Captain. They made a hasty getaway out the window while Captain jumped on the bed to protect me. That's when I woke up. Nothing else makes sense unless you let Captain in my room before you went to bed. If he was sound asleep, he may not have heard anything through the door."

He shook his head. "I didn't ever touch your door after lights-out. With the exception of when Captain was barking."

Her theory sounded plausible enough. "I've already checked that room twice. Now that I know they most likely can't hear us in here, I think we should move you back upstairs into Mom and Dad's room. You're safer there if anyone does get in."

She turned so he could only see the side of her face. She hadn't looked so sad since she'd arrived. "It's certainly better than the basement."

No concerns about the men who came into her room? Something wasn't right, but how to get her to talk to him again? Their trust was broken, and he wasn't sure how to fix it.

He wasn't sure if he was safe to speak in his own house, but judging by the camaras, the kitchen was a safe room. Though he still kept his voice low. "My brother will be here tomorrow. Tonight, he's having a bunch of his friends over for a party. They're all cops. He said I could bring you, if you want to go."

He paused, hoping to see some excitement from her. But she made no response at all. "There's probably not anywhere near Baton Rouge besides the police station that's any safer than that party." If Emily wanted to go, he'd take her. But he didn't want to be there. More likely than not, some of his old team would be there.

"Except getting there." She shivered. "They might know about his house."

He nodded. "I know. But I know you want to see people, and this is the best I can do. I'm trying to give you what you need without sacrificing what you *really* need."

He fought the urge for preservation of his own feelings in lieu of seeing a smile on her face. He pulled her close as he wrapped a gentle arm around her waist. "I know you're trying so hard to do everything right. Stress is making you agitated. I've been there. Let me take you, and we'll see if you feel better."

"This is the party your mother mentioned in her note?" She stiffened in his arms.

He loosened his grip and she stepped away from him, without the smile he'd hoped for. "Yes, she'll be there." Why did it matter? He'd assumed again that he'd make her happy, yet he managed to mess up no matter what.

"Don't you think you should warn your parents that you have a wife? If that's still our story?"

With as chilly as she'd become after shopping, he questioned the logic, but there was no other reason for her to be with him that wouldn't cause suspicion. Though, so would a sudden marriage. The only thing he had going for him was that because he'd shut everyone out, they hadn't seen him in a long time. Probably long enough for him to find a wife. If those things could happen fast. He glanced down into her eyes and his chest ached. Yup, things certainly could happen that fast.

His mind cleared in a split second. Was he falling for Emily? In a real sense? They'd only been together a few days, but they'd been through a lot. He already knew losing her would be hard.

"I think it's a bad time to be coming up with a new story now."

She blushed and stepped back farther, making him want to pull her back in. What had he done? She wasn't responding to him at all anymore. The more he tried, the more she pushed back.

"What should I wear to this party? Is it anything special?" She sounded like dressing was a chore.

He shook his head, thankful she was at least asking questions. "You can just wear something comfortable. You'll be going there as my new wife, since the rest of the people at the party don't know why you're here and we can't tell them. So, just be prepared for lots of congratulations."

She wound her hair into the bun he was growing to dislike and slid an elastic over it. "Might be the only time I get them, so I'd better enjoy it." She headed back toward her room.

"I'm not going to let anything happen to you," he mumbled. Was that why she was so down and defensive? Was she concerned he wasn't capable of the job anymore?

She stopped by her door, tears gleaming in her eyes. "You don't get to control that. You can try to control everything, but in the end, we all have choices. You can't say what others do."

He followed her and turned her to face him because she had to understand. Those men would never get in his house again. He'd go out with Captain later and see if he could find the area where those men were getting on his property and close them off. No one would be getting to Emily.

Ben would be there to help them tomorrow, and then she'd have double the protection. Whatever her attackers wanted, they wouldn't get it. If they'd looked through her drawers, they'd probably been looking for her phone to find out who she told. All they would have to do is scroll through her phone numbers to find out. Her uncle might not want to hurt her, but someone wanted information and probably to keep her from going to trial. Too bad they wouldn't get what they want.

"No. I refuse to give up. Just because those men got close, doesn't mean they'll succeed." For the first time in months, he felt competent and ready to do his job. Because there was no choice in the matter.

Her lips trembled and she gently pushed out of his grasp. "You can't know that. They've already gotten closer than you know."

EIGHTEEN

Ted tapped his foot as he waited for Emily to finish getting ready for the party. Captain lay by his feet, sleeping. His soft snoring would've been comical if there wasn't so much to worry about. Emily needed this break, but he still had to get her there safely and then back home again, breaking his promise to Jake to keep her there on the ranch. Not to mention facing all the people he'd been avoiding for months would be stressful. Once they were at his brothers, anyone trying to reach Emily would be a fool to try. But before he could relax for a few minutes, he had to get the hard part done.

That afternoon, he and Captain had ridden all along his property while Emily stayed with Clara. That wasn't what he wanted to do, but he'd needed Captain to search out any scents. Unfortunately, the men hadn't left anything behind that he could find. There was no way to be certain whether the trail Captain took followed the trespassers or just animals.

The invaders hadn't left car tracks off the main road onto his property, so he couldn't tell where they'd entered.

The men had either walked or covered their tracks well. Captain hadn't alerted while they were out, so the men most likely were not currently on his property, but that could change at any moment. He had no way of knowing if those men could hear what was said in Emily's room if they were on the property, within range of the devices, or if they could listen remotely as well. Some devices had long ranges, others did not. Without the device, there was no way to verify.

Emily finally appeared out of his parents' bedroom, wearing the jeans she'd worn when she arrived and a soft red, off-the-shoulder top with frills that made her look even more feminine than usual. She wore heeled sandals, and her hair was down the way he liked it.

Without thinking, he smiled. "I like your hair like that."

She immediately flipped it over her shoulder and glanced at the floor. "Thank you. It's one of my least favorite things about hiding. I'll be glad when I can have my hair back the way it's supposed to be."

He didn't doubt that. She would be happy to be back with her parents, shopping, closets full of clothes, and not hiding with him. He'd figure out what to do with his life once he got her safely on her own. "I'm sure."

Captain would not be on duty while they were gone, so Ted left him sleeping on the floor as he held the door for Emily. They were both now used to saying little in the house, even though they kept the door to the bedroom where she used to sleep shut all the time. He'd tried having Captain sniff out her room after they had returned, but he'd found nothing. Ted hadn't really expected him to. There was no way Captain could get a distinct scent from sniffing at trees where men had stood the night before. Not when that training hadn't been used in years and there was nothing solid to give him.

He held the door for Emily and waited for her to settle into his truck. To avoid worrying her, he did a quick scan of the perimeter before he joined her. He couldn't see anyone, but if he hadn't zoomed in on the pictures, he wouldn't have seen the men there, either.

Emily broke into his thoughts. "Is Ben your only brother?"

Rambunctious twin brothers had been enough for his parents. He and Ben had been trouble when they were young, or as much as they could be with a father who worked at home and expected his sons' help. His parents had never mentioned wanting more than what they had. "Yes, my only sibling. I never had a sister."

She laughed softly. "I never did either. My mom tried to act as both mother and sister to me. My father is part owner of Deerfield, but he travels a lot for sales and was away from home often. He and my uncle are always competing... Who has the biggest house, who has better stock options..." She shrugged. "I ignore them most of the time."

"Your uncle and your father own Deerfield?" It seemed unlikely, but could her uncle's need to be better than Emily's father have led him down a path to international crime?

"Yes, Uncle Cole." Her mouth snapped shut, and she turned her face to look out the window.

"I know you don't want to talk about him because Jake thinks he's behind your kidnapping. Maybe he's not, maybe he is. I wasn't going to ask."

She shifted slightly. "You can't ask about me, so let's not talk about him. Who else will be at this party?"

Ben hadn't told him any names. He hadn't even realized his parents would be there until his mother had left the note on his door. Which meant it was high time to talk to his whole family again. After such a long absence, and now with a pretend wife, he needed to. The conversation wouldn't be easy, because he didn't want his family to get attached to her. She wouldn't be around long.

"As far as I know, it's Ben, our parents, and some of the guys he works with, plus their spouses."

"Ben is the only one who's not married?" Her wide blue eyes caught and held on his.

Why did questions from her about his brother always give him indigestion? He tried to focus on the road. "Ben is not married. He was almost married, but tragically, she was killed in an auto accident a few weeks before their scheduled wedding day."

"Oh, that's awful. How long ago?" The deep caring in her voice made it easier to answer.

"That was two years ago. Though he still hasn't tried to find anyone else. I don't know that he will." Not that every single woman on the force hadn't tried to get his attention when they'd felt it had been long enough after Sara's death.

A few years sounded like a long time, but it wasn't. Ben had been hurt, but he'd never let on or told anyone. He was more apt to say that he was better off for it. Any woman who chose to try to break through his barriers would have a tough time. That was the closest he'd ever seen his brother to showing honest emotion. Ben usually used arrogance to hide from everyone how he really felt.

"We should've brought Captain. I'm afraid I'll have no one to talk to."

He swallowed hard and remained silent. When had

he turned from being the only one she needed, to nothing? And why?

———

HER STORY WAS SIMPLE ENOUGH, but it still didn't feel real. She was Emily Miller, no not Miller anymore, she would be Emily *Owens*. How could she have missed that? Mia Owens sounded nicer, but that wasn't an option. Emily Owens recently moved to Louisiana from...where? Her pulse throbbed. Why hadn't they gone over this before now? She'd never remember it all with her nerves.

"I'm having trouble remembering my story. We better get it straight together."

He notched his chin slightly in agreement. "You're twenty-eight years old. We went to basic training together, but you dropped out before finishing because of...poor arches."

"When and where did we go to basic? And don't you think that's dangerous in a group of cops? I know nothing about basic." There wasn't a lot she knew about his past, but this was a good opportunity to learn.

"Good point." He pursed his lips and focused on the road. They would be there soon, and her shoulders tensed under the stress. People always asked questions, small talk. She wouldn't know how to answer.

"Okay, we'll just tell people you came from California. I met you through one of my clients. You came out to learn to ride and we hit it off. Fast."

She laughed, because that was true, they had. The closer they could come to the truth without giving her away would be the easiest.

"That way, if people ask me what area of California

you came from, I can say I don't know. Because, once you got here you never went back. The story will be up to you, and we won't tell different versions." He glanced at her quickly as he drove.

She nodded. That plan was brilliant. Plus, everyone would assume since they hadn't known each other long, they wouldn't know a lot about each other. "And how did we fall in love? That's one thing married people seem to ask. That story should match." Not to mention she was curious about what he would say.

He stopped in front of his brother's house. Cars were already parked up and down the street, and she could hear music coming from the backyard. Nervous flutters lit inside her belly.

"If anyone asks when we fell in love, you can tell them the only reason you were sure was when I asked you. Tell them I'm not romantic at all. Then they'll know you're for real."

She opened her mouth to protest, but he got out of the car before she could. That wasn't what she'd wanted to hear. Didn't Ted have an ounce of tenderness in him for anyone but kittens? Why couldn't he treat her like he had the mama cat? Was *fine*, the best he could come up with?

He opened her door and offered his hand to help her out of the truck, then didn't let go as he walked her to the front door. Scattered couples stood on the front porch to greet guests as they arrived. A large man grasped Ted's hand and pulled him into a man-hug, slapping his back, and tugging him free of her. She felt alone the moment the contact broke.

"Booker! I didn't think I'd see you here after the department dust-up. Glad to see you're not in hiding."

Ted backed away a step and gripped her hand once

again tightly. She squeezed back to let him know she was there, supportive.

"I suppose one department's news is another department's gossip." There was an edge to Ted's voice she hadn't heard since the first day she'd arrived.

"Not gossip. Everyone knows you got the short end of the stick. The chief is investigating."

Ted heaved a humorless chuckle. "The chief can investigate, but I was already dismissed."

"But if Captain Boudreaux's negligence doesn't get explored, this could happen to other investigators. There's been a rumor for over a month that Boudreaux got rid of you because he was worried you'd replace him."

"Me?" She'd never heard Ted sound so shocked.

This was the perfect opportunity to not only look like a wife, but to give Ted support. "Yes, you. You're an amazing officer." She cuddled closer to him, and he stiffened slightly.

He stopped talking for a moment then gave her a soft smile over his shoulder. "Thank you. Of course, you're a little biased."

"Who's this lovely lady? I don't think I've had the pleasure of meeting her." The big man held out his hand. Emily had to remind herself that he was a cop and wasn't out to get her. But he was as big as the guys in the red car had been. She came forward to shake his hand.

Ted answered, "This is my wife."

Within moments, she was surrounded and shuffled into the house as all sorts of voices asked questions too rapidly to answer. Ted wandered over to talk to his brother, leaving her with a group of women firing questions at her like popcorn from a frypan.

"When did you meet Booker?"

"He's such a great guy."

"Lucky girl!"

"How ever did you two meet?"

She had no idea who the women were, nor would she remember who asked what later. The words came so quickly she couldn't even catch who'd said each one.

"Uh...thanks." Her heart clenched and sped. They were too close. She couldn't remember what Ted had said. Everything made so much sense in his car, but now she just wanted to scream and run.

"You don't sound like you're from Louisiana. Where did you meet Booker?" A woman in loose jeans and a rose-colored tee asked. She looked to be about the same age as Ted. It was so odd to have everyone calling him Booker, and she wondered if he'd want her to switch. She'd been introduced to him by Jake, but he'd known Ted when they were younger.

"I'm not from here. I'm from...California." There, that was one memory. "We met through one of his clients. My cousin owns Molly Red and told me I should come out and learn to ride. Ted and I fell in love almost right away. At least...I did." There, more truth. She may not be in love yet, but if she had to stay with him, she would. And he wouldn't.

"Ted? Aw...that's so cute. You're such newlyweds. It's a shame what happened to him. Strange, though, that if he wasn't guilty, they didn't let him back." The woman stirred her sweet tea casually, without looking up. Looking for gossip. Emily's internal hackles rose. No wonder Ted felt like he couldn't measure up if these were his friends.

Ted hadn't told her much about the investigation against him, but she wouldn't let the opportunity to support him pass. "I believe he's innocent, and I also believe that all of this happened for a reason. Ted will find a better placement." Like the Marshals, after he protected her and earned it. This woman's head would spin if she knew Ted had a chance to have such a dream job.

"California, you say?" Another woman cocked her head. "What area? I have relatives all over the state."

She knew little about the northern part of the state, but she did know a fair amount about Southern California, since she lived right on the border. But would that give her away too much? Were all these people really safe? "I lived near Verdi Peak."

"Hmm, I don't think I know anyone there, but it's such a huge state. So many people."

Another woman reached out, touching Emily's arm for her attention. She focused on not flinching at the touch.

"You must have had a fast courtship. How in the world did Booker propose when you must hardly know each other?"

They hadn't discussed that question at all, and what if Ted told others something vastly different. Did men ask such questions? "He's not really the romantic sort..."

"Oh, come on. We need details!" The women laughed.

Emily's chest hitched and she couldn't breathe. Her vision blurred and she reached out to gain equilibrium. There were too many questions, and she didn't have the answers. Ben and Ted were still wrapped up in a conversation in the far corner, neither of them realized she was faltering.

A woman in bright red heels opened the kitchen door and rushed toward Ted and Ben with tiny, excited steps.

She was shorter than Emily by a few inches and a little fuller in the hips, but not much. She wore black slacks and a black silk top, making the fabulous red shoes stand out, but something in her made her sure that was Ted's mom.

"Teddy!" She wrapped her arms around him.

He held her close for a few moments and smiled. Really smiled. It took Emily's breath away. When they parted, he pointed in Emily's direction.

The woman turned and faced her, a smile tugging at the sides of her red lips.

She parted the crowd as she came through. "Did I hear correctly? You and my son are married?"

Emily wanted nothing more than to break free from the pack, but facing Ted's mother was even more daunting. She couldn't speak past the lump in her throat and nodded.

Tears gathered in the woman's eyes as she charged toward Emily. "No... no. This is just not how it's done." She blinked rapidly and took Emily by the hand. "We need to do this right proper. You come with me. We need to have a girl talk. Excuse us, ladies."

"Mom..." She heard Ted try to call, but it was too late.

Mom had her by the arm and wasn't letting go.

NINETEEN

Mrs. Owens tugged Emily through the house, dragging her all the way to the back, past a great big gas grill and various couples. Past the older man with close cropped salt and pepper hair tending the grill who might be Ted's father. She finally stopped at a padded swing with an awning in the back corner of the fenced-in yard.

"How did you manage it?" She sat, then tugged Emily down next to her.

She was still so thankful to be rescued from the group of women she couldn't think quite how to answer the question. "How did I do what?"

The woman pushed back on the swing slightly, rocking them forward and back. "Teddy was devastated after they put him on leave. He wouldn't talk to anyone. He was so ashamed, sure he'd done something wrong. And more so that whatever he'd done would cost one of the victims heartache. Teddy has always had a heart full of justice. Fairness. Try raising two boys where their innate language is that of what is fair." She laughed softly.

"Such memories. It was hard then, but I look back on it and see now the men they would become."

She took Emily's hand. "I don't know how you got Teddy to open up to you enough to fall in love, especially in the state he was in. But bless you." A tear traveled down her cheek, and she went for her pocket, drawing a tissue from its depths.

"I..." She hadn't even begun to scrape the surface of Ted's hurt. But she wanted to. Ted deserved a good job, a good wife. He was a great man. "He's an amazing... husband, always putting me ahead of himself." She kept to the theme Ted had set. Truth, as much as possible.

"And he always will. He must have found you just when he needed to pour all of that into someone else, because his job took away the one source he had before. To meet his need to help others. I just wish we could've been at your wedding to support you."

She wished the very same thing, and neither would ever get it. "I think he's still struggling. Maybe, someday, we'll have a full ceremony, where the whole family can come."

The woman took a deep breath and smiled. "I'm Luella, by the way. My husband is Ed." She pointed toward the grill to the man Emily had suspected was Ted's dad. She gave a quick wave to him, then turned back to focus on Emily.

"The important part of a marriage is not *who* attends the wedding, but *what*. If love is there, if *God* is there, then nothing else matters." She patted Emily's hand as Ben approached them.

"Mom, you're keeping the new bride from all my guests. Everyone is curious." He laughed, but his glance never really made it to them. He seemed to distance himself, as he looked over their shoulders. Emily was struck again by the differences between Ted and Ben. Both where handsome men, and Ben certainly had a curious career as a mounted police officer, but Ted was the only brother she felt comfortable with. Identical on the outside, so different on the inside.

"Well, she's my new daughter. You didn't think I was going to let everyone else have a chance to get to know her first, did you?" Luella had that old Southern way of speaking where no one dared question what she said, just because she was the elder in the group.

"Of course." He tipped his chin slightly. "It's just that her groom was concerned about where she'd run off to." His blue eyes met hers for the barest of moments and pain sliced through their depths. They'd hurt Ben with their story of wedded happiness. She wouldn't have understood if Ted hadn't told her.

Luella stood and laid a hand on her son's shoulder. "Don't you worry, Ben. You'll find your own lovely wife in time. That was not 'the end.'"

He shifted slightly, shrugging off her hand. "Not interested. Not in the slightest." He turned his focus to her. "Congratulations." The word wasn't warm, nor honest, and she didn't know how to respond without doing further damage.

Ben had known their story from a few days before, but this was for show, for his mom, to make the story look real. But the pain wasn't fake. Ben hadn't healed in the two years since Beth's death. That was a long time to carry a wound.

She prayed her words wouldn't hurt him. She may like his brother more, but Ben deserved respect and happiness. "Thank you, Ben. Both for the offer of congratulations and for inviting us. Ted has been so wrapped up in his horses lately, he hasn't made time for family. I hope that will change soon." With her leaving and Ted's new job as a marshal, things should go back to normal for the Owens family soon enough. If only she would be there to see it.

Luella and Ed could go back out to the ranch they love. Ted could move where he would be needed. The only drawback would be, of course, that Luella and Ed would assume both of their sons had lost at love. Which was just as much of a lie as Ted and Emily's marriage.

"I'll bring her back in a while. Enjoy the party, Mom." He turned and headed back for the house, motioning for her to follow.

"I...don't really want to go back in there." Emily tried to keep up. Ben didn't adjust his stride to match hers. In her heels, on the grass, she could hardly stay beside him.

"I know. I saw the massacre. Women can be..." He clamped his mouth shut.

"I hope you don't put me in the same pool as everyone else. There are rotten apples in every bunch."

"And sometimes those rotten apples spoil the whole bushel." He kept heading for the house. "Don't take what Madison said too seriously. Her husband is now partners with the man who was probably the one who *actually* mishandled the evidence. He was new and the forensics team thought he'd been sent to help only, not actually do the job. It was a mess. They've shifted people around in the department a lot in the last few months. Hopefully for the better."

"But without Ted," she mumbled as Ben maneuvered her through the house dodging people, then down a hall that had one door. No one was in that part of the house, like it may lead to his bedroom. She bristled at the idea before he opened a sliding door that led into a library. He ushered her inside and closed the door, latching it after them.

"Yes, without Ted. He can't really tell me about what's going on with you while he's here. The only person in attendance who isn't either married or directly related to a cop is you."

She glanced out the window, just as Jake had done way back so long ago in the hotel. She felt watched, even there. "That doesn't mean I'm safe to talk here."

"Exactly. That little initiation Madison gave you is the perfect example. People are people. Trust Ted. Trust me. Trust Jake. That's it."

He knew about Jake? Ted really had shared her story with him. She swallowed hard. If only she'd listened to Ted and Jake about calling her mom. Hopefully they were wrong about her uncle.

"You know, I never thought about it until just now." She lowered her voice and strode close to Ben, needing to flesh out her idea while she still could. Since the attempted abduction, her mind had been so fickle. "Madison's attitude gave me an idea. What if the person who broke into my room wasn't my attacker at all? What if they were really looking for something of *Ted's*? Wouldn't they have just killed me if it were the men looking for me?"

Ben nodded slowly, not really agreeing with her, but obviously considering her words. "If someone was not completely alert to it, they could easily come up to the house and never be seen. There could have been people coming up there the whole time Ted was there. With Ted distracted by his own anger, he didn't notice until your arrival forced him to take note. Speculating...of course."

"So, I might not be in danger at all. And if I'm not, we've got to do something to help Ted." A little flicker of hope lit inside that she hadn't ruined the whole operation by texting her mother.

"You really do care about him. Don't you?" Some of the hardness in his eyes melted.

"I do, but don't you dare tell him." Ben had said she could trust him. Here was his test.

Ben left her side and strode over to his bookshelf, then drew a framed picture off the shelf. He handed it to her. The photo was of Ben and Ted with their parents in front of a group of friends.

"Ted was bitter after he was put on leave. That much you know. He was so angry he shut all of us out, which was bad enough. But he also shut out himself. He doesn't believe in his own ability anymore."

She couldn't imagine facing life without anyone to support her or believe in her. "So, how do we help him get it back?"

He put the picture in its place. "We solve this case and help him go back to doing what he loves. As long as he isn't too distracted." He raised his eyebrows and turned to face her. "I've yet to meet any woman my brother would take under his wing. He's not the type."

She laughed at the absurdity of Ted choosing her. Despite how much she wanted to help him heal and move on, she was nothing to him except a means to a new job. "He didn't have a choice. I was literally dropped on his doorstep."

Ben chuckled as he crossed his arms. She thought he might actually laugh, but it never got that far. "That explains a lot. Sometimes things happen for a reason. I just hope Ted sees it before it's too late."

The small talk sounded like a buzzing in Ted's head. Where was Emily? So many days had passed where he hadn't let her out of his sight that he couldn't stand the idea of not knowing where she was. That had to be the issue. He was still in protection mode and had nothing to protect.

He searched through the whole house, including his brother's bedroom—which he'd thought of in a frantic moment—yet she was nowhere. His mom came up behind him and placed her small hand on his arm.

"Ted, your new wife is such a joy. Did Ben bring her to you? He'd said you were concerned about finding her."

He shook his head and went to the fridge for some tea, poured himself a glass, and downed half of it in a gulp. What could his brother be doing with her and where could they be?

"Did he seem like he needed to talk to her?" Mom wouldn't be an excellent source of information. Ben tended to hide things from her after his fiancée died. There were some things she couldn't fix, even if she wanted to.

"No, he accused me of holding onto her and said you wanted to see her. He brought her into the house."

He thought about all the places Ben could possibly be. His car was still there, his guests were all still there except for Emily. He couldn't ask anyone, or people would take too much notice.

Madison Capri strode into the kitchen and slapped

him with a sickly sweet smile. "Laurence misses you on the team so much, Booker. It really is a shame."

He tried not to bristle. Her husband was always one he avoided. Some men just weren't trustworthy. "Thanks."

"By the way, where did that wife of yours go? We were all asking her about your engagement and speedy wedding when she got pulled away. But she never came back."

"There isn't much to tell about our relationship. She came. She rode horses. I asked her to marry me. That's it." He was ready to be done with the party and get Emily back home where he would know exactly where she was.

Mom leaned close to him and whispered, "Maybe they are in the *pantry*?"

The pantry was the name they had jokingly come up with for Ben's secret office. He stored his personal weapons in a safe in that room, along with his store of specially made chocolate chip cookies. "I don't know how I'd check there with all the guests right at the end of the hall," he mumbled.

His mom smirked. "You leave that to me." She strode a few feet away and cleared her throat. "Everyone! Ed tells me the hamburgers are just about ready out back. Grab a plate and your favorite veggie, then meet him on the porch. Oh, and I need all you burly men to help me set up some tables."

The whole group must have been waiting for the announcement of food. People steadily headed for the plate and side dish line. Within a few minutes, the house was empty and silent. A moment later, the pantry door slid open and Emily dodged out, followed by Ben.

"What were you two up to in there?" He hated that

he sounded jealous, even angry, but of all people, Ben should know better than to keep Emily from him.

"Emily was filling me in on how you two met, since you won't be able to later." Ben leveled him with an ice-cold stare.

So, she'd told Ben about the listening device. He still didn't like that neither of them had thought of including him or at least informing him where they were off to, like they were hiding.

"Ted, is everything all right?" She glanced around. "I didn't think we would be in there so long, but every time we wanted to leave, we could see people standing outside the door on Ben's camera."

"In the future, I'd like to know where my wife is, Ben." Part of him wanted to pick a fight. Ben still worked for the Baton Rouge PD. Ben still had people who looked up to him. No one looked at Ben with suspicion or contempt. No one asked him questions about his past. He had a clean record and he'd had Emily behind closed doors.

"Sorry. I didn't think you'd care so much."

The accusation shot the wind out of his sails. He was supposed to care, but Ben was his second. He would have to trust him and leave Emily with him while he worked in the barn or did anything. Why did it bother him so much that Emily was alone with Ben locked in a room? She would be alone with Ben locked in the house every day.

"You're right. I overreacted. Let's go eat." He reached for Emily's hand. There was a warmth in her eyes he hadn't noticed before. One that made him want to draw her even closer. When she neared him, he felt right again. "Did you both get a lot of talking done?"

She nodded, squeezing his hand slightly. There. Now

everything was right. "Yes. We have a possible theory we can't wait to tell you about. In the meantime, I'm actually pretty tired. I wouldn't mind going home."

He couldn't agree more. "I wanted to give you as much time with people as possible. I know my mom will want more time with you." Though he hoped not enough time to get attached. It was far too easy to get attached to Emily.

"She's welcome to come see me any time at her own house." Emily laughed.

He wrapped his arm loosely around her waist. "Let's say our goodbyes, then I'll take you home." It didn't feel like his parents' house anymore. It felt like his and Emily's, and that was a big problem.

TWENTY

The evening flew by once they got home. The people at the party met her need to socialize, but they'd also worn Emily thin. Ted hadn't asked for her help in getting Ben's room ready, but she wanted to. She'd slipped off to bed a few minutes later.

After the party, she'd been too drained to tell him about her break-in theory, and he seemed to have forgotten she had anything to tell him. Now, in the morning when she was fresh, she could corner him over a cup of coffee and share her idea. With Ben coming, it might be the last chance she got to sit with him alone.

If the people watching them weren't looking for her, she wouldn't have to be as careful. Someone breaking in to get her, then leaving without her, made no sense. Especially when they had come all the way into her room.

She yawned and stretched, glad she'd brought mostly comfortable clothes and hadn't insisted Jake allow her to shop where she normally would. None of the clothes she normally wore would've been right for the ranch. She fit in now, but would she ever fit in back home? Would her old clothes feel right, or foreign to her, when she put them back on?

The hall felt longer than usual as she shuffled toward the kitchen. Ben sat at the table with Ted and she held in a groan. He wasn't supposed to be at the house yet. At least she'd slept well enough she hadn't heard him arrive. Captain raised his head from his fluffy dog bed in greeting.

Ben raised an eyebrow. "Morning."

She didn't want to be cordial when her final private moments with Ted had just been taken, and she'd wasted them with sleep. The loss wasn't Ben's fault, but she still wanted to go back in time and enjoy the last few minutes of peace with Ted all to herself. He was doing what had been asked of him.

"You look like your party lasted all night." She grabbed a mug for her coffee from the cabinet.

"My party ended around eight, then Mom and I cleaned up and I came right out. As soon as I got here, I took the night watch. I'm headed to bed shortly."

So that's how her protection would go from now on. Ted would watch her during the day and leave her with Ben and Captain when he had to work. Ben would be up all night watching. "Did you tell Ted our theory?"

He raked his hand through his perfect hair, then scrubbed his red eyes. "I'll let you tell him. He'll take it better coming from you."

Ted backhanded him on the arm with a loud *thwack*. "He's kidding. He did tell me, and I don't know if I believe it. I didn't see anything before you came. All the activity started once you got here. Just because something makes sense, doesn't make it right." He shrugged. "I'm not discounting your idea, but for now, let's focus on you."

He could, and had, faced his own battles already. She couldn't expect him to just drop a protection order because of a theory, no matter how much more appealing the idea sounded. "Thanks for coming out here, Ben. What does this mean for your job?"

He yawned and set his cup down. "It means that until further notice, I won't be training with my partner for a while. I'm sure the training center will keep Grace running her paces." He stood and stretched. "Now, I hand you over to Ted while I get some sleep." He gave a mock salute and trudged toward the hallway.

"I didn't realize he would be here last night." Having Ben around left her a little nervous. She was sure of Ted, that he would protect her just like he had with the kittens and everything else he'd handled. Ben didn't have the same easy way about him Ted did. "Do you want me to come out to the barn with you so you can work? I don't mind. I find I'm enjoying being out there with you."

Ted didn't answer, making her realize he hadn't said much at all that morning. While she didn't need him to respond to what she'd said, he certainly could confirm he liked to spend time with her. She took a sip of her coffee and gave him a chance to reply. When he didn't, she set down her cup. "Ted?"

He shook his head. "I think it would be best if you stay in here today. Rest and relax. I'll leave Captain with you." He stood quickly, scraping his chair across the floor.

She jumped at the sudden noise. Stay here? With only a guard dog and a sleeping protector? Ted wasn't a man to run from her or anyone else, so why did his abrupt behavior feel like he was trying to escape her? "Are you sure? I don't know if that's safe." Not that she'd really played it safe up until now. He had yet to look at her phone, or he would know she'd sent that text to her mother because the number was locked on the phone screen. The text had been deleted, but the number remained. He hadn't even avoided her like this the first day she'd come.

He didn't look directly at her as he set his coffee cup in the sink. "You'll be fine. Just lock the door, and stay out of your old room. If you see or hear anyone, wake up Ben, but I'll be nearby if you can't."

He strode toward the door and gave Captain the command to get to work. The dog sat up immediately and went to Emily.

She felt both jilted and the immediate comfort of Captain as he sat against her leg, giving her the strength to say what she needed to. "Ted, I really do think you need to consider that you might be in just as much danger as me. What if those men out there really aren't after me? If these are the men who wanted me dead... Well, you said it yourself, they would've killed me."

His face showed a momentary slash of worry, then he nodded but didn't invite her along. "I'll keep my eyes open. Just stay here."

What other choice did she have?

Her phone buzzed in her pocket a moment after Ted closed the door. She smiled, pulling it out to see what he'd said. If Ted changed his mind, she would put her boots on, get Captain and follow.

The text was from her mother, Baby, where are you?

She couldn't tell if the text was actually her mother, or if her uncle had the phone again. She held her breath and pressed the call button. Her mother answered on the second ring, her voice thick with concern.

"Mia! Oh, my goodness. We've been just sick with

worry over you. Where are you? We've looked every-where. The police are involved, but they won't tell us anything."

She couldn't really say. That would be the ultimate betrayal to Ted. He'd potentially risked his life to help her, even if the only threat right now might be his, not hers. "I'm safe. How are you?"

"Worried sick! I'm so frazzled. Your uncle has moved in with us. He had a minor breakdown after you disap-peared. He's been talking to himself. He has severe depression. He's been asking us every day if we know anything or have heard anything from you. He says your disappearance is all his fault for hiring you."

Uncle Cole was living with her parents? So, that's how he'd gotten Mom's phone. There wasn't anything wrong with her uncle replying to her text. He hadn't done anything except worry. When he'd seen her text come through, he must have answered because he was so concerned about her. "Please let him know I'm fine. I just have to be away for a little while."

Mom's voice came quicker over the phone, more agitated. "I don't see why you can't come home. Cole said you would be worried about that woman who committed suicide. It's been all over the news."

She'd stopped watching the nightly news when she'd come to Ted's. Mostly because he had no television. "What are they saying?" If the media had finally taken interest in the case, then it could be almost over. She might be able to leave Ted soon so he could return to work where he wanted to.

"At first, the woman had been missing. Everyone was reporting foul play. She was found a few days later with a note saying she was the one behind the foreign account.

There's one news source that won't drop it, they claim she was poor and there's no connection to the offshore accounts if she obviously couldn't access the money, but we've been ignoring that. Why would she leave a note saying she was the one behind it if she wasn't?"

Which news source was right? The one that agreed with Jake and Ted or all the others who agreed with her? If she was safe to go home, would she go? She wasn't a prisoner, but if she left the protection she had here, and Jake and Ted were right, she was on her own.

"I need to stay here a little while longer, Mom."

She heard something slam in the background. Mom only got angry when she was tested to her very limit. "Mia Fairchild, I don't need to tell you how I feel about your uncle. You know that he creates fights in this house, and I don't like arguing. Your father has said that he can stay until you come home. That should relieve his worry and he'll go back to being his old self. Cole is so concerned that it's his fault you're missing, since he got you the job. Please, please, just come home. I can't take this anymore."

Emily's stomach tied in knots. She wanted to but also didn't. Home meant no more Ted. She would never see him again. He may not care. She might be just a job to him. But to her, he was becoming very important. Uncle Cole had never seemed to care enough about her for her disappearance to cause him mental anguish. Something wasn't right about the story.

"I've got to go." She pressed the end call icon, then went to the settings to make sure once again that the location services were off.

There were too many possible dangers. Too many unanswered questions. Had she just made all the wrong choices?

IGNORING EMILY'S disappointment was one of the hardest things he'd ever done. Ted made it to the edge of the porch before he stopped and considered changing his mind and taking her with him. Leaving her behind was putting her in danger. But if he didn't, he'd only continue to get closer to her.

At the party, when she'd looked at him, she'd cared. Her eyes had softened, she'd leaned toward him, reached for him. The affection he'd found there wasn't an act. No one who saw it would think their marriage wasn't real.

The problem was, no matter how much he might want to pursue those feelings, he couldn't. Her announcement that she liked spending time with him had practically sent him running. She was off-limits. He wasn't just her protector. If he got too close, he could make poor choices.

Poor choices got people hurt or killed.

Between Emily and Ben, he didn't want to see either of them hurt. He strode to the back of his house to the little attached mother-in-law dwelling where Clara lived. She was about as close to unbiased as he was going to get for help in the situation. He knocked briefly on her door, and she came within moments.

She opened and nodded a welcome. "Come in for coffee?" She held the door for him, her colorful skirt swishing over the pristine tile floor.

He accepted, since he'd had to rush through his cup back in the kitchen. Her house smelled of coffee and cinnamon rolls. Like a grandmother's house should, except Clara wasn't a grandmother. Her only daughter was in her forties and had not yet married. Last he'd heard, she wasn't even looking.

"I suspect this is when you tell me I must go find temporary housing with my daughter, in Baton Rouge? For my safety?" She poured the cup and handed it to him. Without telling her much, she seemed to know enough.

He was never sure how she always had some idea of what was going on around his place, but she did. "Yes, and while I'm here. Have you noticed anyone strange coming to the house recently?" Perhaps Clara could put to rest Emily's worry over him. He wasn't in danger. They needed to focus on her. They hadn't stolen *his* photos, they'd taken hers and planted a device in the room she'd been in.

"Other than Emily?" Her dark brows rose.

He chuckled, realizing his question probably did sound strange. "Yes, aside from her."

"I saw a car parked at the end of the drive when I went to visit my daughter about two weeks ago. White car. When I asked if they needed help, they said no. They were going to call a tow truck. I had no reason to disbelieve them. They were gone when I returned."

A white car could be anyone. There were a lot of white cars. It didn't necessarily mean it was the same men who were at Ben's when he'd left Emily there, but it could be. Did they really have two separate groups watching them? If it was the same car two weeks before, that would've been before Emily came. Why would anyone be following him? Now that he'd been removed from his job, he held no power or information.

"Thank you, Clara. I know you probably can't wait for my parents to come back out here. For things to return to normal."

She laughed and ran her cup under the tap. "I was pretty sure they never would. I have my housing here and my social security, so I have nothing to complain about. I'm happy."

He sipped his coffee and took in the small home. The paint was older and could use a new coat. There was a drip from the faucet. He hadn't been a good landlord, though his parents didn't charge Clara rent.

"I'll come over soon and fix that." He nodded at the dripping faucet.

"I figured you'd get around to it, eventually. If it really bothered me, I would've told you." She puttered around, doing little tasks that made him feel as if he should move on instead of just sitting there. He was interrupting her morning routine.

"Thank you for your time, Clara. If you see anything before you leave, please let me know."

He slapped his hat back on and left, heading toward the barn. He'd finally get a full day's work in. More importantly, he'd take a ride to the end of his lane and look for tracks. Not only did he need the ride to clear his head, he had to check the perimeter of his property one more time and check for any signs of people. Or white cars.

TWENTY-ONE

Emily wouldn't meet his eyes as Ted strode through the front door. He toed off his boots and waited for her to say what was clearly on her mind. She quickly hid her phone in her back pocket and turned away from him.

Even her voice quivered with nerves. "I didn't expect you back so quickly, I'll just get something started for lunch."

Despite her arrangement and figuring out a meal plan, she seemed to have no direct course as she moved food around in his cupboards. That wasn't like her.

"Care to tell me what has you so tense?" he asked. "Did someone come up here while I was out?" She hadn't even acted so nervous when he'd shown her the pictures were missing. Then again, she'd been convinced almost from the start that the men weren't after her.

Maybe she was right. If so, what had made her so tense now?

"I..." She slid her phone out of her pocket and juggled it between her hands.

His chest clenched. "What happened?" He'd wanted to keep both her and his brother safe. He couldn't keep his heart from becoming invested if either of them got hurt. He couldn't do either one if she wasn't honest with him.

"My mom called." She laid the phone down on the counter and she walked away from it.

He refused to let anger get the best of him. "How did she get your number?" If he showed anger, she would clam up and he couldn't help anything. He swallowed hard and aimed for calm. As he did, he felt his muscles relax, even if it was only on the outside.

"I sent her a text after I got the phone. She needed to hear from me. She isn't doing well, not acting herself. She's depressed." Emily rushed to justify herself.

Ted clenched his jaw and tried to see the situation from her perspective. "There's no way you could've known that for sure. Any mom would be worried. She's missing her daughter, and that would make anyone scared. That doesn't mean you can call her or rush back."

Emily shook her head and turned to face him. "She's terrified, and there's something I can do about it. She was worried I'd heard rumors about my uncle's last accountant, and I had, but I don't believe them. I still really think that accountant was behind it all. I...may even *want* to go home. They need me. I could help solve all this mess because of what I found while I was working there. They may have my computer, but I saw more than that."

Like the lid on pot with a heavy boil, he felt anger bubble to the surface. He clenched his fists to keep a rein on it. "You want to go home? Just because your mom is depressed. You want to put your life in danger? I know you want to believe the best about your uncle, but that story you heard, is just that. Jake told me they're feeding the media the suicide story and even dropping hints that the accountant was behind some lurid corporate get-rich scheme."

He raked his hand through his hair and tried to regain calm once again. She couldn't just walk away. If she did, he'd have to follow her. Her safety meant too much, more than just a protection order.

"He's my only uncle. I just can't believe he would hurt me." She turned her back on him again.

"The story about the accountant is so that whoever is behind this gets comfortable, makes mistakes, and falls into the FBI's trap. They're watching some prime suspects. I only need to watch you. I can't make you stay here, but it sure would make my job easier."

She slowly shook her head. "No, you can't make me stay, and you probably wouldn't follow me either." She braced her hands on the counter. "I don't want to go, but I can't stand not knowing what's going on."

He wanted to turn her to face him so he could see the emotion on her face. He held his body in check. Touching her now would be too much of a temptation. "If you don't let the FBI finish their investigation, they may never catch whoever is behind the missing money. If your uncle is innocent, and you go home, you could ruin their case."

"You don't think he's innocent." Her spine straightened and he admired her strength to stand up for what she believed, even if he was fairly sure she was wrong.

"I'll admit it. I don't. My gut tells me he's connected in some way. Could be he just found himself in bad company and ended up on the wrong side of the law, but then he never should've brought you into this. It's more likely he *did* know what was going on, and you were just another way to hurt his brother, your father." He knew firsthand what it was like to be jealous of a sibling. He needed to work on that. Ben worked hard. Just because he was still on the Baton Rouge PD payroll wasn't cause for jealousy. Not when Ben was his only brother.

Emily flinched. "You realize that if what you say is true, my family is in terrible danger. I can't just sit by and do nothing while my family is torn apart. I need to call and tell my mother to get him out of their home. I need to give her peace of mind."

He shook his head and finally approached her. He'd gotten through enough with calm words that she wouldn't hurt herself if she tried to go after him. "Your family is safe. They don't know the case like we do. They don't know about the fraud. They don't know he's dangerous, and he has no reason to hurt them unless he finds out your mom has contacted you. He only wants you because of what you know, and he's using your mother and her relationship with you to get to you. Don't let them win. Stay here. Don't put your mom in the danger you were just worried about. If you go home, you will."

He wasn't prepared for her to melt into his arms, but the deep satisfaction of having her there surprised him even more. She wrapped her arms around his waist and laid her head against his chest like she'd been made her just for him.

He wasn't supposed to get attached, but that was becoming more impossible by the moment. Holding her tight and comforting her was the best he'd felt in as long as he could recall.

"I can't lose my mom." Her body shuddered and she sobbed once.

Through all the stress of getting to Shady Creek

Ranch, people following her, being separated from her family, and almost getting kidnapped, Emily hadn't cried. She'd been strong through the whole ordeal. "I don't want you to lose your mom. I just don't want to lose you, either."

"I can't stay here much longer." She gripped the front of his shirt, and her words left a hole in him.

He'd thought he felt more from her. He'd thought she was growing to care for him and that, if given the choice, she might think about staying. He stepped out of her embrace and did his best to hide what her words had done to him.

"Well, I'll do my best to make sure you don't have to." He couldn't just stand there next to her and do nothing. Not when there was so much he wanted to say, but every word would be useless. She'd been shoved on him. She'd had no choice. Of course she wouldn't want to stay. She needed him to protect her. That had made her trust him, that was why she felt close and comfortable. They had to trust each other. Nothing more.

"Ted, I didn't mean..." Her voice cracked and she reached for a tissue.

He wouldn't force her to make him feel better. She didn't need that added to her already full plate. "No, you want to go home. That's as it should be." He took a step back even farther, and her eyes misted again, shiny in the bright sunshine of the kitchen.

He turned from her and grabbed her phone, then set it to block messages from her mother's number. He couldn't erase her mother's ability to call, but he could make sure Emily wasn't tempted to answer anymore. "What did you tell her?"

Emily came alongside him, and her hair smelled like a

bowl of freshly cut fruit. "I didn't tell her anything except that I couldn't come home soon. She was angry about that."

"Does she get angry often?" Though Emily was impulsive, she wasn't the type to get mad. He'd given her plenty of reason to and she hadn't even raised her voice. Since she'd said her mother was her best friend, it would stand to reason they were similar.

"No. Her behavior was very strange for her." She cocked her head, then frowned as she glanced around the room. "The other thing that was odd was Milo wasn't there." She wiped her eyes and took her phone back.

"Milo?" He wasn't sure why that information was important. She'd never mentioned Milo before.

"Milo is her little yorkie. He's loud and she's never without him. If she's excited, he is. If she's frustrated, he barks. She was mad so I should've heard him fussing." Emily raked her hair behind her ear. She'd been wearing it down since their trip to the mall, despite the annoyance it caused her.

"Do you think something happened to the dog?" He couldn't press too hard. Emily wanted to go home. Too much push and she might do something she shouldn't, just to help.

"I don't know. I should've asked. Now that I'm grown and moved out, the dog became like a child to her."

He'd tell Jake everything he could and try to save the situation. The fact was, it wasn't good. Emily had put them in a compromising position. Saying as much wouldn't help. He knew her stance and an argument over what was already done wouldn't lead them to answers.

"Emily...talk to me."

He couldn't seem to bring Emily back to engage with

him. Her voice, face, even manner seemed to pull away with every breath. He was losing her by the second and there was no way to change her mind.

EMILY CROSSED her arms over her stomach and hoped Ted didn't look too deeply into her eyes. She'd never been good at keeping secrets. Giving Ted what he needed, a solid record of success so he could have his job, would be impossible if she didn't work with him. Yet, staying put her heart at risk and put her up against her uncle. She desperately wanted him to say she hadn't ruined everything, and they could work together...that she was welcome to stay...that he wanted her.

None of those things could ever happen. Her hope didn't hold up. She'd managed to find the perfect guy, who she could never be with.

Captain nudged her behind the knee and she reached for him. He always seemed to know just when she needed him, when she was at her weakest. His cold nose nuzzled her palm. While Mom's dog was small and annoyed her, mostly because the dog had taken her place somewhat, Captain wasn't pushy or loud. He was a gentle, quiet animal and she would miss him when she left.

"I don't know what would've happened to Milo, but it probably isn't connected to this case. In fact, it seems like we have a lot of disconnected information. Forget I even mentioned him," she replied, trying to turn the conversation around.

Now that she'd admitted she'd talked to her mom, she wished she hadn't. He was only more convinced he was right, not less. He regarded her with his dark blue eyes, but none of his questions seemed to be about the case. He wanted her to trust him, to believe him. But that would mean admitting she was wrong and admitting her uncle was a monster.

Ted pursed his lips. "We know, for a fact, that right after you gave your statement to the FBI and told your uncle about the fraud, you were targeted. Whether or not the people here are after you doesn't matter. Even if they're after me, you're still in danger, and I will protect you from that." His logic was sound.

She shivered inside but refused to let it show. "If Jake or the FBI or whomever is investigating this case focuses on my uncle, it may never be solved. He's not guilty. I don't think he even knows who is. They can't just leave me here indefinitely." She couldn't stay, falling for Ted, and watching him from afar. He didn't want her there.

"If he's not a part of this, then why is he suddenly with your parents? You said there was a lot of sibling rivalry."

She bristled at his assessment. "A little back-and-forth doesn't mean he'd try to kill me to one-up my dad. That's just..." She couldn't even think of a word. Her uncle had never acted that invested over their petty arguments.

"I think it's amazing that you always see the best in people. I don't know what Jake's long-term plan is for you to stay here. I can't answer that."

Ted had indicated he didn't even want her to consider staying. He'd said as much when she'd tried to explain herself. She'd wanted to say she couldn't stay there much longer, or she wouldn't be able to leave, but tears wouldn't allow her to finish her thought. Then he'd finished it for her. He wanted her to go home. Out of his life.

You want to go home. That's as it should be.

If that was how it should be, then she would spend as little time with Ted as was possible, given the situation? Her heart pulled to opposing sides. Did she help prove her uncle's innocence, or did she try to show Ted how she felt? He was convinced she was wrong, no matter how often she told him her uncle would never do anything. So she couldn't have both. Ted wouldn't help her find evidence to prove Cole had nothing to do with the fraud.

She would have to be the one to prove her uncle wasn't in the wrong, and that the accountant really had done everything. Despite what Ted said. The only way to do that was to get herself caught and pray they didn't kill her right away. Then, when they saw her uncle had nothing to do with her real kidnapping, they could find the real culprit...and hopefully her.

If the people coming around really were after Ted, they wouldn't bother with her anyway. Just like that night when they'd broken in. Tomorrow, she would sneak out, saddle up Molly Red, and go for a ride looking for whoever was watching the house. If she got caught, then she would be on the inside, able to find out more information. She could then try to pass it on to Ted or Jake. If she didn't get caught, she could prove to Ted he was in danger.

Either way, the time had come for her to make a move.

TWENTY-TWO

Ben went to bed the next morning just as Emily had expected him to. Ted would go out to work with the horses, and he would then ride off to exercise one of them about two hours later. If he didn't take Molly Red, that would be her chance.

Once he was gone, he couldn't see her leave. He wouldn't know which way she went and wouldn't be able to follow her. She sat on the bed and stared at the scrap of notebook paper sitting on her nightstand. If she left him a note, there would be a better chance of him or Jake finding her more quickly. But if they came too soon, she wouldn't be able to find out any information to help save Uncle Cole. Then her risk would be worthless, and Ted would be angry.

Since he usually turned the other horses out to pasture in the morning, he might not even notice one of the horses was missing when he rode back up. If he didn't notice until evening when he brought them back in for their evening feed, all the better. But how was she going to keep him from noticing her absence...

She stayed away from Ted as he finished his breakfast, keeping herself curled up on the couch with Captain. The dog would be one of the biggest obstacles, because going anywhere without him was almost impossible. The only way to assure he wouldn't escape out the front door with her would be if she locked him in a bedroom or bathroom. Even then, he would make a lot of noise and might wake Ben.

"I think Captain needs some exercise. He seems...anxious."

Captain's head remained on her foot where it had been for the last twenty minutes.

Ted narrowed his eyes but didn't ask her the question she saw in his eyes. "I'll let him run when I get back. I just let him out, so you shouldn't need to open the door for any reason. Stay inside."

She swallowed hard. How had he learned to read her? He had to know she was planning something if he told her that. "Where would I go?"

His lips flattened. "I don't want to argue with you. Just stay put. Let me do my job so you can get back to your mom."

She flinched, and the realization was like ice over her head. Mom wasn't as compelling anymore. In the last day, she'd lost Ted and he was more important. She wanted him more than she wanted her old life. But she couldn't just abandon her family.

"I won't take chances." At least, not too many.

Ted finished his coffee and cleared his throat. "You're sure you'll stay put?"

Did the possible last words between them have to be questions of character? He didn't trust her after her mother had called. When he discovered she was gone, she didn't want him thinking she was being rash or wild, just determined. "I will. You don't have to worry about me."

He crooked an eyebrow as he flipped his hat off the coat tree. "That's my job at the moment, so forgive me if I don't give up on it so easily." He cracked one of his rare smiles and her heart broke. If her day went according to plan, she might never see another one.

"Goodbye, Ted."

He stopped short, his hand gripping the knob. "Goodbye?"

She hadn't ever said anything like that, and she bit her lip. "Yes, you'll be gone all day. So, have a good one. Goodbye." She wasn't made for acting, and this wasn't easy.

He didn't move and his eyes bored into hers. Pinpricks of perspiration broke out across her forehead and neck. Did he really know her so well in such a short time that he could read her? She certainly knew his nuances. They'd been through so much in the last week, she felt as if she'd known Ted her whole life.

"Not goodbye. See you later." He finally shifted his gaze off her and to Captain. "Work."

Captain immediately sat up straight, his attention focused on Emily. Drat. Now it would be even harder to get Captain to stay behind. He always put more weight on orders from Ted, and the dog seemed to have an infallible memory.

As soon as Ted closed the door, she cleaned her room. Nothing could be left out of place for Ted and Ben. But she had to keep her phone. That could go with her at least. She checked the phone to make sure Ted had put his, Ben's, and Jake's numbers on it, then she turned it to silent and verified again that the location was turned off.

It was only a no-contract phone, but if Ted could track it, he would. That would be dangerous for him.

The goal was to glean information, not to wind up dead, so bringing in police would be hazardous. Once she was caught, she'd have to figure out her own escape. A nervous laugh tickled her throat. That should be easy compared to escaping Captain.

The handsome German shepherd sat at her feet and glanced up at her with his huge brown eyes. She would miss him and his companionship. "I wish I could take you with me. But they would hurt you for sure, and I can't have that. Ted will be mad enough with me. I don't need him to hate me. You'll take care of him when I'm gone, right?" Tears formed unexpectedly.

She fell to her knees and hugged the dog close, keeping her voice quiet in case Ben wasn't sleeping deeply.

Ted would never treat her like those kittens in the barn, except that, like them, he would let her go. He hadn't wanted her in his barn near as much as he wanted the kittens, nor had he snuggled her in, like he'd put them in his hat. She'd craved that kind of care, but Ted wasn't ready to care for anyone. He was still so broken after what his department had done.

The people at Ben's party had known that. Without directly speculating about it, they had known Ted wasn't ready for love, so they'd all been surprised. Not just about the sudden change, but that it could happen at all. They knew Ted better than she ever would. They'd seen through the ruse but had enough respect for Ted not to outwardly call their relationship a lie. From that moment on, it would be.

"Maybe one of those kittens will stick around and

take my place." She ruffled Captain's ears as he snuggled in close to her neck. Sandy Creek Ranch had come to feel like home. Even the basement no longer frightened her. Even Ben, with his attitude and barriers, was now like family.

A plaque on the wall caught her attention. It was a tree with another smaller tree beside it. *Thou shalt leave thy father and mother and cleave to one another.* She wasn't meant to stay with her parents forever any more than Ben or Ted were meant to be alone.

She couldn't stay with Ted. She could give him the information he needed for Jake to see him as an undeniable asset to the Marshals. Then at least he would never forget her. Despite how he felt about his own abilities, she saw him as a success. He was an excellent officer who cared about people and justice. Fairness, just as his mother had said.

It was only fair that she help him as much as possible, since she would never forget him. Emily stood and headed to the kitchen to fix herself a sandwich. The small meal would have to last. She may not get another one for a while... or ever. If she stuffed herself now, her nerves would make her sick. Those were already plentiful. Her stomach had been in knots all morning and even the sound of birds made her jumpy.

Emily paced, trying to force time to go faster. The plan had seemed so easy yesterday when she'd formed it. Wait for Ted to leave. Listen for Ben to snore. Sneak a horse, then ride out. Get caught if the men out there were after her, and bring back information for Ted if they weren't. Then get out of Ted's hair for good. Now, so many doubts whispered in her ears.

What if the men tried to kill her without kidnapping

her? What if they nabbed her and she wasn't able to escape? What if she was wrong and the men were after Ted, but they decided to take her hostage since she would then know about them?

Despite all of that, what worried her the most was how angry and possibly hurt Ted would be if he discovered what she planned to do. He'd done a good job of hiding his disapproval the day before when she'd owned up to talking to her mother, but it had still been evident in subtle ways. Oddly, his displeasure bothered her more than the worry that she'd potentially put herself in danger. She wanted him to remember her in a good light.

Two hours had passed, and if she was going to go out to the barn, she had to go now. Ted wouldn't ride for long. There was also the chance he may have ridden in the same direction she had planned to go. So much of her strategy relied on chance, but just sitting there, waiting for something to happen, would drive her crazy. She was already falling in love with Ted. Months of staying there would seal her heart.

Captain glanced up at her as she stood. Ben would be tired, and he'd sleep through a lot, but not if Captain barked or made too much noise. She'd never tested him to see what he would do if she tried to separate herself from him. It was probably similar to what he'd done when Molly Red's owner had grabbed her.

With quick jogging steps, Emily led Captain to the end of the hall, then raced into each room, running around in circles, then to the next. The goal was to make Captain get confused, but he only seemed to get more worked up, and louder, with each circle. He barked and jumped at the new game.

She sprinted into the room she'd been sleeping in.

Since Captain slept there with her, maybe he would calm down faster if she locked him inside. Captain rushed in and bounded to a stop by the bed, waiting for her to continue the chase. She felt horrible for tricking him, but he couldn't come with.

She turned on her heel and stepped back out of the room, shutting the door behind her. Without making noise, she locked him in. He whined and clawed to get out, but he wasn't howling yet. "Sorry, boy," she whispered. "At ease."

She'd hoped by giving him the off duty command that he would go rest, as he often did when he was relieved of his obligation. He was an older dog. Instead, he seemed to double his efforts, as if she'd reminded him he was supposed to be working, and he was now mad he'd been tricked.

"Shh. Don't wake up Ben," she hissed through the door. She had to get out fast. Captain was making such a racket. Even Ben, who was exhausted from the shift in schedule, would hear the commotion.

She quickly let him out and ruffled his neck fur, quickly quieting him. "Let's go take a bath." The idea had struck quickly and now wouldn't let go. It would kill two birds with one stone. If she ran water in that huge tub without plugging it, she might buy some time. Ted would wait a long time before venturing into the bathroom. She hated using his honor against him, but she had to use whatever devices she could.

Captain raced to the big bathroom, but never let Emily out of his sight. She made sure the tub was unplugged, then dug around in the bathroom closet for a few water dog toys she'd noticed in there before. They must use the tub to give Captain baths. "Here you go, boy!" She tossed the toys under the stream of warm water.

Captain looked at the toys, then her, and whined. He knew he wasn't supposed to do anything fun when he was on duty. She cleared her throat to speak clearly. No matter how often she'd tried, she'd never successfully given him a work command. "At ease." She prayed she had enough authority to make him listen.

With a tilt of his head, he relaxed slightly, then dove into the huge tub with a splash. "Please don't get hurt on the slippery tub," she whispered as she quietly ducked out the door and closed it behind her.

Grabbing her hat, Emily dashed for the door and made it outside. The grasshoppers and cicadas filled her ears with noise as soon as she was outside. Since Ted had insisted on using the air conditioning and locking all the windows, she could hardly hear Captain, so Ted wouldn't either. Ben would be the real issue. His room was right next to the bathroom, but all the rooms were close together. The only place that might have been quieter would be the basement.

She glanced all around to make sure no one had come up the driveway, nor could she see Ted. Within a few running steps, she'd made it to the barn. Cat met her just inside the door with a soft meow. Emily jumped at the noise from the shadows.

The kittens still lay in the nest of hay where Ted had placed them days before. In the few times she'd been back to the barn to help, she'd ignored them. When Ted had been there, he'd put her to work. She wasn't there to stand and didn't enjoy just watching him. Now she could see each gray tabby had slightly different markings. They were happy just where Ted had put them.

All the boarded horses were still in their stalls. Emily held her breath for a moment as she searched the wide-open space for Ted. If she'd scheduled wrong, he could still be in the barn. Heidi, his horse, was gone, but that was no guarantee. He sometimes let her out to pasture in the afternoon. She strode to the other end of the barn and glanced off into the pasture, but neither Ted nor Heidi was within sight. She was in luck.

If she acted quickly, she'd have Molly Red saddled fast and could be gone before Ted even realized what she was doing. Unfortunately, with all the boarded horses stabled, he would notice Molly's absence immediately. But if she headed out by way of the exercise arena, he would never pick up her trail in all the hoof prints.

Molly didn't complain, even as Emily felt like she'd probably put the saddle on wrong. The knots alone were harder than she remembered. When Ted had been right there to help her, it seemed like an easy task, like a child could do it, but she hadn't been out there in days. Now she wished she'd ridden more than once. If she didn't need the horse to get across the ranch, she would avoid it and just walk.

As she led Molly out of the barn and into the arena, she listened for anything that might mean her absence had been noticed. Ben couldn't sleep through Captain's noise indefinitely, and he would deal much more harshly with her than Ted would. Ben would be furious and probably try to make her feel guilty for wanting to help Ted and her parents. Ted had tried but hadn't pushed when Jake had told him there were no other options. There were always other options.

She swung onto Molly Red's back and clicked her

tongue as she'd been taught. The horse headed off at canter toward the east end of the ranch where the driveway went through the property. Her plan was to find the river, then follow it to the fence line near the bayou, which would lead her to the driveway. That should take her to the men who'd been listening in on them. If they hadn't given up since Ted had insisted they keep her door shut.

The ground spread flat ahead of her with tufts of long grass poking out in odd places. The trees made shade easy to find, and she wove her way in them, trying to avoid any obvious path. Her phone was hidden under her shirt, in her belt. If she was taken hostage, they probably wouldn't find it as long as riding didn't shake it loose.

A hint of shiny white paint glinted in the sun and she reined in. A small clutch of trees ahead would make the perfect place to hide, and if she remembered the area correctly, the trees were close to the road. But Ted had said there should be a fence in the way.

After swinging down, she flipped the reins over a low branch, hoping Molly Red would eventually get tired of standing there and would walk back up to the barn. She could hear a radio hum with soft, crackly chatter and a muffled dog barking. She crept closer to the trees but stayed hidden as much as possible.

Two men sat in a white sedan. Windows open. They seemed relaxed, obviously comfortable in the knowledge that they wouldn't be seen or get caught. That meant they had been sitting there long enough to *get* comfortable.

"You think someone's ever going to get that dog? I can't hear a thing." One of them pulled an ear bud from his ear.

The other shifted and turned a dial on a device sitting on the dash. "Don't know. They usually don't let it bark. It must have to go outside or something."

Someone shouted, making the two men jump and both reached for the radio at once. The yell sounded familiar, like Ben. The driver leaned forward in his seat and righted the device. The dog had stopped barking and she realized they were listening at Ted's house.

"Where is she, Captain?" Ben's voice carried easily through the couple trees separating her from the car. A few moments later, he spoke again. "Yeah, Ted. Get back up here. She's gone."

Both men sprang to attention at that, then glanced at each other. "Mia's gone? If she isn't there, where could she be?" The driver rested his head against the backrest of the seat.

This was her chance to see her captor's faces. She'd never recognize the men who'd tried to kidnap her the first time, but these men could be identified. She unfastened her belt and dug for her phone under her shirt. She could take pictures of the vehicle and text them to Ted later.

She leaned out slightly from the tree and zoomed in to get a good shot of the license plate then clicked the button. The sound of the phone camera carried just as well as the radio had, and the driver swung his head to glance in the rearview mirror, and locked eyes with her.

She froze. Knowing she needed to get caught and actually letting it happen weren't as easy as she'd thought. The huge man opened the door of the car, and red, cinnamon gum wrappers fluttered to the ground. Cinnamon, just like the men who'd tried to kidnap her.

These men weren't after Ted. They were definitely her attackers. She hid behind a tree to plan her getaway as a bullet whizzed by where she'd just been standing.

Maybe escaping Captain wasn't going to be the hardest part of her plan.

TWENTY-THREE

Bullets cracked in the distance, close enough that it couldn't be neighbors. Ted only stopped for a moment to consider where they could be coming from, then he heard someone running from the house.

He'd rushed in from the pasture when he'd gotten the call from Ben to tell him Emily was missing. They'd done a quick search around the house and barn and found Molly Red was gone. Then Ben had gone back inside to look for anything she may have left behind, until moments later, rapid shots sent him back.

Ben raced toward him, Captain on his heels. "I didn't see anything in the house, but I barely had a minute to look."

His brother, though tired, was wide awake and ready to face whatever had happened. Ted just hoped Emily hadn't put herself in whatever situation she was in. After hearing she'd called her mother, and the way she'd been acting, he couldn't discount the idea. What he didn't understand, was why.

Captain barked and took off running west. "Captain!"

he yelled. His dog never disobeyed. But Captain ignored Ted's order, racing for the sound of the shots. There wasn't time to grab Heidi, he had to catch up with Captain and find Emily. The bullets had stopped. Were they too late? What would make her leave?

His legs ached as he ran after the agile dog. Even with the dog's arthritic hips, he wasn't about to let Emily be in danger, not after she'd become his job. Poor Captain would run himself into the ground before he let Emily get hurt. A crashing noise heading straight for them stopped Ted, and he ducked behind a tree. There was no way to know if the noise was friendly or not until they came into view. Molly Red hurtled through the trees, faster than he'd ever seen her go. Her chest heaved with the strain and her eyes rolled wildly.

"Run!" Emily's eyes were wide, as she whipped Molly to go faster.

He couldn't see well, but if she was injured, thankfully it wasn't enough for him to see. He held his position and waited for whoever was chasing Emily. He had to at least slow them down.

Captain slid to a stop, landing on his haunches, then took up the chase, nipping on Molly's heels and yapping to get her to run faster. A man leaned from behind a tree and leveled a pistol at Emily. Ted held his position and his breath as he yanked his gun from the holster. He barely had time to get a good bead, and his shot went left, landing solidly in the tree, narrowly missing the assailant's head.

Emily's attacker turned and took off back into the safety of the trees. Ted's blood pumped in his ears. His adrenaline pumped too hard to quit running. He took chase, trying to catch up with the shooter.

An engine revved, and tires spit dirt as a white car bumped and pitched over the rolling ground until it pulled into the ditch, then back onto the road. As Ted made the clearing, it raced off, leaving nothing but a few gum wrappers.

Ted stood, catching his breath and leaning against a tree. A stitch in his side kept him from drawing a full breath. His investigator's mind tried to figure out what could possibly have happened. No matter what scenario he came up with, he kept coming back to Emily. She should've been in the house but wasn't. He needed answers.

Without paying attention to his footsteps, he followed the path Emily and Captain had taken back to the barn. If he weren't so glad she was still alive, he'd probably scream. When he made it to the barn, she was already taking off the saddle with shaking fingers.

"Go in the house." He couldn't talk to her just yet. If he did, he'd give away his feelings. At some point, he'd grown to really care for her. For some reason, she'd decided throwing her life away was better than staying with him. Safe. Where she belonged. She'd decided that going with her attackers was better than staying with him, and he couldn't handle the rejection. It was too close to what his team had done.

He wouldn't allow her to know how he felt, because she wanted to go home. That much was obvious after she'd ridden out to meet the men who were sure to drag her right back there, if they didn't just kill her. But he couldn't force her to choose him. He couldn't lay that guilt on her. Love wasn't about guilt. Love was sacrifice. So, he would give up his happiness to make sure she had her own.

"I can do this," she snapped, shoving the leather through the buckle of the girth strap and refusing to leave.

"I don't want you to. You've done enough. Go in the house," he shouted, too angry to rein it in any longer.

Her lip trembled, and she leaned against Molly for a just a moment as her shell of strength broke away.

"Are you hurt?" He stepped forward to catch her if she was weak. He might be angry, but if she hurt herself, he'd never forgive himself.

She shook her head. "No, not physically."

Captain whined and Ted could feel it too. There were too many things unsaid between them, and Captain could feel the tension. But what could he do? They'd tried talking. She wanted what she wanted, and it was in direct opposition to him. There could be no compromise.

"I'm going to go back out there on Heidi and see if I can find any evidence other than the papers left behind, then call in the police. I need to know you're fine."

She didn't respond right away. Her eyes glazed over, and she captured her lip between her teeth.

"Em, go in the house with Ben. I'll be in there as soon as I can."

She slowly closed her eyes and ran her fingers through Molly's mane. "I didn't *want* to be fine, Ted. But I was too frightened to complete what I'd set out to do. He wasn't supposed to try to shoot me. He was supposed to try to kidnap me like before, or ignore me because he was supposed to be...after you." The words tumbled from her.

He couldn't believe what he was hearing. "Wait." He paused, making sure he understood what she'd said. "You *wanted* them to catch you?" She'd done all of this to try to get kidnapped, after all the US Marshals had done to protect her and what *he'd* done...

This whole setup, all the hiding and making up stories, all the missed work and time spent together was to keep her from getting caught. Didn't she realize how important she was? Without her, her uncle would go free. He gripped the nearest wall as he realized that was exactly why she was involved. She was literally walking right into her uncle's trap and there was nothing he could do to stop her.

"Yes, I tried to get caught. I'm tired of being in your way. The only thing stopping you from getting the job you want is me. The only thing stopping me getting what I want is me. So I decided to do something about it."

"By taking my horse and riding into a gun fight?" He hated to point out just how dangerous the situation was and how lucky she was to be alive.

"The FBI won't find anything if they keep focusing on my uncle. He isn't the key, but these guys are. I got photo evidence to prove it." She tugged out her phone and handed it to him.

He opened up the recent photos. There was only one, a blurry but readable Nevada license plate on a white car. "This was theirs. I saw it pull away before I could get close enough."

She nodded. "It's a different vehicle than the one they used when they first tried to kidnap me. It's not the white car that was at your brother's either. But I think it's the same man who tried to kidnap me the first time."

Could it be the same white car Clara had seen on the driveway? But if it was, how could they know Emily would be here? If these men were after Emily, who were the others? "How do you know for sure? You said they wore masks, and I hope you didn't get close enough this time to smell them." He remembered her mentioning a car air freshener.

"I didn't have to. When the driver opened his door to come after me, I saw the red gum wrappers."

"Those are still out there. I saw them. I need to go right away and get them before they blow away or lose too much scent. It's a long shot, but between the plate and potentially getting fingerprints, this might be enough to open up the case." Not that he was through arguing with her about her motives and plans.

"I don't want you to hate me, Ted." She wasn't crying, even though she had every right to. Even some of the strongest men cried after the stress of being chased by a gunman. He touched her arm with as much tenderness as he dared. Too late, he realized he needed the contact as much as she did.

Her eyes followed his hand and locked on to where he touched, then up to his eyes.

"I don't hate you, Em. I just want you to be safe. That's all I've ever wanted." He brushed her hair behind her ear, then thought better of letting that be it and pulled her near, tucking her into his chest. He'd come so close to losing her. Her lips parted slightly as she tilted her head to look up at him. He didn't want to argue with her. He brushed his lips over hers and she gasped, gripping him tighter.

The moment lingered and she pressed in nearer. That was all he needed for invitation, and he deepened the kiss, tasting her, experiencing her. All too quickly, he let go of his hold on her lips, but still cradled her face between his hands.

"Don't you dare let them catch you, Ted Owens." Her face was so close to his, he could feel the warmth of her breath on his cheek. She leaned in and kissed him one more time, then took Captain by the collar and headed for the door.

Instead of rushing out, she waited, scanned the yard, and then left. At least one thing he'd taught her hadn't fallen on deaf ears. Though he couldn't complain too much. He loved her stubborn independence, even if he didn't understand why she did the things she did.

Gathering Heidi's reins, he swung into the saddle and headed in the direction Emily had come. He listened and kept his gun drawn, waiting for the sound of bullets and hoping none would hit their mark before he could find cover.

Molly Red had left divots in the lush grass from her run, and it was easy to follow her trail. As he passed trees, he could see the damage from the pistol. Whoever the men were, they weren't trained. As Emily had directed Molly in a zigzagging pattern through the trees, her follower had easily been able to keep pace. But hadn't been able to shoot her. If the men were from Deerfield Electronics, they only had greed fueling them.

Ted heard an engine roar to life ahead. He whistled, and Heidi sped to a lope. He couldn't go much faster or he'd risk hitting a tree. She could accidentally unseat him and then he'd be without his horse with murderous kidnappers close by.

He heard the scrape of wheels on gravel as the car sped onto the side of the road, then up on the pavement and gunned the engine, leaving Ted in the dust. Unease settled over him. Why had they returned so quickly?

They were headed toward his driveway. Though they probably wouldn't be so brash, and Ben was with Emily. He didn't want either of them to face an attack unprepared and without him. After collecting a few of the discarded wrappers in a paper bag, he mounted, whipped the horse around, and headed back for home.

Emily had gotten their plate numbers, though she'd done it in the most dangerous way possible. Hopefully she would give that information to Ben so he could call it in to Baton Rouge. The police would be out shortly, and they wouldn't be alone for long. They would need all the help they could get. Soon.

Those men had seen Emily's face, knew she was there, and knew she had their picture. Hiding was no longer an option.

CAPTAIN RUSHED into the house just before Emily, and she slammed the door shut, leaning against it as her heart slammed into her chest. But there was no way to tell if it was because she'd been frightened or because Ted had kissed her. Her bet was on both.

Ben sat at the table, his head braced by his hands. He looked as if he hadn't slept in days as he glanced up at her and raised an eyebrow. "Where's Ted?"

"He went after the men in the car." She yanked out her phone and showed him the image. "Those are the men who were listening to us. I heard them. They had a device that could hear everything in the house. I could hear Captain barking from down the hall, and I heard when you woke up and discovered I was missing. There has to be a device somewhere outside of my room, or they've figured out how to make it more sensitive."

He glanced at the picture then used his fingers to zoom in on it. "The make is just visible at the top of the image and the plate is barely legible." That picture could've cost her everything, but she was proud she'd been able to get it.

A long silence stretched as Ben stared at the image, as if to memorize it. "I'm going to call this in. You...don't move. I'm not finished with you yet."

Ben's anger was expected. He was the brother with the shorter temper and was by far less warm. Frankly, she'd been shocked Ted hadn't been more so. He was too glad that she hadn't been hurt to be angry, but once he'd had a chance to think a little, it would come. Both brothers could be dealt with once they understood. She probably deserved it. No matter how much the information helped the case, she'd still put herself in danger.

Ben finished on the phone, then indicated she should sit. "Since I'm not going to run you out to the barn to talk, we'll have to keep our voices down. I've had them put out an APB for the car and let them know there were two men inside. The dispatcher looked up the owner. He's got no record. It's not registered as stolen, and he works for your uncle. This means the corruption goes deep. There are quite a few people benefiting from the return scheme."

Ben knew? Ted hadn't wanted to know anything about the case, but Jake had brought him up to speed anyway. Now they all knew. "So, Ted was right. It really wasn't the accountant."

If the last accountant had been murdered, then that explained why they would shoot at her now when she was far away from home. In Reno, they would've had to hide her body. In Louisiana, there would be no trace of her. Especially when no one knew she was there.

"I still don't understand why they didn't just kill me

when they planted the devices." Not that she wanted to think of her own death, but it was the one piece of the puzzle that didn't fit. "Something changed over the course of a few days. They went from just listening...to shooting. And why have they still stayed hidden after they shot at me?" She shivered. The case was so much different now that she'd made a move.

"Unless your uncle was the one who hired the wire taps but wasn't the one to hire the hit men. Same group, but someone's not telling everyone everything. Maybe they were originally planning to cut you in on the money, but you went to the feds instead. It is possible your uncle's hands are dirty with fraud, but not your attempted murder." Ben folded his hands over his notes and stared at her. "I don't know if that's the case, but that seems to make sense. And it would mean you were at least in part correct, your uncle isn't corrupt enough to want you dead."

"Ted isn't in danger then." That fact made her breathe easier. At least one theory could be tossed out. She was getting used to being hunted. The thought that they both might be had made the situation almost unbearable.

"Maybe. We still have the issue of the other white car. Ted told me this morning that a white car was seen at the end of his drive a week before you came. Since we didn't know you were coming and I doubt Jake knew, the only option is that someone is also after Ted."

How could he defend himself and her? "What could they want?" If she'd never come to make him more aware of his surroundings, they would've gotten to him.

Ben shrugged. "It could be anyone. My brother put away a lot of criminals. When they get released, they usually haven't gotten over the fact that they were there in the first place. Being a cop is hard, being an investigator or judge is even harder."

"I don't suppose people take the time in prison for self-examination." If Uncle Cole was captured and put there, she doubted he would either. He would blame whoever caught him.

"No. More often than not, prison just makes criminals better at what they do. Rarely do people come out reformed."

Ted's team had turned on him, hadn't helped him when there had been false charges lodged against him. Someone had to stand up for what was right. "I helped get my case moving by finding this information. What can I do to help Ted? There must be some way to find out what they want or have them arrested for something."

Ben laughed and tugged a set of handcuffs from a junk drawer. Emily sucked in a breath as he quickly, though loosely, cuffed her to her chair before she could even coherently realize what he was doing.

"Nothing. You're going to stay right there while I finish my nap. And you're going to be quiet. That's for leaving me with the dog." He laughed as he headed down the hall.

TWENTY-FOUR

A scraping noise coming from the kitchen drew Ted's attention as he raced up his front steps to check on Emily. His own pasture had seemed much bigger as he'd ridden back to the house than usual, and it had taken him longer than he'd wanted to be gone. The sound conjured images in his mind of someone wrestling Ben to get to Emily.

The scratching continued as he tried to find the keys to unlock the front door. If he called out, he would alert whoever was inside that he was there, and he'd lose the element of surprise. A muffled yelp, then a crash, pushed him to move faster. Whatever was behind that door needed his attention. The lock gave and he rushed in.

Emily lay on her side, her wrist cuffed to the back leg of the chair, now facing him. He froze where he stood, trying to figure out how Emily had tipped the chair and who could've locked her to it. She glanced up at him and sighed in relief.

"Thank goodness, you're back. I couldn't sit like this for another minute. I had hoped I could slide the cuff down the leg of the chair, but there's a cross piece and it won't go further. I'm completely stuck, and your brother will pay for this."

If she'd been cuffed by someone meaning to hurt her, she would be more panicked than angry. She wasn't scared at all, just relieved to see him. "Ben did this?" His brother had done some strange things, but this went beyond the norm.

She growled as she leaned as far down as she could in the uncomfortable position, trying to guide the cuff off the leg of the chair and jiggling it once it stuck. "Of course. He seemed to think I couldn't be trusted not to leave if he went back to sleep. He shouldn't have gone back to bed. And just so you know, I won't go again."

He stood for a moment, speechless, though he agreed. Ben should've stayed awake with Emily until he returned, but Ben wasn't attached to her like he was. Nor did he have the benefit of a potential promotion. Though that offer didn't matter anymore. He would protect Emily even if they took away the promise of a job. Bracing his feet to the floor, he righted Emily's chair, then dug his spare key out of the junk drawer in the kitchen.

"You keep a set of handcuffs and a key in your kitchen?" She gave him a sideways glance.

He shrugged. "Where else do you keep spare things? Did Ben call in to the station?"

She nodded, rubbing her wrist. He knew it hadn't been tight and that she wasn't hurt, but Ben shouldn't have cuffed her. He was too cold after Sarah's death. Someone needed to warm him back up, remind him that women were human.

"One of Ben's buddies will call him back or come out

here. I need to call Jake and fill him in on what happened. Then you and I need to talk."

Emily bit her lip and her cheeks bloomed pink. "He's going to be mad, isn't he? And so are you...aren't you?"

Jake would be furious, which was why he was glad he'd be making a phone call and not having Emily tell him in person, if that were even possible. "That you didn't trust him to work the case or let the investigation happen as it should? That you didn't trust his gut about your uncle...? Yes. He will."

He'd expected his own anger to consume him just talking about it, but instead, he only wanted to hold her and make sure she was there and all right. He'd had the need since he'd seen her racing through gunfire back to his barn. While he didn't agree with her methods and didn't agree with her assessment of her uncle, he understood where she was coming from. She just couldn't act on those beliefs. Not now.

"Ben doesn't think my uncle is behind this." Emily gripped the back of the chair and stood tall. He was again surprised by her willingness to defend the man. If only he'd had someone like that in his corner when his department was lodging its complaint against him.

"He doesn't, huh? What's his new theory?" The man hadn't slept well in days. He had to be losing his mind.

"Ben thinks that my uncle is an unwitting participant. He thinks Cole hired me with the intent to cut me in, not realizing I would never take it. Whoever he's working with is the murderer, and my uncle is now in too deep to get out. He has his own theory about why they didn't kill me when they came to plant the bug in my room. His theory makes sense."

Resting a hand on her shoulder for support he didn't

need, he took a moment to think. Thank the Lord she had some sense of self-preservation instinct, or her willingness to defend her uncle would've gotten her killed. "I'll get Ben's take on it tonight when he joins us for supper. For now, I want you to take this into your old room." He held out a paper bag that held one of the paper gum wrappers. He had more in other bags, but this one he'd kept separate. "Open the bag, let Captain sniff it, then tell him to *find*. Say it with power. That might lead us to this device. If that works, we can at least have our home back."

She took the bag and called for Captain. If there was anything to scent in that small room, it wouldn't take the dog long. He may be retired, but he was one of the best dogs he'd ever known on the force.

Ted pulled up Jake on his phone and pressed call.

"Jake." The man answered without any preamble.

Ted filled him in on the day's events, including the car's description and plate number.

"You had it right. The first accountant was no suicide, though they tried hard to make it look that way. The angle of trajectory is the only way we can prove it. FBI forensics has already determined she wrote her own suicide note. The note is almost certainly in her own handwriting."

That made Ted sick to his stomach. These people were the sickest kind of greedy. "She must have been the one to first report the crime, because everything was in motion when Emily got involved."

"Yes, Courtney was set to go under protection the night she disappeared. I showed up to collect her and the house was a mess and empty. As soon as Emily showed up with the same story, I had to get her protection order drawn up quick."

"They didn't even try to kidnap Em this time, they

tried to shoot her as she ran away." He swallowed hard, forcing himself to stop thinking about *what if*.

"Thanks to the information she gathered, we can connect the attempt on her life to Deerfield. That car shouldn't have been in your pasture, and it was owned by someone from Deerfield. It may be a loose connection, but it's there. Sometimes these little clues are the ones that break cases open. In the meantime, I want to propose a way to kickstart what we have. Normally, if someone is under protection, we would never ask them to do this, but Emily has broken every rule we've given her. Obviously being seen brought us some information. Being seen again might draw these guys out and force them to do something stupid."

Ted found himself shaking his head even before he had a chance to speak. "No. I don't like it. They shot at her. I can't ask her to risk her life. What if they succeed? Then you have no one to take to court." And he would never outlive his grief, not if he was the one to ask her to do it.

"We've been watching Emily's parents' house and her uncle's. He's missing. No sign of him. We're concerned that he's dead. Our eye on the foreign account says that the refunds have increased. Deerfield's tech stock is plummeting as word is getting out. Whoever is in charge is killing the company, and I expect them to cut out of the country soon. Our window is closing. We need her to do this."

"He's not missing. He's with them. That's where you'll need to look. I can't dangle her like a carrot. You asked me to protect her." There wasn't even a question. He wouldn't do it.

"Then protect her, but let her do as she would

anyway. I'm not giving you a choice. Consider it an order."

He wasn't sure he had it in him.

CAPTAIN SHOVED his snout in the bag and snuffled deeply, taking his time. "Find." She ordered, trying to pull the bag away. She attempted to make her voice sound like Ted's. Captain raised his head, and his eyes narrowed as if he questioned whether she was going to trick him again.

She'd never witnessed a dog concentrate before, but that appeared to be exactly what he was doing. He took deep, short sniffs as he slowly swung his neck from left to right with his lips raised like a snarl, but not. His intelligent brown eyes missed nothing. With tentative steps, he crossed the room, then sniffed more. His head stopped moving as if he'd found a target and then he strode forward with confidence, taking deep inhalations.

The dog seemed to come into his own at the challenge. He started at a corner of the window and slowly made his way up the outside of the casement trim until he stood on his back legs then could go no farther. When he could reach no higher, he went to the other side of the window and at about the height where a man would grab if he were trying to climb in, Captain alerted.

"Good boy." She'd kept back to let him work without distraction or contaminating the area with the scent Captain was supposed to find. She craned her neck to see the side of the thin strip of wood, and there, embedded in where no one would notice, was a device. It was small and white, about the size of a tack.

Sending her mother that text may have been foolish,

but with that device, they would've found her anyway. Most likely because they'd followed her first phone. But was Ben right? Was her uncle guilty of money laundering, but not murder? Was this any different? Both were terrible crimes that destroyed lives. The refund amounts weren't small. A woman had already died.

She stared at the device and what it meant. Was her uncle after her now, or was he truly just worried that he'd put her into this mess? He would go to jail for conspiracy to commit murder or maybe second-degree murder if there was a connection between the fraud and the accountant's death. Her heart clenched recalling all the times she'd come to her uncle's defense.

She went back into the kitchen, and Ted sat at the table, a notebook in front of him. She didn't want whoever was listening to know what they'd found. "Captain found something." She tugged on his arm. The moment she touched him, she could feel the sweet buzz of tension through her. That same buzz that filled her head when he'd kissed her.

He stood, went to the bathroom first, found tweezers, then followed her to the bedroom. Carefully, he pulled the device from the wood and put it in a bag. "Most likely, it's not working anymore."

He took a deep breath and laid a reassuring hand on her arm, then shoved the device in a drawer and closed it. "Jake wanted me to use you as bait to draw these guys back out, but I suspect losing their ears on the inside will do the same thing. We should probably prepare for them to show up."

Emily pursed her lips but refused to cower. "Do you really think that will be enough? How long should we wait?"

He shrugged and stepped closer, filling her with a strength she'd had before but didn't realize.

"Until they come? Who knows? I'll wake up Ben again. We're going to need him, and hopefully his friends are on the way."

Captain barked from the living room. Ted brushed past her, out to follow the sound and see what had Captain agitated. She followed close behind. The dog sniffed an area right behind the couch. Ted got there and Captain nosed the screen. Next to a very small tear in the metal weave, there was another device.

Emily couldn't hold back a shocked gasp as Ted plucked that one off the wall as well and put it into the bag.

She felt her jaw slacken in shock. "They've heard everything we said except when we were in the barn. You were right the whole time."

TWENTY-FIVE

A black van rumbled up the driveway and Captain growled, his hackles making his neck look hunched. He moved in front of her and took up a defensive stance. Emily felt just that same tension. Three days before, Ted had told her to be ready, and they had done what they could to prepare. She'd actually been shocked she'd had that long.

Ben sat at the kitchen table with Ted, and he sat up straight in his chair. Both men jumped to their feet and reached for their guns. "Emily, get away from the window." Ted waved her back as Captain nudged her hard in the thigh.

The van stopped right out front, and the driver got out. Jake appeared as he rounded the front of the van. His dark sunglasses and hat hid most of his face, but his hard jaw and rigid stance made him stand out. That, along with his black bulletproof vest that read US Marshal across the front, put her at ease. Two other officers got out from the passenger side.

Jake had told her the next time she saw him would mean the end of her need for protection. She'd prayed for a short stay when she'd arrived. Now, she wanted more time. The last few days had been too busy preparing for an attack that hadn't come. She hadn't spent a minute alone with Ted.

When Ted answered the door, Captain resumed his low growl. She laid a hand on his head, but it didn't stop him. He wouldn't cease until Ted gave him the order.

Ted sighed. "I didn't expect you to actually come. You usually just give orders over the phone."

Tension rippled up her spine. Ted never spoke to Jake that way over the phone, which meant they all knew something she didn't. He hadn't wanted her to be in any more danger than she already had been, but secrets had yet to help in this case.

"I had to. You were too stubborn to consider my suggestion. Things have gotten worse. We've not been able to find that car near Baton Rouge. There are just too many places it could hide. Who knows where they go when they aren't sitting out in your pasture listening."

"And why did they listen so long?" Emily needed to be part of the conversation. "If they want me dead, they know where I am. They've known for a long time. They had the perfect opportunity to shoot me when they placed the devices. Ben had an idea about that, but no one is listening."

Jake gave her an encouraging nod. The two men with him seemed to fade into the background like they weren't there at all. "We have been listening. I'll tell you what I think." He motioned for her to sit, and then joined her on the other end of the sofa, sitting on the edge like he was ready to jump at any moment. Captain's low growl didn't seem to bother him at all.

Ted finally gave the order for Captain to stand down, and he laid at her feet.

Jake's mouth flattened as he took his time before opening his mouth. "I don't think Cole Fairchild wants you dead. That's why you're still alive. Even when those men chased you, they didn't hit the mark. Ted said they could've easily shot you from that range."

She swallowed hard. Could her uncle be both the reason she was in so much danger and the reason she was alive?

"He's paying a lot of money to make sure you're followed. We know this because we can see large sums leaving his bank account and going to the bank account of the car owner. Those funds are being used for gasoline and food, but interestingly enough...no rent or hotel. So we don't know if they're on the move or not."

She considered that all those gum wrappers from the truck could mean they spent a lot of hours there. "Maybe they're just living homeless for now? Though I can't imagine trying to sleep in there."

Ted came and stood next to her. "It wouldn't surprise me. As long as they don't have to do it for months, it wouldn't be comfortable but could be done. It's also a car, so they could take turns sleeping in the back."

She hadn't considered that they may have been camping in her back yard since she'd arrived. How had they found her when Jake had been so good at watching everyone as they'd meandered their way to Ted?

Jake continued, "We'd like to set up our base here, probably in your basement so we're out of your way, since you have one. We'll monitor what's going on and try to set up some kind of trap. We need to catch these two men. I believe once they're caught, they'll talk, and the whole scheme will come crashing down."

They still couldn't admit her uncle might not be the leader. Murder, money laundering, attempted kidnapping, trespassing... So many crimes and the only motive that even made sense was greed. Though her father and Cole had always fought about who was the more accomplished brother, she didn't believe Cole would go to such lengths to win the argument. Especially if he would have to leave the country to ever see his ill-gotten riches.

Even if he wasn't guilty of all that they accused, he couldn't be completely innocent. Not after Jake had tied payments from her uncle to the owner of the white car. His hands were dirty, and she'd tried to prove him innocent. A woman was dead, and she'd almost ruined the case.

Emily rubbed her arms, remembering a light cashmere sweater Uncle Cole had purchased for her for Christmas the year before. He'd joined them for holidays, bought gifts, even offered to send her to college. He'd insinuated that her father had held her back by not wanting to part with the money, when she was the one who'd wanted to go to tech school for accounting. Solely so she could stay near Mom.

Now, she didn't crave cashmere, college, or acceptance from her uncle. So many things were different with her now. Flannel, not cashmere, was comforting. The fabric was not only soft, but she didn't have to worry about snagging it or ruining it in the washer. Not to mention what a sweater like that would look like if she snuggled with Captain.

Which life would she be forced to choose? Because

she suspected she wouldn't really get a choice. She wouldn't be able to snuggle Captain if she went back to her cashmere life. Without having the option, thinking about Ted and Captain didn't matter.

Ted sat distant from her, engrossed in conversation with Jake and the other two Marshals. Ben sat across from him intently listening, taking in everything the Marshals talked about but remaining separate and his usual aloof self.

Being on the mounted police, she guessed he didn't often work the night shift, and the change hadn't treated him well. He looked like he could sleep for a week. If any links were weak in their chain of defense, it was Ben. Though now, that mattered less since Jake was there.

No one needed her or her opinion just then, and she wandered into her old room. There was nothing of hers left in there, and she flopped on the bed. Fatigue pressed down on her. She could sleep for a week when this was all through.

Being back in there reminded her that the pictures of her and Mom together had disappeared. When she'd been so sure the men were after Ted, she'd forgotten that fact. They had to have been after her. They had to have known about the pictures, so they'd probably followed her all the way from Reno. They had to have somehow seen or known she'd printed them. All this time, she'd thought she was sneaky in getting them, yet everyone had known. Even Jake had known. He'd told her by his actions that he had.

But if her uncle knew where she was, why was he so nervous? Her mother had said he was depressed and couldn't leave. Couldn't...or *wouldn't*. Ted could be wrong. Her parents could be very much in danger if he was willing to kill the other accountant to keep his name from being known. Not to mention, with her father out of the way, Deerfield would be Cole's.

Cole's potential guilt left her sick to her stomach. He'd thought she would be willing to be just as dirty and corrupt. Maybe he'd even gotten her involved in case her father had left his portion of the company to her in his will, eliminating them both. Captain sensed her unease and he whined, jumping up next to her on the bed and resting his huge head on her stomach. His softly pointed ears and deep brown eyes didn't seem to miss anything.

"When I first got here, I would've gladly made myself bait to draw out these men. Now, I don't know. I guess I didn't fully trust Ted until now. He wouldn't put me in danger, and he believes Cole is guilty. I can no longer defend him. I have to believe that Ted could be right."

Captain shifted his head so he looked at her face, his warm chocolate eyes blinked softly as he cocked his head. The dog had always seemed as smart as anyone else. Even now, he acted as if he understood her.

"I just worry that Jake will push for me to do this, and I'll never have the chance to tell Ted how I really feel. I'll never be able to show him that he's not what his former team made him out to be. I'll never get to tell him that I'm falling head over heels for him because of the man he is. What if something happens to me and I never get that chance?"

She wasn't expecting Captain to answer, but she dearly hoped for both time and the strength to tell him. Even if he didn't feel the same way, he had to know she would always look up to him. She would always think he was the best protector and officer, no matter what he thought.

She heard men moving equipment into the house and was thankful the entrance to the basement was over by the kitchen, not the bedrooms, so she could stay out of their way and they could be away from her. Her private time with Ted was over.

TWENTY-SIX

Emily's phone buzzed and Captain sat up to stare at her. She rolled slightly and pulled it from her back pocket. Ted had blocked the number, but she'd wanted to know if her mother tried to call, so she'd changed the setting. She recognized the number as her mother's immediately. But was the call really Mom, or Uncle Cole looking for information?

Three days had passed since Ted had run those men off his property. They'd returned once right away, but then hadn't been back. If Jake wanted to draw out the criminals, and he believed the criminal *was* her uncle, then she should take the call. Hiding wouldn't help, they already knew where she was. Answering the call could only get them more information.

"Hello?" She tried to keep her voice down and not sound nervous. She'd been told so many times not to talk to anyone. Even though it might help the case, she still felt like she shouldn't announce her actions.

Her mother's voice trembled over the line. "Sweetie, I can't take this anymore. You need to come home. I can't stand what this is doing to our family. Your uncle has taken over the house, giving everyone orders, and making veiled threats. He locked poor Milo out when he first got here, and no one has seen him since. He's crazy."

Mom loved Milo, which meant she did too, but her fear was more for her parents. "What kind of threats?"

Her mom made a slight choking sound. "I don't know, vague threats like he knows people who can get things done if we don't do as he says. Not only that but he never leaves the house. He keeps all the blinds closed and insists on darkness everywhere. He stays in our guest house mostly, but I know I'd better get out of his way if he comes through the breezeway."

The guest house was attached to the main house and had room-darkening shades. Perfect for someone who never wanted to be seen. "Has he directly threatened you? Could you call the police?" She didn't want to alarm her mother any more than she already was, but if she called the police, her uncle could be taken in for questioning. That would effectively end the case.

"Donald won't let me. He says Cole has always been strange. But *he* works all day. He doesn't see what I see. Please, Mia, come home. Stop all this madness. I need my house back. He's so worried about you. Nothing is more important than coming home."

She wouldn't ever agree to anything like that. "Did he say he would leave if I came home?"

Mom stalled. "Not directly, more like hinted at it. He wants me to get confirmation that you're coming home soon. Something happened in the last few days to make him go into a frenzy. You're all he'll talk about. Donald thinks it's the cars he sees parked outside all night, but I don't think Cole even cares about those. I thought he was just worried before, now I think he might be a little crazed about it. He needs to see you and know you're safe."

The cars had to be the FBI, but why wouldn't they be more...clandestine? The way they were handling the investigation was putting her parents in danger. It had to end.

"Did they ever update the story on Courtney, on the news?"

Her mom was silent, then there were scratches on the other end of the line. "No, Cole, it's not what you think. This is Mia. Here, talk to her yourself!" Her mother sounded frantic.

Talking to her uncle was the last thing Emily wanted to do, and she smashed the end call icon. Her mother had sounded shaken, both verbally and physically. Cole was much bigger than Mom, and she would be pliant without her dog in the hopes of getting him back.

A man who was innocent wouldn't be threatening her family. He wouldn't be hiding in their home behind curtains. He wouldn't have scared off the dog so that her mother wouldn't have to let him out every few hours, thus opening the door.

Emily curled her knees up and covered her face with her arm. Other than her parents, she had no other family. Uncle Cole was unmarried and the only sibling to her father. Her mother had been an only child. All her grandparents were gone. How could he do this to her? How could he do this to their family? Ted's family and friends cared about him. They didn't compete and fight. The realization had been simpler to accept when it wasn't in her face. He was treating her parents as if he was guilty, not innocent. They mattered much more to her than Cole. If only she could be a part of Ted's family.

Except that wasn't possible. She came from a completely different world, and Ted had yet to indicate in any way that he wanted her as part of his. He'd held her a few times, and that one kiss had been amazing. But stress could bring two people together, and life would most likely break them back apart. They both came from different worlds that weren't meant to mix.

She hadn't been sure before that her uncle was living with her parents, but now she knew. That would be information Jake would want to know. The cars were already watching her parents, so it wouldn't take them long to find Cole. Once he was in custody, Ted could then make plans to move his parents back out. He and Captain could move back into town. To his house. Where he could start his new career. Without her.

He would have all kinds of things to keep him busy and not think about her. She would go back to Reno and deal with the mess her uncle had made of her family. She'd have to go back to her lonely apartment, where her attempted kidnapping had happened at the bus stop just outside. There would be no job waiting for her. Before, she'd been so excited to return. Now she never wanted to leave.

But leave she must.

Someone knocked lightly on her door. She got up and checked her eyes in the mirror. They were a little red, her skin a little too pale, but there was nothing she could do about that. Jake hadn't given her time to buy new makeup, and she hadn't been anywhere that sold it since. She'd been clean faced for two whole weeks.

"It's open." She sat back on her bed.

Jake opened the door but lingered outside her room. "Since I have this with me, and we already know they're aware you're here, it makes no sense to keep you from your friends. If there's anyone you want to talk to..." He handed her the familiar device. Ted had a similar phone, and he'd charged it before giving it to Jake. It was now dead.

"Thanks. I appreciate it. I actually need to come out and talk to you and Ted in a little while, but I need to collect my thoughts first."

"Thanks to you, we were able to identify the cinnamon man. I have to admit, I never thought that clue would amount to anything, but with that much gum, the man and the car, were bound to smell like it. We think the original dark red sedan you described belongs to the accomplice, Phil Vinton. He has one registered to his name that matches the description."

"How did you find an accomplice just from the license plate?" That was some real detective work.

"That was easy, actually. Once the plate was reported to the Baton Rouge PD, they put out a bulletin to all the local gas stations. One of them found a video of the white car on their security camera. It was clear enough that we were able to identify the passenger. The driver wore a cap into the store to pay with cash, but the guy who stayed in the car apparently thought he was concealed enough and didn't hide."

Taking her life into her own hands had led to that information. If she'd told Ted or Jake that she was planning to do it, they wouldn't have let her. But now that it was done, they would accept her help and her information. "You're welcome. Ted says you might need my help again."

He laughed. "And he's still saying no to my demands. He's taking this protection order very seriously. Don't get too comfortable in your role as undercover agent. This is only temporary."

The reminder made her eyes burn. Everything was temporary.

TED FOLLOWED Emily's every move as Jake led her from her room. He felt better when she was within his sight. Those men had broken into his house before, they could do it again. Emily shouldn't have to face them alone. He trusted her, but she was in too much danger, and knowing where she was made his emotions easier to control.

She sat next to him, and their eyes met for a bare moment. A tense sensation passed between them, straining his shoulders. She'd been crying, or close to it. He wanted to reach out to her, to find out what had bothered her. But with Jake there, he didn't want anyone asking questions he couldn't answer. Jake would accuse him of taking advantage of her if he thought there was anything between them.

He couldn't put words in Emily's mouth, so he would stay silent. So far, she'd needed him for occasional comfort, but she hadn't trusted him enough to tell him right away when her mother had called, or that she was going to risk her life to break the case open. They weren't ready for anything yet.

She cleared her throat and wove her fingers together in front of her at the table, then looked at each man in turn. "My mother just called me. My uncle is living there in secret and he's threatening her. My father doesn't see it, but he isn't home all day."

Jake sat up straight in his chair and whipped out his

phone, setting it on the table. "Hold on. Let me record this." He pressed a few buttons, then motioned for her to go on.

"I talked to my mother for just a few minutes. She told me that my uncle, Cole Fairchild, was staying with them, has vaguely threatened them, keeps all the shades drawn, and won't go out. She insists that I come home so he'll leave and she won't feel threatened anymore. I heard him possibly attack her."

Though he wasn't supposed to be part of the interview, Ted couldn't keep quiet. Just because Cole had acted up wasn't a reason to put Emily in danger. "We're not sending you home yet. If he's doing anything to your mother, she needs to call the police there."

Jake shook his head. "No, we're not. But this is good information. The FBI has been watching the place, but there's been almost no movement other than your father going to work and coming home every day. Grocery delivery just started to the house, so they knew more than just your father was there. One of our agents even talked to the delivery guy, but he saw nothing strange within the house, and no sign of Cole."

Emily nodded and licked her lips, she glanced at him, and he nodded that she should go on. "He did something to their dog, Milo. But other than that, he hasn't physically harmed either of my parents according to what my mom says. I'm not so sure I agree with her, but that's where he is."

Her hands trembled just slightly where she clenched them, and he reached for her. If Jake knew how he felt, so be it. So would Emily. She took the offer of comfort with a slight smile and squeezed his hand in return.

"What made you change your mind about Cole?" he

asked. She had denied his involvement so heatedly, this change was drastic.

Slowly shaking her head, she muttered, "He threatened my parents. If he was willing to do that, then it's also possible he's done all this to me. Whether he was the one who prevented the guys who planted the listening devices from hurting me or the one who gave the order for them to scare me away, but not shoot me...it doesn't matter. He still put me in danger. People don't always follow orders."

Both Ted and Jake snorted, drawing Emily's attention. She'd proved that was true. She'd yet to follow any solid order they'd given. He couldn't fault her. He would've fought just as hard if his own family had been accused of any crime.

Jake drummed his fingers on the table and took a minute to speak. "You've been so adamant your uncle was innocent that when we thought he disappeared, we thought maybe he'd fallen victim to the real culprit. We thought, maybe, whoever was really pulling the strings, pulled one on your uncle."

Ted squeezed her hand to give her a little support. Hearing that the uncle she'd defended was most likely guilty couldn't be an easy pill to swallow. He was so proud of how she handled the discovery.

"No, it would appear he's more in control of those strings than I ever dreamed. I guess what I'm saying is, if you still need me to do anything, I'll do it. I want this to end. Both for me and my family. I don't just let people hurt those I love."

He wanted to be one of those people, counted among the few. The way she turned her bright blue eyes on him, he dared to hope he could be. Once this was over, before Jake took her back, he would tell her how he felt. She still didn't fit with him, but maybe after he'd been a marshal for a while and had something to offer her... Women wanted men who were established, who could provide. Men who didn't say *fine* when they meant amazing...

"We don't know if those men are still sitting out there or not. If there are other devices we don't know about, then maybe. We have to assume they are at least watching the driveway closely so they can tell when and if you leave. Probably from a distance. I'll have my guys canvas the nearby properties for them."

With this part, Ted could offer help. He'd been fairly quiet when they were talking about things he couldn't control. "I'll call my neighbors and give them a warning, ask if they've seen anything."

Jake gritted his teeth, then laid his palms flat on the table. "I think what we need is to stage a strategic mistake. One that doesn't look like a goof, but that will give them information they want. Then, thinking they've won and pausing for celebration, we snap our trap."

Ted hated the idea. "I know just what you're thinking. I don't like putting her back in the line of fire. I won't allow it." Not that he could stop her if she volunteered, but she was still on his property. That left him responsible.

Jake ignored him. "If we fake a transfer, make it look like we're trying to get her out of here—" He tapped his chin. "We could put you in the van and head for town, that might draw them out if they weren't watching too closely. We've got five men to their two. Good odds."

Ted refused to let this go. Not when it could mean life or death for Emily. These men had shot at her. She'd never taken an oath, and she shouldn't be asked to perform like she had. "No. There are too many ways this could go wrong. Emily or any one of us could get hurt."

Emily's blue eyes met his and silenced him. "And if I don't, my parents could be the next one's hurt. I refuse to let my silence be the reason they're hurt. I have to do this. I have to be the one to pull the plug."

"He knows you have the evidence against him!" If she left the house now, there was no telling what might happen. She may never even make it to the van. The FBI had evidence, but juries liked witnesses. Emily was the only living witness unless they took one of the kidnappers into custody and they were willing to talk.

Ben leaned against the counter and poured a mug of coffee. "Until we come to an agreement on this. We can't move forward. You're inviting these guys onto our property. That means we need to approve of the plan."

Those words sounded good, but Ted wasn't sure if they were true or not. Jake could probably do as he pleased, especially if Emily volunteered. He hadn't gotten justice for the people hurt by the doctor after the evidence was mishandled. People he'd sworn to protect. Even though he hadn't directly hurt them, they would never see justice because of what had happened in his department. Emily's uncle would be brought in, whether she put herself out there or not. They knew where he was. Catching the lackeys who had been watching them didn't seem enough of a reason to put a key witness—a witness he had strong feelings for—in grave danger.

"I just can't agree, and since we're on my property. It isn't going to happen."

TWENTY-SEVEN

Emily's mind flitted back to the week before, to the time when she and Ted had been alone. He'd said everything she had to say that was important should be said in the barn. There were lots of important issues she needed to talk about, and the barn was the place to do it away from Jake and his team. The Marshals wouldn't follow her there, and she'd yet to see Ben go to the barn even though he worked with horses. That made the barn *their* place.

"Ted, I'd like to visit Molly Red, if you would come with me." To everyone else, her request probably seemed out of place, but Ted would understand.

He squeezed her hand tightly and stood, then pulled her in closer. He narrowed his eyes and mumbled for only her ears, "If you leave this house. You put yourself in danger."

If she could just get him somewhere private. Those men hadn't come in days, though the arrival of the big federal van would most likely stir them into action just as much as anything they could ask her to do.

"You've told me before I'm not your prisoner. Please. I just need to *see the horse*." She stood her ground and didn't release his hand. He could argue with her, but he wouldn't win this battle. She was too determined to tell him what he needed to hear. She loved him. And she would let him go. Every man deserved that woman who would support him no matter what. She would be that someone, even if it had to be from afar.

His jaw tightened, flattening his lips into a hard line of concern. She could see the war in his mind. He didn't want to let her go but didn't want to make a scene either.

"We can't talk in here because we don't know if there are more devices in here."

Jake's dark eyebrow rose as he scanned the room. "I thought you had checked everywhere?"

Ted gritted his teeth and barely opened his mouth to speak. "I did, and so did Captain. But without a way to really scan for the tech out here, I could've missed some."

"We should've taken that into account. I assumed the place was cleared." Jake swiveled his head as if he could sense the devices himself.

Emily took a step closer to Ted, and she felt the tension coiling off him like jellyfish tentacles ready to sting.

"I can escort you both out there, if that would make it easier." Jake drew his pistol and flicked the thumb release, checked the cartridge, then palmed it back in place.

Ted nodded then took a deep breath but didn't let go of her. He'd held her hand through the whole argument. No matter what, he wasn't letting her go. Though he loosened his grip, she refused to release him. He might not be behind her choice to put herself in danger, but she wouldn't give up on him.

He followed her to the door, then whistled for Captain. The dog had been lounging on the couch, letting everyone else work and taking a much-deserved break. She hadn't really noticed his age before, but his snout was flecked with gray. Ted and his faithful dog would stay on her mind and heart long after she left Louisiana.

Ted drew his gun, opened the door slowly, then she hung to his side as he inched his way forward through the door. He glanced in all directions, then carefully pulled her out. Jake followed right behind her, his gun sweeping the area.

Her heart raced as she kept up with Ted yet watched all around her. The silence surrounding the ranch had always been peaceful, but now it hid sinister things. She kept close to Ted's back all the way across the yard. Once they made it to the barn, Jake made his exit, confident no one waited outside for him.

She strode to Molly's pen and patted the horse's rump. She'd missed the horse, all of them really. The story had been a ruse, and Ted knew it. "Ted, you have to let me help. You can't keep protecting me."

He slid his gun back into the holster and crossed his arms. Defiance in every beautifully muscled angle. "No, I don't. I've been protecting you as best I can since you got here. At least as well as you'll let me. I can't just shut that off and say, 'Okay, well if you're going to get shot at, so be it.' That's not how this works. I protect you. That's my job."

One of the gray kittens, so much bigger after just two weeks, hopped out of the little nest Ted had made for it. The little kitty's tail stuck straight into the air, and Emily scooped it up for something to do besides talk to Ted. Now that he was here and listening, what she had to say seemed like the hardest thing in the world to speak. But she couldn't go forward without his blessing. He had to believe in her.

"I want to be like this kitten." She rubbed the tiny white spot on its forehead. "I want for someone to make a nest for me, tenderly tuck me in and care that I won't get trampled." Not her body or her heart.

"I thought you were looking to get back to your mom for just that reason." Ted didn't come close. He seemed to be hesitant to go anywhere near her.

"I thought I did, too. But then I realized my mother won't be there forever. I realized my needs are different from before."

He snorted slightly and scuffed his boot in the hay. Emily held her breath and tried another way to get through to him. "It's true. I need to know she's all right. I need that relationship, but things have changed. *Nothing in Reno will ever be the same again. There isn't one bit I'm excited to return to."

He shook his head slowly and ducked his head, hiding his eyes from her. "I'm sorry. I wish you'd never been brought into this." Ted's voice was strong, sure, yet quiet. He was holding back, and she didn't want him to.

She took a step forward and felt the imaginary wall between them. But which one of them had built it, and could she tear it down? "I need you to know. If I really *had* come here to learn to ride and your job wasn't chang-ing, the story we told everyone could've easily been real. In some ways, it was real. To me."

She turned away from him and cuddled the kitten close. Here was where he would tell her they wouldn't work. Here was where he would run. Here was where her heart would be broken, allowing him to tell her to do what she must.

"I'm not right for you, Em. I have nothing I can offer you. You're too amazing to be with someone who may have no future. Jake told me I might be in the running for that job if I did well enough with you. But I haven't. You've managed to out-maneuver me at every turn. What does that say about my ability? I didn't do this job well. Just like I didn't do the other job well." His low voice melted her heart.

She set the kitten down and faced him, ready to obliterate the lies he told himself. "That's not true. You protected me and did everything you could for me. As far as your last job, Ben told me it wasn't you. Captain Boudreaux was looking to get rid of you because you scared him. It was office politics, plain and simple. That's why I didn't bat an eyelash when we thought that car might be someone after you. Your team didn't stick up for you. But I will. What they did was wrong."

He swiped his thumb over his lip and avoided looking her in the eye. "You weren't there. They couldn't just make something up to get me to lose my job."

"The truth will come out. Ben has reported it, and he's ready to leave the department if something doesn't get done." Ben had asked her to keep that private, but Ted needed to know. He wasn't alone.

He looked momentarily shocked, then went on. "That may be, but I still have nothing to offer you. I have no job. No future anywhere except this ranch if Jake doesn't come through. My record won't allow me to get another position as a cop in any capacity. They'd be taking too much risk. I might be able to work in the prison system, but I'll admit, I don't want to." He turned from her and leaned against the railing of an empty stall. "If I have to choose between working in the prison or just staying here with the horses, then here it is. But this won't provide for you. This will never make me a wealthy man."

She shivered. Prison work was probably even more dangerous than that of an investigator. Emily approached him, feeling like she was about to hug a brick wall. He didn't want to open up to her, but it was time. She wrapped her arms around his waist and waited for him to either push her away or accept her love. He didn't drive her away or prevent her from doing so. His arms lay loosely at her back but gave enough warmth that she could keep going. His heartbeat throbbed under her cheek.

"Ted, even though you don't want me here. I think you were the best man for this job. I think the Marshals will be glad to have you. I think you're going to do them proud. I think the horses will miss you... I know I will."

He choked slightly. "You don't have to say any more. I know you want me to let you do what you want. I don't like it. I won't say what you want to hear, but you don't have to try get it out of me by saying what you think I want to hear." His voice was rough like sandpaper.

Even if he didn't realize what she *really* wanted to hear, he was at least being honest. Her request had nothing to do with his blessing to offer herself as bait. She would do that anyway. What she needed to hear was that he loved her, too, and he'd been unwilling. He thought she was trying to manipulate him. "I know. I guess...I just wish, through all that I've told you, you would realize if you were available to me, I would always be here for you."

EMILY WASN'T MAKING any sense. Of course he was available. It wasn't as if he'd been married or lost his love like Ben. Ben was unavailable. "I don't know what you mean. I'm right here."

She laughed softly but shook her head. "You aren't. Your heart has to be open for someone to come inside. You have to believe you're worth the time and effort. Without that, you aren't available."

She tried to step back, but now that she was there, he wasn't ready to let go. Especially not with the discussion he needed to have, which was to convince her to stay in the house. They would find some other way to trick those fools into believing she was on the move.

"Whether I'm available or not changes nothing. I still won't let you risk your life. I would die of guilt if you were hurt and I could've stopped it." Even considering that she could get shot left his chest aching and his body heavy. She meant too much. Didn't she realize what she was doing to him?

"I want you to do for me what you did for the kittens, not just protect me."

He hadn't really realized she'd been talking about him. He'd thought she meant her family. "How so? I made them a home and I protected them. That's what I've done for you."

"But with them, you did it because you cared that they survived. For me, you did it because Jake hired you."

He held her tighter and breathed in the fresh scent of her hair. "Maybe at first, but not now. I'm sorry I acted so put out by your arrival."

How could he tell her without forcing her to stay where she didn't want to? He couldn't make her choose him. "Now I protect you because I couldn't imagine ever letting you get hurt."

"Then don't hurt me." She tipped her face up, and the tears in her eyes burned his battered heart.

"But..."

She stretched on her toes and kissed the words from his lips. His worries died as his focus shifted to only her. Not the danger. Not what he couldn't do. Just them alone in the barn. He cupped her cheeks and let the moment last as he held her close. Who was ever going to make this woman do anything? She'd even managed to evade getting kidnapped twice.

Her fingers splayed across his chest, and she sighed. "I'm going to help Jake. I'm going to miss Ben, and I hope he finds true love again."

That sounded way too close to a goodbye, and he wasn't having it. He opened his mouth to deny what she was getting at. She met his gaze and her lips flattened. "But I'll miss you most of all. There's nothing for me back home. Just an apartment full of bad memories. No job. And a family who thinks the reason they have to put up with my uncle is me. If you change your mind, and decide you need a Calamity Jane to go with your Wild Bill, I'm here. I love you, Ted Owens." She pressed her lips to his again, not even long enough for him to register what she was doing, then she turned and walked out of the barn.

He took two breaths, then realized she'd just done exactly what he'd begged her not to do. Go alone.

"Emily! Stop!"

TWENTY-EIGHT

With almost no time to react, Emily screamed as the first bullet sounded.

"Emily, drop!" Ted's voice behind her made her skid to a stop, and she fell to her knees, then her stomach as another bullet cracked from somewhere close by. A moment later, the door of the house swung open with a *bang,* and Captain rushed to her, laying on top of her, a low growl rumbling through his heavy chest.

Bullets pinged off buildings and cars as Emily held her eyes closed. No sound penetrated her thoughts but the loud rapport of shots and the sound of bullets finding purchase in something solid. She tried to shift from under Captain and risked a glance around her. Two men crouched behind a well house, but she was too exposed to move. She was an easy target in the middle of the driveway.

Captain shifted on top of her, giving her a better line of sight. One man was injured, the other staying better hidden. He was obviously still able to shoot since the bullets kept coming. Captain's weight kept her pinned to the ground, preventing her from trying to belly-crawl to escape.

Jake's van rumbled to life behind her, and it slowly crept toward her. Bullets dinged the side and she prayed they wouldn't ricochet into her as the wide door slid open. Someone's hands reached down and pulled Captain off her then dragged her inside.

"Ted!" She turned toward the barn just in time to see a bullet hit him in the shoulder. Red splotched down his front and she screamed, lunging for the door as someone held her back. He reached for the wound as he dropped to his knees.

"No!" She fought against the strong hands that held her as they slid the solid door shut, closing off her view of Ted. Those men would kill him, and it would be her fault. She'd known how dangerous it was to go out but had insisted on talking to him where it was private. He'd begged her not to do anything dangerous, to let him protect her. If he died, she would never forgive herself.

A moment later, an eerie silence hung over everything. The marshal who'd been holding her finally released his grasp, and she flew to the door of the van to get to Ted. "Someone, call an ambulance." She didn't even bother to turn back to see if anyone heard her, she had to get to Ted.

He lay on his side, hunched, protecting his shoulder, his breathing was shallow through the pain. She didn't speak to him, didn't need to hear his voice. She only wanted to check his pulse and make certain it was still strong. She'd sit next to him and protect him if he needed it.

Captain lay by her side, whimpering. "We'll help him as much as we can, boy." All of her clothes were covered in dirt. Anything she could use to cover his wound might make it worse.

Ben appeared at her side and landed on his knees. He pressed a kitchen towel against Ted's shoulder. "If we can stop this, there's a better chance of him making it." Ben looked pale and, for the first time she'd ever seen, scared.

He wouldn't do Ted or himself any good. He needed to be up and part of the action so he didn't think about Ted. "I'll take over. You can go help Jake." She slid closer to Ted, and Ben helped to roll him on his back. There was no exit wound, so the bullet was still lodged in his body. Ted winced and sucked in a huge breath. She was actually thankful to hear it. That breath proved he was still alive.

"Don't leave me, Em." He reached for her hand over his chest. It was covered in blood, but she propped his head in her lap and held him tight.

"I won't. Not ever. You can't make me. You know you can't." Tears burned her eyes because she'd wanted him to ask her to stay, but not because of pain. She'd wanted a profession of love from the heart.

Sirens called in the distance, and the whir of helicopter blades joined the din. At least they had plenty of room to land on Ted's huge spread. If only they could get close enough that they wouldn't have to cart him too far. Just breathing made him pant and wince.

Emily didn't know what else to say, so she just kept talking, hoping it would help Ted. "Don't worry about your ranch. I'll take care of your horses. I'll take care of Captain. He was such a good boy." She choked on her words. Captain had protected her at the risk of his own life. She couldn't ever leave either of her two brave officers.

"Ben is here, your parents should be here soon. I saw one of the shooters was shot. I haven't seen the other." She craned her neck to see the whole scene, hoping that if she kept blabbering on, he would have something to think about other than blood and pain. There were about a half dozen bullet holes in the van. It had to have been made to withstand this type of situation, because none had reached inside. The barn wasn't so lucky, and she prayed none of the horses had been injured.

"Oh, no..." She whispered, then remembered Ted could hear her. She called for Ben to come back.

He finished talking to one of the officers, then jogged over to her. "The chopper is here for Ted. They'll be over to get him in just a few seconds."

She nodded toward the barn. "You need to check in there." Her heart hurt. If the boarded horses had been injured or killed and the Owens family was sued over the loss, they could lose their whole ranch.

He glanced up and seemed to notice the holes for the first time. "I'm on it. You stay with him. No matter what they say, stay with him."

The paramedics brought a gurney and lifted a board with four handles down next to Ted first. "Sir? Can you hear me?" The woman began, her bright flight suit far too chipper for the way Emily felt.

Ted mumbled something, and the woman put her head down by his chest to hear him.

"Don't you worry, sir. Everyone here has had the best care possible. Right now, you're the man of the hour."

Emily prayed that the woman's lighthearted banter meant Ted wasn't as bad off as it appeared. Ben gripped her elbow. "The horses are fine. I'm going to take Captain back into the house. Suspect one is dead, suspect two is in custody now. Jake had already called the team back in Reno to tell them to move in carefully on your parents' house. This should be over soon."

Though it mattered, it didn't feel like it should. A man was dead, she should feel horrible about it, but she couldn't. He'd put himself in that position when he'd broken the law. Ted hadn't broken the law and he'd been hurt. For her. Her heart only had room for Ted and what would happen in the next few hours. Ben walked up to the gurney and gripped his brother's hand, he said a few words, then turned to the paramedic. "She goes with him. They are a package deal. No one says otherwise."

"Yes, sir." The woman nodded and finished strapping Ted to the gurney.

Emily closed the distance and touched his shoulder. His eyes opened slightly, though he seemed in a daze.

"Em, in case I never get to see you again... I love you." His eyes closed and they carried him toward the chopper.

Her heart stuttered. He'd finally said what she'd needed to hear...but would his love be too late?

TWENTY-NINE

Ted stared at the news ticker flashing across the screen of his hospital room. He'd gone through surgery and four days of recovery, but they weren't quite ready to turn him loose just yet. Emily had been there almost constantly, only going home to sleep.

Home. She thought of the ranch as home, too. His mom had even told her where the spare set of keys were for his truck, and she drove it every day to come see him. She hadn't mentioned the case at all, only that he needed to get better. Soon enough, she would have to go home to testify, and he was still worried that the reminder of her real home would make her realize what she was giving up to be with him. Even after he'd pestered her to tell him about the case, she'd just smiled and changed the subject.

All that would change when they let him loose. At some point they had to face the reality that she could be giving up too much to stay with him. She'd claimed there was nothing left for her at home, but now that the threat was gone, would she still believe that?

He flexed his shoulder as pain sliced down his whole

arm. He glanced at the IV stand nearby, and the drip had slowed to almost nothing. He'd need pain medication soon, but only after Emily left. He wanted every moment she was there to remain firm in his memory.

The doctor had said with physical therapy he might be able to return to work in six months at the earliest. Probably closer to a year if he didn't sit still, which was unlikely. He never sat still. The bullet had done more harm than his surgeon had thought, and he'd had to go through two surgeries to repair the damage. Jake had yet to tell him if he'd earned a spot or not. While that mattered, he'd do it all over again in a heartbeat.

Emily strode in with Captain on a leash like a burst of sunshine. His trusty dog wore his retired police vest that had been in a hall closet back at home. "What's that?"

She laughed. "I know he's not on the force anymore, but once a police dog, always a police dog. He wanted to come and check on you, and the vest was the only way they would let me." She lowered her voice and giggled. "I talked to the nurse about it yesterday."

Captain didn't tug on his leash, but he wanted to. The muscles in his shoulders quivered in excitement to get near the bed and see his owner. Ted snapped his right hand to keep Captain on that side, away from his injured shoulder. Captain put his front paws on the bed and nosed his thigh with a soft whine.

"I miss you, too, buddy. Is Mia taking good care of you?" He'd had to get used to calling her by her real name. He still slipped up once in a while and called her Em, but at least that was the letter of her real first name. She'd told him the first day, after he'd come out of surgery. He'd needed to know something, and that's what she'd given up about the case. Since he couldn't know her name before, it was an odd way to consider the job done but had a finality to it, too.

She laughed and crossed her arms in mock displeasure. "You don't think I'd take good care of the dog who risked his life to save me?" She raised her eyebrows, as if waiting for him to rise to her baiting.

"Never. What about the *guy* who risked his life to save you?"

She released Captain's leash and reached for his hand, gripping it tightly. "He's in good hands, too."

Ben, Dad and Mom came through the door bearing real food and a little noise. He'd missed all of them. Captain, his family, the food, the noise, the feeling of belonging. He'd sacrificed all of it when he'd let himself fall into depression after losing his job. Now he knew the job wasn't nearly as important as all of them.

Mom handed him a plastic container, then opened it for him since he only had one hand. Captain whined, taking immediate exception to being ignored. "Hold on, buddy. Let's see what's in here. I'll share if you can have any."

Mom sighed deeply and rolled her eyes. "I didn't go to all the trouble to make beef stew just so you could give it to the dog."

Mia ruffled his ears. "But he's such a good dog." Captain sat at her feet and stared at him hard. Though he couldn't claim the dog was begging. Mia stroked Captain's head. She fit perfectly in with his family, and he never wanted her to be apart. He couldn't even picture his life without her in it anymore.

Ben stood with his legs spread and crossed his arms, like he was uncomfortable. Or a drill sergeant, which wouldn't be a bad job for him. It wasn't the company he was with, so Ted suspected it was the show of affection between himself and Mia.

"I got word today from Jake," Ben said to direct them to a conversation where he would feel safest.

Dad growled slightly. "Not now, Ben. He's recovering. He'll need to go back to work soon enough. Let him rest while they're forcing him to."

Ted held up his hand to stop them both. He'd been curious about his future. Would it be full of horses or danger? "Please, don't worry, Dad. I can listen and heal. I want to know. I've been wondering for days."

Ben didn't waste any time once he'd been given the floor. "Mia's uncle has been caught and is now being held in a secure facility. He tried to flee, but our men were already there. We're not sure how he knew it was time to escape. We suspect one of the kidnappers called him in the middle of the gun battle and told him they were losing. There's been no new activity with the foreign bank account, so we think Cole Fairchild was behind it all. The feds have frozen his accounts here, so any new activity would be an accomplice."

Ted watched Mia for any sign of resignation. She'd been so sure about her uncle. Her face only held sadness. He had to tell her none of this was her fault. "It wasn't you. The greed got to him. Don't let his actions make you feel anything."

She stared at his coverlet and didn't look up. "It's still hard to process that I would've done almost anything to prove him innocent. I believed in him. I almost lost all of this...for someone who thought I could be controlled. For someone who thought I was expendable."

Ben's mouth flattened, and Ted tried to give him a look to hold his tongue. That didn't work when they were younger, and it certainly didn't work now. "Your uncle was so jealous of everything your father had that he wanted to be better. But the money wasn't enough. Your father was still happier. So, he tried to take that away, too."

She tucked her chin to her chest. "I hope he gets justice...and help."

Ted agreed completely. He wished he could be the one to go after him. But even as a marshal, that wouldn't be part of his job.

"I noticed you keep saying 'we.'"

Ben laughed and shrugged, but held his tongue.

"And? What else did Jake have to say? I can see you want to say more, so out with it."

Ben leaned against the wall, the closest he'd come to looking relaxed since he'd gotten there. "Before I get to that, we have one more white car to discuss. The one out there a week before Mia showed up."

"The one Clara saw?" He eyed Mia, but he wasn't surprised this didn't seem to be new to her. She already knew what Ben was about to say.

"Yes. After some hunting around, I found out that the chief had a flat at the end of our driveway. He was too ashamed to come up and ask you for help after what they'd done to you. Afraid you'd say no and try to get information out of him. That prompted me to ask what information he had." Ben paused for effect, and Mia punched Ben lightly in the shoulder.

"Just tell him already." She laughed, giving him a warm smile.

"He's under investigation for misconduct, and I don't want to work for a department so full of people I can't trust, I had to turn in my saddle. We were both offered deputy positions with the US Marshals."

Ted was sure he'd never see the day his brother would give up the crowd herder and people pleaser job on the mounted force. Though he would only tease Ben about that in private, he'd never thought Ben would ever give up the job he loved. He'd always been proud of the work his brother did and his ethics. "I'd be happy to work with you." He frowned as he glanced at the IV tower one more time. "When they let me out of here."

"Well, you may not be able to do much for a while, but the job is yours when your doctor clears you. Jake mentioned a desk position until you can be out in the field."

Mia stepped forward and clutched Ted's hand, then glanced at Ben. "Did the second suspect ever tell you who else was behind the money laundering scheme and who killed Courtney?"

He'd been wondering the same thing. Though he'd never met Cole Fairchild, Mia hadn't painted him as a murderer, especially one so planned. Ben avoided eye contact and crossed his arms again. "No, as soon as he learned Cole was arrested, he clammed up. We're still hunting for more connections. But for now, the trail has gone a little cold and Cole isn't talking. Unless we get any action on the foreign account or something happens, she'll be able to be on her own without protection. Jake ordered us to loosely keep an eye on her in case someone else knows where she is. It's completely precautionary and shouldn't change the way she lives much at all. No one has followed Mia at all the last few days."

That would make her feel more at home. Maybe she wouldn't leave so quickly if she had no reason to believe her freedom might disappear. That had been a thorn in her side since she'd arrived. "I plan to make following her my personal mission."

Mom laughed and collected Captain's leash. "With that, I think we should leave these two alone for a little while, don't you think? Don't worry about the ranch, Ted. We're taking very good care of the horses. None of them were hurt at all, just spooked. Your dad loves the work, and we're in no rush to give it up. You get better, and then accept that job where your heart is."

Dad nodded his agreement and draped an arm over Mom's shoulder. "When I get to an age where I can't handle it, I'll retire. For now, this gives me something to do."

He hadn't worried about his parents or their happiness at all. They had managed all on their own before he'd lost his job. They would manage. If possible, they even seemed happier now.

As soon as they were alone, he tugged gently on Mia's hand, leading her close to him, until she was face to face with him. "Well, it's a loose protection order, but I'm up for the job. Do you accept?"

"Accept that you'll boss me around, or accept that you'll make a little nest for me in the hay and care for me?" She raised her eyebrow with a slight grin.

"Maybe a little bit of both?" He laughed and kissed her hand. He couldn't help who he was. Protection was in his very blood. He might always be a take-charge guy and she might always argue with him a little over it.

"I can take it." She kissed him, and he loved the feel of her hair as it brushed over his shoulder. Hair that he realized was three shades lighter than the day before. He ran his fingers through it. "It looks nice."

She blushed slightly. "The salon wasn't able to get it all out...but it's better."

He hated that he couldn't get down on one knee from where he had to stay in bed, but the question couldn't wait. "Mia... I want you to stay here with me. Always."

She kissed him softly but didn't linger, nor did she pull away, and he loved that she liked to be near him. "I'll marry you. What would you like my name to be this time?" Her impish grin almost did him in.

"I'll just be happy with Mia Owens. How does that sound?"

She laughed and kissed his nose. "I think it sounds...fine."

THIRTY

A year later

Captain's specially made tuxedo had arrived just days prior to the wedding. Mia handed the child-sized hanger to Luella, knowing she could get him into his suit with ease. She was a woman who got tasks done. Ted had told Mia that was a quality he loved about his mom and that attracted him to his future wife.

Her. In a few hours, she'd be his wife. For real this time.

"Did you order one for Milo?" Mom squeaked from where she sat on the sofa, snuggling the tiny dog. Though her mom had always been her best friend, lately they hadn't gotten along as well. Mom saw Ted as a threat to the status quo. The whole reason she'd never returned to Reno. And a reminder of Uncle Cole. Things would never be the same for them. They couldn't.

"I'm sorry, Mom. I didn't. Captain is a highly trained, retired police dog who is like our baby. He's part of the wedding party. Milo is your baby." And she still hoped

Mom didn't bring Milo into the service, though she probably would. The dog could be loud, and she wanted a calm wedding day.

To prove the truth of that statement, Mom picked up the little dog and made smoochy lips at him while the dog whined and growled to be put back down.

"Your father should be flying into Baton Rouge shortly. I hope he makes it here in time for the ceremony. He'll have to hire a driver..." She rolled her eyes, then dug in her purse for the lipstick she'd already reapplied twice.

Dad was busy. That was the way of life. After a lot of reflection on her childhood, Ted had helped her to see what a healthy family looked like. Her own hadn't been what she'd always thought it was. Her dad cared about her but was still dominated by money. He wasn't as bad as Uncle Cole, but they were from the same branch of the family tree.

"I'm glad *you* could make it." Mia poured herself one final glass of sweet tea before she'd go back to Luella and Ed's room to get dressed.

The ranch was decked out and polished to perfection. Ben and Ted had set up rows of rented chairs. Gauzy fabric floated on the breeze like clouds from an arch at the front. White vining roses clung to the wooden slats of the porch trellis, placed there months in advance to make sure they covered the arch properly. Ed had made it and was going to gift it to them after the ceremony.

"Mia..." Mom spoke but didn't look up. She reached over to snuggle the struggling dog. "I never said I was sorry. I...knew in my heart something wasn't right with Uncle Cole. Yet, I wanted to believe that if you came back, everything would go back to normal. That's all I ever wanted, for life to return to normal."

The topic had been an elephant in the room since her mother had shown up a week before to help with the final wedding preparations. But no one had wanted to push the issue. That she would bring it up on the day of the wedding was telling.

"You couldn't have suspected he was as bad as he was. I certainly didn't." Her heart still ached that she had almost lost Ted to go back home. She'd wanted to believe in family, and what she thought to be true, so much that it would have cost her everything.

"Be that as it may, that knowledge wouldn't have mattered if you'd come back like I asked you to. If you'd listened to me, the guilt would've been on my head. You knew well enough to leave, or at least tell the people in the right places. I didn't see it." She ruffled the dog's head. "I would've just died if anything had happened to you."

For so long she'd wondered if the feelings of friendship and love had been one-sided. Mom seemed to love Milo more and she'd been left as the tag-along. "Mom—"

"No. I know you don't believe me. Your father asked me a few years ago to let you go. He told me that if I continued being your best friend, you'd never move on and have a fulfilling life. And what would you do when I die?" She sniffled.

"Mom—" she tried once more, but Mom interrupted again.

"I was so deeply saddened at the loss that I got Milo."

"So, you did replace me with the dog." She'd always known it to be true, but now she knew why. And she was actually thankful for it. Mom and Milo were bonded very well, and she wouldn't miss Mia as much now. The deep tie they'd had before was still there, but not what it was.

"I didn't mean to hurt you, but I saw what your father

said was wise. I just wish you'd reached out to more people in the last year. If you had also found others, then this might never have happened. I hate that you're going to live so far away."

Mia gulped her tea to give herself a minute to think. Mom did love her in her strange way. Once Cole had been arrested, they'd resumed talking daily. The only difference was now they talked over states, not a few miles. The phone calls were the same.

"Mom, I love Ted. I love him more every single day. He fills a part of me I didn't even realize I was missing. I know you're sad that I'm not coming back to Reno, but aren't you glad that you raised a daughter who isn't afraid to fly out of the nest anymore?"

Luella returned with Captain in his black and white tuxedo, looking dapper. He seemed to walk taller and hold his head higher. "We practiced having him hold the basket with the rings and walk up the aisle the last few days. He does it perfectly in training...which means when it's time to do it for real, he'll probably bolt." Luella laughed and let Captain go. He sat at Mia's feet, looking up at her with eyes that begged for reassurance that he was, in fact, a good boy.

Mia pressed her eyelids with her thumbs. She loved the idea of Captain as their ring bearer, but she'd been worried about him deciding at the last minute that everything was a game and he'd take the rings for a run. "Ted said no leash. So, I've got to trust his judgment. He said Captain can do it."

Luella pursed her lips slightly but not enough to crease her makeup. "No one knows that dog better than Ted. I just hope he's right. Your makeup artist is all set up in my room and ready for you. Why don't you go and get ready, dear?"

She pushed away from the counter and put her glass in the sink. The rest of the day was planned to the minute, if only that meant she didn't have to worry about it.

***

TED ADJUSTED his bow tie and ignored Ben's pacing. Today was not the day to be stressed over a case, but criminals never seemed to understand wedding days. Ben was already dressed and ready. Though he'd agreed to play the part of the best man, he hadn't actually done anything to help the wedding process or planning. Neither of them had. The wedding had been left in Mia's capable hands since he'd returned to work and had been traveling a lot.

He hadn't actually laid eyes on her in three days since they'd been off in Baton Rouge rescuing a group of immigrants from their handler. He loved the new job, but he couldn't wait to have a wife to return home to where he could relax.

"Have you told her yet?" Ben leaned against the wall and crossed one foot over the other, finally looking calm, but never relaxed.

"I haven't and I won't. Not today. I'll tell her tomorrow, or the next day. I'm not ruining this for her and you'd better not either." Cole Fairchild had ruined enough of Mia's life. He would not allow the man to have a part of this day.

"All I'm saying is that it might actually be good, so she doesn't worry about it anymore." Ben pressed the issue.

"No. End of story. Not today. Drop it." He gave up on

his tie. If he hadn't tied it well enough, his mom would fix it anyway.

"You don't think she'll want to know that the trial date has finally been set and it's only a month away?"

It had taken a year for the case to come to trial. In all that time, neither Cole nor his lawyers had tried to contact them. There was no question about it, the state of Nevada would subpoena Mia as a witness. He couldn't stop it, no matter how much he didn't want her to have to face her uncle. He wished he could be there, but since he'd only just been cleared for field duty, that wasn't likely. At least she would be near her mom.

"I ask that you let me tell her when I'm ready. Don't take this matter into your own hands. I know her better than you do."

Jake came in from the back deck and sat down on Ben's couch. "I just got here from the ranch. Everything is about ready. Your future mother-in-law is driving your mother crazy. They are so opposite that I almost wish I could stay longer to watch the fun."

Ted snorted softly and knew just what he meant. "Mia's mom is heading back to Reno this evening with her father. She's been here a week, and that's long enough. She's nice, she just makes Mia tense, and I'm ready to see that gone. We've had enough tension."

Jake chuckled. "I'm sure her nerves and tension had nothing to do with getting ready for a wedding to a guy who's traveled all over the state of Louisiana in the last three days. She wasn't even sure you'd be here for your wedding day."

"I promised her I would. When it matters, I'll be here for her." Never again would he put his family second. His job was important. All those people he helped made his life fulfilling again. But nothing could replace his family.

"Good to hear. You both ready for your escort?" Jake stood and checked the room. Ted did the same thing. The action came as natural as breathing.

Ted glanced around Ben's house and hoped he hadn't forgotten anything. "I think I am." He patted his suit coat and felt the ring box where he'd left it.

"I think it's well past time to see this done." Ben headed for the door.

Ted couldn't agree more, but he and Mia had needed a full year of just living life as a couple to know for sure this was absolutely right. He wouldn't go back and do it differently now. "Agreed."

THE MUSIC STARTED and everyone stood. Sunbeams poured through the roses on the trellis, creating lovely dancing shadows near the pastor's feet. Mia watched, waiting in the back as soft music played while the guests took their seats.

Mom set Milo on the ground and slowly walked up the aisle, signaling the beginning of the procession.

"You got this, kid?" Mia's father chucked her chin softly. "I wish I could've come sooner. I just want you to know I'm proud of you. Of everything you've done."

Tears gathered in her lashes and Dad scrambled to find a tissue. "Thank you, Daddy." Cole had been his brother, and she would be the one to give the evidence to hopefully convict him. She'd needed to know he approved of her.

The groomsman and bridesmaids lined up next and

slowly walked down the aisle, taking their time. Her heart beat even faster. Her time was almost here. Finally, Ben and the maid of honor, who was a friend of Ted's, made their way to the front. Last—and she had to admit he upstaged her a bit—was Captain. He calmly strode to his master, then sat for Ted to take the rings.

"Now it's our turn. Are you ready?"

She smiled as she took in all the people in attendance. People who had become her friends over the last year. She was getting closer and closer to them. Mom stood, and the guests all followed her lead.

"Yes, I've never been more ready for anything."

ALSO BY KARI TRUMBO

Don't forget to join me for future books! There will be more US Marshals! Also, coming late 2023, Deadly Yellowstone Secrets from Love Inspired Suspense will hit the shelves.

To learn more, follow me HERE: https://landing.mailerlite.com/webforms/landing/k4x2p2

Want more right now? *Love's Security* might be just what you're looking for. You can find it at: https://books2read.com/LovesSecurity-Trumbo

ABOUT THE AUTHOR

 Where western meets happily ever after.

Kari is a *USA Today* best-selling author who writes swoony heroes and places that become characters with detail and heart.

Her favorite place to write about is the place her heart lives, (even if she doesn't) South Dakota.

Kari loves reading, listening to contemporary Christian music, singing when no one's listening, and curling up near the wood stove when winter hits. She makes her home in central Minnesota, land of frigid toes and mosquitoes the size of compact cars, with her husband of over twenty years. They have two daughters, two sons, one cat, and one hungry wood stove.

facebook.com/KariTrumboAuthor

instagram.com/karitrumbo

amazon.com/Kari-Trumbo/e/B015IJOLN4

bookbub.com/authors/kari-trumbo

goodreads.com/karitrumbo

www.ingramcontent.com/pod-product-compliance
Lightning Source LLC
Chambersburg PA
CBHW021422150726
47989CB00001B/82